MRS. RED PEPPER

"He moved his head and tried to speak naturally: 'I am —
rather — ashamed of myself ——' "

Mrs. Red Pepper

By Grace S. Richmond

Author of
"Red Pepper Burns," "The Indifference of Juliet,"
"With Juliet in England," "Strawberry Acres,"
Etc.

With Four Illustrations
By W. H. D. KOERNER

A. L. BURT COMPANY
PUBLISHERS   NEW YORK

CONTENTS

LIST OF ILLUSTRATIONS

MRS. RED PEPPER

CHAPTER I

THE Green Imp, long, low and powerful, carrying besides its two passengers a motor trunk, a number of bulky parcels, and a full share of mud, drew to one side of the road. The fifth April shower of the afternoon was on, although it was barely three o'clock.

Redfield Pepper Burns, physician and surgeon, descended from the car, a brawny figure in an enveloping gray motoring coat. He wore no hat upon his heavy crop of coppery red hair — somewhere under the seat his cap was abandoned, as usual. His face was brown with tan — a strong, fine face, with dark-lashed hazel eyes alight under thick, dark eyebrows. From head to foot he was a rather striking personality.

"This time," said he, firmly, "I'm going to leave the top up. It's putting temptation in the way of something very weak to keep lowering the top. We'll leave it up. There'll be one advantage." He looked round the corner of the top into the face of his companion, as his hands adjusted the straps.

3

"When we get to the fifty-miles-from-the-office stone, which we're going to do in about five minutes, I can take leave of my bride without having to observe the landscape except from the front."

"So you're going to take leave of her," observed his passenger. She did not seem at all disturbed. As the car moved on she drew back her veil from its position over her face, leaving her head covered only by a close-fitting motoring bonnet of dark green, from within which her face, vivid with the colouring born of many days driving with and without veils, met without flinching the spatter of rain the fitful April wind sent drifting in under the edge of the top. Her black eyelashes caught the drops and held them.

"Yes, I'm going to say good-bye to her at that stone," repeated Burns. "She's been the joy of my life for two weeks, and I'll never forget her. But she couldn't stand for the change of conditions we're going to find the minute we strike the old place. It's only my wife who can face those."

"If the bride is to be left behind, I suppose the bridegroom will stay with her? Together, they'll not be badly off."

Burns laughed. "Ye gods! Is that what I've been — a bridegroom? I'm glad I didn't realize it; it would have made me act queerer than I have. Well, it's been a happy time — a gloriously happy time, but —— "

He paused and looked down at her for an instant, rather as if he hesitated to say what was in his mind. He did not know that he had already said it.

But she knew it, and she smiled at him, understanding — and sympathizing. "But you are glad you are on your way back to your work," said she. "So am I."

He drew a relieved breath. "Bless you," said he. "I'm glad you are — if it's true. It's only that I'm so refreshed by this wonderful fortnight that I — well — I want to go to work again — work with all my might. I feel as if I could do the best work of my life. That doesn't mean that I don't dread to see the first patient, for I do. Whoever he is, I hate the sight of him! Can you understand?"

She nodded. "It will be like the first plunge into cold water. But once in —— "

"That's it. Of course, if he happened to be lying on my lawn, all mangled up and calling for me to save his life, I'd welcome the sight of him, poor chap. But he won't be interesting, like that. He'll be a victim of chronic dyspepsia. Or worse — she'll be a woman who can't sleep without a dope. I have to get used to that kind by degrees, after a vacation; I don't warm up to 'em, on sight."

"Yet they're very miserable, some of those patients who are quite able to walk to your office, and very grateful to you if you relieve them, aren't they?"

Red Pepper chuckled. "I can foresee," he said, "that you're going to take the side of the unhappy patient, from the start — worse luck for me! Yes, they're grateful if I can relieve them, but the trouble is I can't relieve them — not the particular class I have in mind. They won't do as I order. And as long as I can't get them comfortably down in bed, where the nurse and I have the upper hand, they'll continue to carry out half of my directions — the half they approve, and neglect the other half — the really important half, and then come round and tell me I haven't helped them any — and why not? Oh, well — far be it from me to complain of the routine work, much as I prefer the sort which calls for all the skill and resource I happen to possess. And the dull part is going to take on a new interest, now, when I can escape from the office into my wife's quarters, between times, where no patient can follow me."

She smiled, watching a big cloud, low on the horizon before them, break into fragments and dissolve into blue sky and sunshine. "I hope," said she, "to be able to make those quarters attractive. You remember I haven't seen them yet — not even the bare rooms."

"That's bothered me a good deal, in spite of the assurance you gave me, when we discussed it by letter. If I hadn't been so horribly busy, and had

had the faintest notion of what to do with them —
or if you had wanted Martha and Winifred to put
them in shape for you —— "

"But I didn't! It's going to be such fun to work
it out, you and I together."

He shook his head. "Don't count on me, dear.
I probably shan't have time to do more than take
you in to town and drop you in the shopping district.
You'll have to do it all. You've married a doctor,
Ellen — that's the whole story. And it's the
knowledge of that fact that makes me realize that
I may as well leave my bride at the fifty-mile-stone.
It'll take my wife that fifty miles to prepare herself
for the thing that's going to strike her the minute we
are home. And, by the fates, I believe that's the
stone, ahead there, at the curve of the road!"

He brought the Green Imp's pace down until it
was moving very slowly toward the mile-stone.
Then he turned and looked steadily down into the
face beside him. "Shall you be sorry to get there?"
he asked.

"No."

"Why?"

"Because I don't want to be a bride. They are
useless persons. And I don't care much for bride-
grooms, either. I prefer a busy husband. And
I shall enjoy getting those rooms in order, quite by
myself. To tell the truth I'm not at all sure I don't

prefer to do them alone. I've had one enlightening experience, shopping with you, you know."

"So you have." He laughed at the remembrance. "Yet I thought I was pretty meek, that day. Well, so you don't mind getting to the mile-stone?"

"Not a bit."

They were beside it now. Burns stopped the car. It was a country road, although it was the main highway between two large cities, and on this April afternoon it was deserted by motorists. Only in the distance could be discerned anything in the nature of a vehicle, and that was headed the other way.

"I suppose I'm a sentimental chap," he observed. "But in one way I've been rather dreading getting home, for your sake. It's come over me, since we turned our faces this way, that not a thing has been done to make my shabby old place fit for you — except to clean it thoroughly. Cynthia's seen to that. Does it seem as if I hadn't cared to give you a fit welcome home?"

His eyes were a little troubled, as they searched hers. But they grew light again as they read in her serene glance that she did not misunderstand him.

"Red," said she — and her hand slipped into his — "I like best to come into your house, just as it is. Take me in — that's all I ask — and trust me to make my own home there — and in your heart. That's all I want."

"You're in my heart," said her husband, "so close and warm there's not much room for anything else."

"Then don't worry about the house. It will be a dear delight to fill the empty rooms; I've a genius for that sort of thing. Wait and see. And meanwhile" — she smiled up into his nearing face — "say good-bye to your bride. She's quite ready to go — and give place to your wife."

So Redfield Pepper Burns kissed his bride, with the ardour of farewell. But the next minute, safe in the shelter of the deep-hooded top, he had welcomed his wife with his heart of hearts upon his lips, and a few low-spoken words in her ear which would make the fiftieth-from-the-office mile-stone a place to remember for them both.

Then he drove on, silently, for a while, as if the little roadside ceremony had left behind it thoughts too deep for expression. And, quite unconsciously, his hand upon the throttle was giving the Imp more and more power, so that the car flew past the succeeding mile-stones at such short intervals that before the pair knew it they were within sight of the city on the farther side of which lay the suburban village which was their home.

"I might stop at the hospital and see how things

are," said Burns as they entered the city's outskirts. "But it would be precisely my luck to find something to detain me, and I think I owe it to you to take you home before I begin on anything else."

"Stop, if you want to, Red," said Ellen. "I expected you would."

"But I don't want to. I might have to send some one else to drive you out to the house, and that would break me up. I want to see you walk in at the door, and know that you belong there. Then, if you like, and not till then, I'll be content to go on duty at the old job."

So he took her home. As they approached the village the ninth April shower of the afternoon came blustering up, accompanied by a burst of wind and considerable thunder and lightning, so that when they caught sight of the low-lying old brick house, well back from the street, which was Red Pepper Burns's combined home and office, after the fashion of the village doctor, it was through a wall of rain.

But the house was not the only thing they saw. In the street before the house stood a row of vehicles. One electric runabout, hooded and luxurious; two "buggies," of the village type, drawn by single horses standing dejectedly with drooping ears and tails; one farmer's wagon, filled with boxes and barrels, its horses hitched to Burns's post by a rope: this was the assemblage.

Red Pepper drew one long, low whistle of dismay, then he burst into a laugh. "Confound that blundering angel, Cynthia," he ejaculated. "She's let it out that we're coming. And Amy Mathewson — my office nurse — not due till to-morrow, to protect us! I was prepared, in a way, to pitch into work, but, by George, I didn't expect to see that familiar sight to-day! Hang it all!"

"Never mind." Ellen was laughing, too. "Remember you've left the bride behind. Your wife will soon be used to it."

"We'll run in by the Chesters' driveway, and sneak in at the back door," and Burns suited the action to the word by turning in at the gateway of his next door neighbour. "I rather wonder Win or Martha didn't go over and drive away my too-eager clientele."

"Possibly they thought it would look more like home to you with an office full of patients."

"It certainly will, though I could dispense with them to-night without much sorrow. But — where am I going to put you? You can get to my room, but you won't want to stay there. The part of the house that will be the living part for you is either empty or cluttered up with wedding presents. By all that's crazy, Ellen, I'm just waking up to the fact that there isn't any place to put you, when there are patients in the house — which there everlastingly are — except the dining-room and kitchen! Lord Harry! what am I going to do? And what will you think of me? Dolt that I am!"

He had heard her laugh before. A low and melodious laugh she had, and he had often listened to it and joined in with it, and rejoiced at the ability she possessed to laugh where many women would cry. But he had never heard her laugh as she was laughing now. Her understanding of the situation which had only just struck him was complete. She knew precisely how busy he had been in the weeks preceding the wedding, and how thankfully he had accepted her suggestion that she come to his home just as it was, and plan for herself what disposal she would make of the empty rooms in a house of which he had used only the wing. Until he had seen that row of vehicles before the gate he had not comprehended the fact that almost the entire furnished portion of the house was the public property of his patients whenever they chose to come. And they were there now!

The car stopped behind the house, close by the French window opening upon a small rear porch. The window led to the large, low-ceiled room which was Burns's own, leading in turn to his offices, and having only these two means of entrance. Burns looked down at his wife, her expressive face rosy with her laughter.

"I'm glad you see it that way," said he. "That sense of humour is going to help you through a lot, tied up to R. P. Burns, M. D. Will you go into my room, by this window? Or will you accept Cynthia's hospitality in the dining-room? Or — maybe that's the best plan — will you just run over to Martha's? I remember she begged us to come there, and now I see why. Want to stay there a couple of weeks, till we can get your living-rooms straightened out?"

She shook her head. "I've come to your home, Red," said she. "I'm not going to be sent away! Go in and see your patients, and don't bother about me. Cynthia and I will discover a place for me."

His face very red with chagrin, Burns took her in. The downpour of rain had covered all sounds of the car's approach, so that neither the Macauleys on the one side, the Chesters on the other, nor the housekeeper herself, were aware of the arrival of the pair.

"For mercy's sake, Doctor!" cried Cynthia, and hurried across the neat and pleasant kitchen to meet them. "I wasn't expecting you yet for an hour. Mrs. Macauley and Mrs. Chester wasn't either. They was over here ten minutes ago, planning how to get rid o' the folks in there that's insisting on setting and waiting for you to come."

"Never mind them, Cynthia," said her new

mistress, shaking hands. "The Doctor will see them and I will stay with you. I've so much to plan with you. What a pleasant kitchen! And how delicious something smells! Cynthia, I believe I'm hungry!"

"Well, now, you just come and set right down in the dining-room and I'll give you something," cried the housekeeper, delighted.

"That's right, Cynthia," approved Burns, much relieved. "Look after her till I'm free." And he vanished.

"I reckon that'll be a pretty steady job," Cynthia declared, "if I'm to do it 'till he's free.' He won't be free, Mrs. — Burns, till the next time you get him out of town."

She led the way into the dining-room.

"Mrs. Macauley wanted to have you come to dinner there, to-night, and Mrs. Chester wanted you, too. But Mr. Macauley said this was the place for you to have your first dinner in — your own home, and he made the women folks give in. So the table's all set, and I can hurry up dinner so's to have it as soon as the Doctor gets those folks fixed up — if there ain't a lot more by that time. Since Miss Mathewson went I've been answering the telephone, and it seems 'sif the town wouldn't let him have his honeymoon out, they're so crazy to get him back. Now — will you set down and let me give you a bit o' lunch? It's only five o'clock, and I've planned dinner for half-past six."

"It would be a pity to spoil this glorious appetite, Cynthia, though I'm sorely tempted. I think I'll use the time getting freshened up from my long drive — we've come a hundred and sixty miles to-day, through the mud. Then I'll find Bob and be ready to have dinner with the Doctor."

"I'll have to take you round by the porch to get to the Doctor's room — you wouldn't want to go through the office, with such a raft of folks."

Ellen's bag in hand, Cynthia led the way. In at the long window she hurried her, out of the rain which was dashing against it.

"I expect you'll think it smells sort o' doctorish," she said, apologetically. "Opening out of the office, so, it's kind o' hard to keep it from getting that queer smell, 'specially when he's always running in to do things to his hands. But, land! his windows are always open, night and day, so it might be worse."

"I think it's beautifully fresh and pleasant here. Oh, what a bunch of daffodils on the dressing-table! Did you put them there?"

"I did — but 'twas Mrs. Macauley sent 'em over. You'll find clean towels in the bathroom. Oh, and — Mrs. Burns," — Cynthia hesitated, — "the Doctor forgot to say anything about it, but I've fixed up this little room off his for Bobby.

He used to have the little boy sleep right next him, in a crib, but I knew — of course,"— her face crimsoned,— "you wouldn't want ——" She paused helplessly.

But Ellen helped her with quick assent. "I'm so glad the little room is so near. Bob won't be lonely, and I shall love to have him there. I can hardly wait to see him."

Cynthia went away, rejoicing that her arrangements were approved. She was devotedly fond of little Bob, Burns's six-year-old protégé, by him rescued, a year before, from an impending orphan asylum, and now the happy ward of a guardianship as kind as an adoption. She had been somewhat anxious over the child's future status with her employer's wife, but was now quite satisfied that he was not to be kept at arm's length.

"Some would have put him off with me," she said to herself, as she returned to her kitchen, "though I didn't really think it of her that took so much notice of him before. She's a real lady, Mrs. Burns is — and prettier than ever since she married the Doctor, as why shouldn't she be, with him to look pretty for?"

Left alone Ellen looked about her. Yes, this was the room in which he had lived the sleeping portion of his bachelor's life, so long. It gave her an odd sense of what a change it was for him, this having a woman come into his life, share his privacy,— he had so little privacy in his busy days and nights,— and occupy this room of his, this big, square, old-fashioned room with its open windows, the one spot which had been his unassailable place of retreat. She felt almost as if she ought to go and find some other room at once, ought not to take even temporary possession of this, or strew about it her feminine belongings.

The room was somewhat sparsely furnished, containing but the necessary furniture; no draperies at the open windows, few articles on the high old mahogany bureau, an inadequate number of nearly threadbare rugs on the waxed floor, and but three pictures on the walls. She studied these pictures, one after another. One was a little framed photograph of Burns's father and mother, taken sitting together on their vine-covered porch. One was a colour drawing of a scene in Edinburgh, showing a view of Princes Street and the Castle,— one which must have become familiar to him from a residence of some length during the period of his studies abroad. The third picture — it surprised and touched her not a little to find it here — was a fine copy of a famous painting, showing the Christ bending above the couch of a sick man and extending to him his healing touch. The face was one of the best modern conceptions of the Divine personality. She realized that the picture might have meant much to him.

She could hear his voice, as she set about her dressing. He was in his private office, talking with a patient whose deafness caused him to raise his own tones considerably; the closed door between could not keep out all the sound. She felt her invasion of his life more keenly than ever as she realized afresh how close to him her own life was to be lived. Marrying a village doctor, whose home contained also his place of business, was a very different matter from marrying a city physician with a downtown office and a home into which only the telephone ever brought the voice of a patient. It was to be a new and strange experience for them both.

She sat before the dressing-table, having slipped into a little lilac and white negligée. The half-curling masses of her black hair covered her shoulders as she brushed them out — slowly, because she was thinking so busily about it all, and had forgotten to make haste. Suddenly the door leading into the office flew open — and closed as quickly. Steps behind her, pausing, made her turn, to meet her husband's eyes.

He came close. An unmistakably "doctorish" odour accompanied him — an odour not disagreeable but associated with modern means for securing perfect cleanliness. He wore his white jacket, fresh from Cynthia's painstaking hands.   His eyes were very bright, his lips were smiling.

His arms came about her from behind, his head against hers gently forced it back to face the mirror. In it the two pairs of eyes met again, hazel and black.

"To think that I should see *that* reflected from my old glass!" whispered Red Pepper Burns.

CHAPTER II

THE WAY TO ATTAIN AN END

MRS. REDFIELD PEPPER BURNS stood in the doorway of her living-room and studied it with a critical eye. Within the room, on either side, stood her sister Martha, Mrs. James Macauley, and her friend Winifred, Mrs. Arthur Chester. In precisely these same relative positions were they also her neighbours as to their own homes. Their husbands were Red Pepper's best friends, outside those of his own profession. It was appropriate that they should have stood by her during the period of fitting and furnishing that part of the old house which her husband had termed her "quarters."

"It's the loveliest room in this town," declared Winifred Chester, "and I'm going to have all I can do not to be envious."

"I doubt if very many people in this little town will think it the loveliest," said Ellen's sister. "Its browns and blues will be too dull for them, and Ellen's old Turkey carpet too different from their polished floors and 'antique' rugs. By the way,

Ellen, how old do you suppose that carpet is, anyhow?"

"It's been on Aunt Lucy's floors since before the
Civil War. Isn't it beautifully faded? — it fur-
nishes the keynote of the whole room. Isn't it
fortunate that the room should be so long and low,
instead of high and square? Is it a restful room,
girls? That's what I'm after."

"Restful!" Mrs. Chester clasped her hands in a
speaking gesture. "Red will forget every care, the
minute he steps into it. When are you going to
show it to him?"

"To-night, when the fire is lighted and evening
office-hours are over. If he hadn't been so busy
it would have been hard to keep him away, but he
hasn't had an hour to spare even for guessing what
I've been doing."

"I hope he'll have an hour to spare, to stay in it
with you. How you both will hate the sound of
the office-bell and the telephones!"

"I'm going to try hard not to, but I suppose
I shall dread them, in spite of myself," Ellen owned.

"This great couch, facing the fire, with all these
lovely blue silk pillows, is certainly the most
comfortable looking thing I ever saw," sighed
Winifred Chester, casting her plump little figure
into the davenport's roomy depths and clasping
her hands under her head in an attitude of repose.

"If Red doesn't send out word that he's not at home and can't be found, when a call finds him stretched out here, he's a stronger character than I think him."

"Now let's go up and look at the guest-rooms." Ellen led the way, an engaging figure in a fresh white morning dress, her cheeks glowing with colour like a girl's.

"If you didn't know, would you ever dream she had been wife and widow, and had lost her little son?" murmured Winifred in Martha's ear.

Martha Macauley shook her head. "She seems to have gone back and begun all over again. Yet there's a look —— "

Winifred nodded. "Of course there is — a look she wouldn't have had if she hadn't gone through so much. It's given her such a rich sort of bloom."

The guest-rooms were airy, attractive, chintz-hung rooms, one large, one somewhat smaller, but both wearing a hospitable look of readiness.

"I like the gray-and-rose room best," announced Winifred, after a critical survey, as if she were inspecting both rooms for the first time instead of the fortieth. She had made the gray-and-rose chintz hangings herself, delighting in each exquisite yard of the fine imported material.

"I prefer the green-leaf pattern, it looks so cool and fresh." Martha eyed details admiringly. "This is your bachelor's room, you say, Ellen? Oh, you've put a desk in it! The bachelor will want to stay forever. Who do you suppose he will be?"

"The first friend of Red's who comes. He says he's always wanted to ask certain ones, and never had a place to put them, except at the hotel."

"He'd better be careful whom he asks — now. They'll all fall in love with you. By the way, do you know Red has a terribly jealous streak?" Winifred glanced quickly at Ellen as she spoke.

"No — what nonsense! How do you like my idea of a book-shelf by the bed, and a drop-light?"

"Pampering — pure pampering of your bachelors. You'll never be rid of them. But he can be jealous, Ellen."

"What makes you think so? I never saw a trace of it," cried Martha Macauley.

"It's there — you mark my words. He couldn't help it — with his hair and eyes."

Ellen laughed. "Hair and eyes! What about my black locks and eyes? Shall I not make a trustful wife, because I happen to have them? Oh!" — she ran to the window — "there comes the Imp! You'll excuse me if I run down? Red's been away all night and all morning."

She disappeared as the Green Imp's horn vociferated a signal of greeting from far down the road.

"They'll never get time to grow tired of each

other," commented Martha, as the two friends descended the old-time winding staircase. "Isn't this old hall delightful, now? I never realized the possibilities of the house, with this part closed so long."

"One more peep at the living-room, and then we'll go. Isn't it just like Ellen? Such a charming, quiet room, without the least bit of ostentation, yet simply breathing beauty and refinement. She is the most wonderful shopper I know. She made every dollar Red furnished go twice as far as I could. I don't suppose he would let her spend a penny of her own on this house."

"He's too busy to know or care what she does — till he sees it. I'll venture she has slipped in a penny or two. That magnificent piano is hers, you know, — and two or three pieces of furniture. All he'll realize is that it's delightful and that she's in it. It's all so funny, anyhow,— this bringing home a bride and having her fall to work to furnish her own nest."

"She's enjoyed it. I'd like to be on the scene to-night, when she shows it to him."

"No chance of that. When Red does get her to himself for ten minutes he quite plainly prefers to have the rest of us depart. Have you noticed?"

"Yes, indeed. I only hope that state of things will last." And Winifred smiled and sighed at once, as if she were skeptical concerning of the permanency of married bliss.

Office-hours were full ones that evening, and it was quite nine o'clock before R. P. Burns, M. D. closed the door on the last of his patients. The moment he was free he turned to Miss Mathewson, his office nurse, with a deep breath of relief.

"Let's put out the lights and call it off," he said. "Run home and get an hour to yourself before bedtime, and never mind finishing the books. Do you know," — he was smiling down at her, where she sat, a trim white figure at her desk, an assistant who had been his right hand for nine years, and who perhaps knew his moods and tempers better than anybody in the world, though he did not at all realize this, — "do you know, I find it harder to settle down to work again than I thought I should? Curious, isn't it?"

"Not at all curious, Doctor Burns." Miss Mathewson spoke in her usual quiet tone, smiling in return. "It is distracting, even to me, to know that a person so lovely as your wife is under the same roof."

This was much for this most reserved associate of his to say, and Burns recognized it. He regarded her with interested astonishment. "So she's got you, too!" he ejaculated. "I'm mighty glad of that, for it will tend to make you sympathetic with my wish to have an hour to myself — and her —

now and then. I'm to see my home to-night, for the first time, — if —— "

Steps sounded upon the office porch. Burns made a flying leap for the door into his private office, intent on getting to his room and exchanging his working garb for one suited to the evening he meant to spend with Ellen. When he had swiftly but noiselessly closed the door, Miss Mathewson answered the knock.

A tall countryman loomed in the doorway.

"Doctor in?"

"He is in," said the office nurse, who would tell lies to nobody, "but he is engaged. Office-hours are over. Please give me any message for him."

"I'd like to see him," said the countryman, doggedly.

"I don't wish to disturb him unless it is quite necessary," explained Miss Mathewson.

"I call it necessary," said the countryman, "when a fellow has a broken leg. Got him out here in the wagon. Now will you call the Doctor?"

"I surely will," and Miss Mathewson smiled sympathetically.

She called her employer, who came out, frowning, still in his white coat.

"Confound you, Jake," said he, "don't you know it's against the law to break legs or mend them after office-hours?"

Miss Mathewson, in the brief interval consumed by the men in bringing the injured man in from the street, slipped across the hall.

"It will be another hour, Mrs. Burns," said she, at the door of the living-room. "But after that I shall not be here to answer the door or the telephone, and the Doctor can ignore them, if he will."

Ellen rose, smiling, and came across the room to her. The two figures, one in the severe white of a uniform, the other in the filmy, lace-bordered white of a delicate house gown, met in the doorway.

"You dear, kind little person," said Red Pepper's wife, with her warm hand on the nurse's arm, "how good it is of you to care! But I can wait. Can't you stay in here with me, while the Doctor sees his patient?"

"I must help him. It's a broken leg, and I must go this minute," said Miss Mathewson. But she paused for an instant more, looking at Ellen. The nurse was the taller, and looked the older of the two, but the affectionate phrase "little person" had somehow touched a heart which was lonelier even than Ellen guessed — and Ellen guessed much more than Red Pepper had ever done. Red Pepper's wife leaned forward.

"You and I must be good friends," said she, and Miss Mathewson responded with a flush of pleasure. Then the nurse flew back to the office, while Ellen, after listening for a little to the sounds of footsteps in the office, turned back to the fire.

"How does it happen," said she musingly to herself, as she stood looking down into the depths of the glowing heart of it, "that one woman can be so rich and one so poor — under the same roof? She sees more of him than I,— lives her life closer to him, in a way,— and yet I am rich and she is poor. How I wish I could make her happy — as happy as she can be without the one thing that would have made her so. O Red! — and you never saw it!"

The hour went by. The broken leg was set and bandaged, the injured man was conveyed back to the wagon which had brought him; and Red Pepper Burns took a last look at his patient, in the light of the lantern carried by the countryman.

"You've been game as any fighting man, Tom," said he, cheerily. "The drive home'll be no mid-summer-night's-dream, but I see that upper lip of yours is stiff for it. Good-night — and good luck! We'll take care of the luck."

As he turned back up the path the front door of his house swung open. It was a door he had never entered more than once, his offices being in the wing, and the upright portion having been totally unused since he had owned the place. With an exclamation he was up the steps in two leaps, and standing still upon the threshold.

"Come in a little farther, please, dear," said a voice from behind the door, "so I can close it."

Burns shut the door with a bang, and turned upon the figure in the corner. But his extended arm kept his wife away from him. "Let me go and refresh," he begged. "I can't bear to touch you after handling that unwashed lumberjack. Just five minutes and I'll be back."

He was as good as his word. In five minutes he was no longer a busy professional man, but a gentleman of leisure, with hands cleaner than those of any fastidious clubman, and clothes which carried no hint of past usage in other places less chaste than his wife's private living-rooms.

"Now I'm ready for you," he announced, returning. "And I'll be hanged if I'll see another interloper to-night. A man has some rights, if he is a doctor. Morgan, up the street there, is the new man in town, and he has a display of electric lights in front of his office which fairly yells 'come here!' Let 'em go there! I stay here."

He took his wife in his arms and kissed her hungrily, then stood holding her close, his cheek against her hair, in absolute contentment. He seemed to see nothing of the new quarters, though he was now just outside the living-room door, in the hall which ran between the two parts of the house. Presently she drew him into the room.

"Look about you," said she. "Have you no curiosity?"

"Not much, while I have you. Still — by George! Well!"

He stood staring about him, his eyes wide open enough now. From one detail to another his quick, keen-eyed glance roved, lingering an instant on certain points where artful touches of colour relieved the more subdued general tone of the furnishings. The room suggested, above all things, quiet and repose, yet there was a soft and mellow cheer about it which made it anything but sombre. Its browns and blues and ivories wrought out an exquisite harmony. The furniture was simple but solid, the roomy high-backed davenport luxurious with its many pillows. The walls showed a few good pictures — how good, it might not be that Red Pepper fully understand. But he did understand, with every sense, that it was such a room as a man might look upon and be proud to call his home.

But he was silent so long that Ellen looked up at him, to make sure that there was no displeasure in his face. Instead she found there deeper feeling than she expected. He returned her look, and she discovered that he was not finding it easy to tell her what he thought of it all. She led him to the couch and drew him down beside her. He put his arm about her, and with her head upon his shoulder the pair sat for some time in a silence which Ellen would not end.   But at length, looking into the fire, his head resting against hers, Burns broke the stillness.

"I suppose I'm an impressionable chap," he said, "but I wasn't prepared for just this.   I knew it would be a beautiful room, if you saw to it, but I had no possible notion how beautiful it would be.   There is just one thing about it that breaks me up a bit. Perhaps you won't understand, but I can't help wishing I could have done the work for you instead of you for me.   It isn't the work, either, it's the — love."

"And you couldn't have spared enough of that to furnish a room with?"

He laughed, drawing her even closer then he had held her before.   "I'll trust you to corner me, every time," he said.   "Yes, I could have spared love enough — no doubt of that.   But it seems as if it were the man who should put the house in order for the woman he brings home."

"You have excellent taste," said she demurely, "but I never should credit you with the discriminations and fastidiousnesses of a decorator.   And why should you want to take away from me the happiness of making my own nest?   Don't you know it's the home-maker who finds most joy in the home?   Yet — it's the home-comer I want to have find the joy. Do you think you can rest in this room, Red?"

He drew a deep, contented breath. "Every minute I am in it. And from the time I first begin to think about it, coming toward it. Home! It's Paradise! This great, deep, all-embracing blue thing we're sitting in — is it made of down and velvet?"

"Precisely that. Velvet to cover it, down in the pillows. I hope you'll have many a splendid nap here."

"You'll spoil me," he declared, "if you let me sleep here. I'm used to catching forty winks in my old leather chair in the office, while I wait for a summons."

Her face grew very tender. "I know. James Macauley has told me more than one tale of hours spent there, when you needed sounder sleep. It's a hard life, and it's going to be my delight to try to make it easier."

Red Pepper sat up. "It's not a hard life, dear,— it's one of many compensations. And now that I have one permanent compensation I'm never going to think I'm being badly used, no matter what goes wrong. Come, let's stroll about. I want to look at every separate thing. This piano — surely the sum I gave you didn't cover that? It looks like one of the sort that are not bought two-for-a-quarter."

"No, Red, that was mine.   It came from my old home with Aunt Lucy — that and the desk-book-case, and two of the chairs.   And Aunt Lucy gave me this big rug, made from the old drawing-room carpet.   I built the whole room on the rug colour-ings.   You don't mind, do you, dear? — my using these few things that belonged to me in my girlhood, in South Carolina?"

"In your girlhood?   Not — in your Washington life?"

"No, Red."

She looked straight up into his eyes, reading in the sudden glowing of them under their heavy brows the feeling he could not conceal that he could bear to have about his house no remote suggestion of her former marriage.

"All right, dearest," he answered quickly.   "I'm a brute, I know, but — you're mine now.   Will you play for me?   I believe I'm fond of music."

"Of course you are.   But first, let's go upstairs. I'm almost as proud of our guest-rooms as of this."

"Guest-rooms?" repeated Burns, a few minutes later, when he had examined everything in the living-room and pronounced all things excellent. "We're to have guests, are we?   But not right away?"

"I thought you'd be eager to entertain those

bachelor friends you mentioned, so I lost no time in getting a second room ready for them."

"Well, I don't know." Burns was mounting the stairs, his arm about his wife's shoulders. "By the way, Ellen, I don't believe I ever went up these stairs before. Comfortable, aren't they? I'm glad there's covering on them. I never like to hear people racketing up and down bare stairs, be they never so polished and fine. That comes of my instincts for quiet on my patients' account, I suppose. About the guests — we don't need to have any for a year or two, do we?"

"Why, Red!" Ellen began to laugh. "I thought you were the most hospitable man in the world."

"All in good time," agreed her husband, comfortably. He looked in at the door of the gray-and-rose room, as he spoke. "Well, well!" he ejaculated. "Well, well!"

And again he was silent, staring. When he spoke:

"Would you mind going over there and sitting down in that willow chair with the high back?" he requested.

His wife acceded, and crossing the room smiled back at him from the depths of the white willow chair, her dark head against its cushioning of soft, mingled tints of pale gray and glowing rose. Red Pepper nodded at her.

"I thought so," said he. "This is no guest-room. This is your room."

"Oh, no, dear. My place is downstairs, with you — unless — you don't want me there."

He crossed the room also and stood before her, his hands thrust into his pockets. "This is your room," he repeated. "It's easy enough to recognize it. It looks just like you. I've been uncomfortable about you downstairs, whenever I had to leave you. You'll be safe here, with every window wide open."

She looked up at him, mutely smiling, but something in her eyes told him that all was not yet said. Red Pepper leaned still lower and kissed her.

"It will be easy enough to have an extension of the telephone brought up here," he added — and found her arms about his neck. But she shook her head. "Don't settle it so quickly," she urged.

"You said there was another guest-room," he reminded her presently. "The bachelor's room. Is it next door?"

They went together to look at the bachelor's room. Burns surveyed it with satisfaction.

"The jolliest room for the purpose I ever saw," he confessed. "And I know the bachelor who will sleep in it. He's downstairs now, in the small room out of ours."

"Bob? Why, Red —— "

"We'll have a door cut through. The telephones shall be in there, then they won't disturb you. They won't bother Bob a minute. And when I come in at 2 A. M. I can slip in here, shove the boy over against the wall, and be asleep in two minutes."

"Red! All my preparations for the bachelor! The desk,— the reading-light by the bed —— "

"They suit me admirably. I never saw a better arrangement. The two rooms together make a perfect suite — when the door is cut through."

"And where will you put our guests? There's only one more room on this floor, of any size."

"Let's go and see."

Catching up a brass candlestick from the bachelor's desk, Burns lit it and proceeded to explore, Ellen following. There were dancing lights in her eyes as she watched him.

"Here's your fourth room," said he, throwing open a door at the back of the hall.

"This box? It can't be made a really comfortable room, even if I do my best with it. Your bachelor will not stay long."

"Best not make him too comfortable. Nobody wants him to stay long." And Red Pepper closed the door again, with an air of having settled the matter to his entire satisfaction. "Besides," he added, "if he's really a desirable chap, and we want him around more than a day or two, he can bunk in my old room downstairs. When he's not there I'll use it for an annex to my offices. Somebody's always needing to be put to bed for an hour or two. Amy Mathewson will revel in that extra space. Her long suit is making people comfortable, and smoothing the upper sheet under their chins."

"Redfield Pepper, please consider this carefully," said his wife, as they returned to the gray-and-rose room. "Remember how long you have had that downstairs room,— you are attached to it, perhaps, more than you think. You have been a bachelor yourself a good while —— "

"And am supposed to be old and set in my ways," interpolated her listener. He stood before her with folded arms, a judicial expression on his brow. Beneath his coppery hair his black eyebrows drew together a little above a pair of hazel eyes which sparkled with a whimsical light which somewhat impaired the gravity of the expression.

"You are wonted to your ways — naturally," Ellen pursued. "It will not be so convenient for you, having your rooms up here. I am quite contented there, with you, and not in the least afraid with Cynthia sleeping down there too — and the little bachelor. Think twice, Red, before you decide on this arrangement."

He glanced at the wall between the two rooms. "Where would be a good place to have the door cut through? What's behind that curtain? A clothes-press?"

He advanced to the curtain and swept it aside. It hung in a doorway, and was of a heavy gray material, with an applied border of the gray-and-rose chintz. As he moved it light burst through from the other side of the wall, and Burns found himself looking into the "bachelor's room" next door.

He turned, with a shout of laughter. "You witch!" he cried, and returning to his wife laid a hand on either richly colouring cheek, gently forcing her face upward, so that he could look directly into it. "You meant it, all the while!"

"Don't be too sure of that. If this room looks like me, the one downstairs certainly looks like you. I don't want to take you out of your proper environment."

"My environment!" he repeated, and laughed. "What is it, now, do you think? Not bachelor apartments, still?"

But she persisted, gently. "Keep the downstairs room, dear, just as it is. Don't make it a public room, except for necessity. Sometimes you'll be glad to take refuge there, just as you're used to doing. Leave those three pictures on your walls, and look at them often, as you've always done. And be sure of this, Red: I shall never be hurt, when you show me that you want to fight something out alone, there. It must be your own and private place, just as if I hadn't come."

Sober now, he stood looking straight down into her eyes, which gave him back his look as straightly. After a minute he spoke with feeling:

"Thank you, dearest. And bless you for understanding so well. At the same time I'm confident you understand one thing more: That by leaving a man his liberty you surely hold him tightest!"

CHAPTER III

BURNS DOES HIS DUTY

"EXCUSE me for coming in on you at breakfast," Martha Macauley, Ellen's sister and next-door neighbour, apologized, one morning in late May. "But I wanted to catch Red before he got away, and I saw, for a wonder, that there was no vehicle before the door."

"Come in, come in," urged Burns, while Ellen smiled a greeting at her sister, a round-faced, fair-haired, energetic young woman, as different as possible from Ellen's own type. "Have a chair." He rose to get it for her, napkin in hand. "Will you sit down and try one of Cynthia's magnificent muffins?"

"No, thank you. And I'll plunge into my errand, for I know at any minute you may jump up and run away. You may, anyway, when you hear what I want! Promise me, Red, that you won't go until you've heard me out."

"What a reputation I have for speed at escape!" But Burns glanced at his watch as he spoke. "Fire away, Martha. Five minutes you shall have —

and I'm afraid no more. I'm due at the hospital in half an hour."

"Well, I want to give a reception for you." Martha took the plunge. "I know you hate them, but Ellen doesn't,— at least, she knows such things are necessary, no matter how much you may wish they weren't. I don't mean a formal reception, of course. I know how you both feel about trying to ape city society customs, in a little suburban village like this. But I do think, since you had such a quiet wedding, you ought to give people a chance to come in and greet you, as a newly married pair."

Burns's eyes met his wife's across the table. There was a comical look of dismay in his face. "I thought," said he, "you and I agreed to cut out all that sort of thing. As for being a newly married pair — we aren't. We've been married since the beginning of time. I can't conceive of existence apart from Mrs. Redfield Pepper Burns, nor recall any period of my life when she wasn't a part of it."

"You've been married just seven weeks and three days, however," retorted his sister-in-law, with a touch of impatience, though she smiled, "and not a quarter of the people in town have ever met Ellen. You'll find that it's not the same, now that you're married. They won't flock to your office, just out of admiration for you, unless you show them some attention."

Burns chuckled. "Won't they? By George, I wish they wouldn't! Then I could find time to spend an uninterrupted hour with my wife, at least once a day."

"Do be reasonable, Red. Ellen, will you make him see it's a very simple thing I'm asking of him? Just to stand by you and shake hands for a couple of hours. Then he can go out and stand on his head on the lawn, if he wants to."

"To relieve the tension?" her victim suggested. "That's an excellent idea — real compensation. But as the blood will be all at the top, anyway, after two hours' effort at being agreeable, saying the same idiotic things over and over, and grinning steadily all the time, I think I'd prefer soaking my head under a pump."

"Do what pleases you, if you'll only let me have my way."

Burns looked at Ellen again. "What do you say, dear? Must these things be? Do you want to be 'received'?"

"Martha has set her heart on it," said she, gently, "and it's very dear of her to want to take the trouble. She promises really to make it very informal."

"Informal! I wish I knew what that word meant. Don't I have to wear my spike-tail?"

"I'm afraid you do — since Martha wants it in the evening. The men in a place like this are not available for afternoon affairs."

"If I must dress, then I don't see what there is informal about it," argued her husband, with another glance at his watch. "My idea of informality is not a white necktie and pumps. But I suppose I'll have to submit."

He came around the table, and Ellen rose to receive his parting kiss. With his arm about her shoulder, and his chin — that particularly resolute chin — touching her hair, he looked at Martha. "Go on with your abominable society stunt," said he. "I'll agree to be there — if I can."

His eyes sparkled with mischief, as Martha jumped up, crying anxiously:

"Oh, that's just it, Red! You *must* be there! We can't have any excuses of operations or desperately sick patients. We never yet had you at so much as a family dinner that you didn't get up and go away, or else weren't even there at all. Even your wedding had to be postponed three hours. That won't do at this kind of an affair. Ellen can't be a bridal pair, all by herself!"

"Can't she?" His arm tightened about his wife's shoulders. "Well, I'll tell you what I'll do. If I have to leave suddenly I'll take her with me. That'll make it all right and comfortable. If you and Jim will retire too, the company can have a glorious time talking us over."

He stooped, whispered something in Ellen's ear, laughing as he did so, then kissed her, nodded at Martha, and departed. From the other side of the closed door came back to them a gay, whistled strain from a popular Irish song.

"He's just as hopeless as ever," Martha complained. "I thought you would have begun to have some effect on him, by this time. The trouble is, he's been a bachelor so long and has got into such careless notions of having his own way about everything, you're going to have a bad time getting him just to behave like an ordinary human being."

"What an outlook!" Ellen laughed, coming over to her sister, and stopping on the way to help little Bob insert a refractory napkin in its silver ring. "Perhaps I'd better not waste much time trying to make him over. He really suits me pretty well, as he is,— and it doesn't strike me he's so different from the average man, when it comes to receptions. Is Jim enthusiastic over this one?"

"Oh, Jim isn't making any fuss about it," evaded Martha. "He'll be good and amiable, when the time comes. Of course, any man likes better just having a group of men smoking round the fire, or sitting down to a stag dinner, but Jim understands the necessity of doing some things just because they're expected. I really think that having a perfectly informal affair of this sort is letting them off easily. They might have had to stand a series of 'At Homes.'"

"Not in this little place. Everybody would have come to the first one, and there would have been nobody left for the rest. As it is, you will have a houseful, won't you? It's lovely of you to do it, Martha dear, and Red and I will be good, and stand in line as long as you want us."

"And you won't let him get away?"

"He won't try,— though if an urgent call comes, it's not I who can keep him. But don't worry about that. It doesn't always happen, I suppose."

"Pretty nearly always. But I'll hope for the best."

Mrs. Macauley went away with her head full of plans for the success of the affair she was so sure ought to take place. It was difficult for her to understand how Ellen, who had known so much of the best social life in a city where there is no end to the round of formal entertaining, could be now as indifferent as Martha understood she really was to all experience of the sort. It was association with Redfield Pepper Burns which had done it, Martha supposed. But was he to do all the influencing, and Ellen to do none? It looked like it — to Martha.

Left alone with Bob, Ellen made him ready for

the little village kindergarten which he had lately begun to attend. Before he went he put up both arms, and she bent to him.

"I'm going to be a pretty good boy to-day, Aunt Ellen," said he. "I promised Uncle Red I would. But I don't like to skip in the circle with girls. Why need I?"

"Would you rather skip with boys, dear?"

"Lots rather. But the girls keep asking me. Why do they, when I don't ask them?"

Ellen smiled down into the questioning little face, its dark eyes looking seriously up into hers through long and curly lashes. Bob was undoubtedly a handsome little lad, and the reason why the girls — discerning small creatures, true to their femininity — should be persistent in inviting him to be their partner was obvious enough.

"Because that's part of the skipping game, Bobbsy. I'd ask the girls sometimes — and, do you know, I think it would be fine to ask some of the little girls whom the other boys don't ask. Do you know any?"

Bob considered. "I guess I do. But why do I have to ask them?"

"Because they're not having as much fun as the others. You wouldn't like never to be asked by anybody, would you?"

"I don't care 'bout any girls ever asking me,"

Bob insisted stoutly. "I like boy games better —
'circus' and 'grandfather's barn.' Only they let
the girls play those too," he added, disgustedly.

He started away. But he came back again to
say, soberly, "I'll ask Jennie Hobson, if you want me
to, Aunt Ellen. She's some like a boy, anyway.
Her hair's cut tight to her head — and her eyes are
funny. They don't look at you the same."

"Do ask her, Bob. And tell me how she liked it."
And Ellen looked affectionately after the small,
straight little figure trudging away down the
street.

Martha's plans for her reception went on merrily.
On the day set she came hurrying over before breakfast, to administer to her brother-in-law a final
admonition concerning the coming evening.

"I hope this isn't going to be the busiest day of
your life?" she urged Burns.

"It's bound to be, — getting things clear for
to-night," he assured her, good-humouredly.

"Promise me you won't let anything short of
a case of life or death keep you away?"

"It's as serious as that, is it? All right, I'll be
on hand, unless the heavens fall."

He was good as his word, and at the appointed
hour his hostess, keeping an agitated watch on her
neighbour's house, saw him arrive, in plenty of time
to dress. She drew a relieved breath.

"I didn't expect it," she said to James Macauley, her husband.

"Oh, Red's game. He won't run away from this, much as he hates it. Like the rest of us married men, he knows when dodging positively won't do," and Macauley sighed as he settled his tie before the reception-room mirror, obtaining a view of himself with some difficulty, on account of the towering masses of flowers and foliage which obscured the glass.

When Burns and Ellen came across the lawn, Martha flew to meet them.

"You splendid people! Who wouldn't want to have a reception for such a pair?"

"We flatter ourselves we do look pretty fine," Burns admitted, eying his wife with satisfaction. "That gauzy gray thing Ellen has on strikes me as the bulliest yet. If I could just get her to wear a pink rose in her hair I'd be satisfied."

"A rose in her hair! Aren't you satisfied with that exquisite coral necklace? That gives the touch of colour she needs. The rose would overdo it — and wouldn't match, besides." Martha spoke with scorn.

"Yes, a rose would be maudlin, Red; can't you see it?" James Macauley gave his opinion with a wink at his friend. "With the necklace your wife is a dream. With a rose added she'd be a — waking up! Trust 'em, that's my advice. When they get to talking about a 'touch of' anything, that's the time to leave 'em alone.   A touch of colour is not a daub."

"Who's lecturing on art?" queried Arthur Chester, from the doorway.

His wife, Winifred, entering before him, cried out at sight of the pale gray gauze gown.

"O Ellen! I thought I looked pretty well, till I caught sight of you.   Now I feel crude!"

"Absurd," said Ellen, laughing.   "You are charming in that blue."

"There they go again," groaned Macauley to Burns.   "Winifred feels crude, when she looks at Ellen.   Why?   I don't feel crude when I look at you or Art Chester.   Neither of you has so late a cut on your dress-coat as I, I flatter myself.   I feel anything but crude.   And I don't want a rose in my hair, either."

"You're a self-satisfied prig," retorted Burns. "Hullo!   Somebody's coming.   Tell me what to do, Martha.   Do I run to meet them and rush them up to Ellen, or do I display a studied indifference? I never 'received' at a reception in my life."

"Get in line there," instructed Macauley.   "Martha and I'll greet them first and pass them on to you. Don't look as if you were noting symptoms and don't absent-mindedly feel their pulses.   It's not done, outside of consulting rooms."

"I'll try to remember." R. P. Burns, M. D. resignedly took his place, murmuring in Ellen's ear, as the first comers appeared at the door, "Promise you'll make this up to me, when it's over. I shall have to blow off steam, somehow. Will you help?"

She nodded, laughing. He chuckled, as an idea popped into his head; then drew his face into lines of propriety, and stood, a big, dignified figure — for Red Pepper could be dignified when the necessity was upon him — beside the other graceful figure at his side, suggesting an unfailing support of her grace by his strength to all who looked at them that night. He had declared himself ignorant of all conventions, but neither jocose James Macauley nor fastidious Arthur Chester, observing him, could find any fault with their friend in this new rôle. As the stream of their townspeople passed by, each with a carefully prepared word of greeting, Burns was ready with a quick-wittedly amiable rejoinder. And whenever it became his duty to present to his wife those who did not know her, he made of the act a little ceremony which seemed to set her apart as his own in a way which roused no little envy of her, if he had but known it, in the breasts of certain of the feminine portion of the company.

"You're doing nobly. Keep it up an hour longer and you shall be let off," said Macauley to Burns, at a moment when both were free.

"Oh, I'm having the time of my life," Burns assured him grimly, mopping a warm brow and thrusting his chin forward with that peculiar masculine movement which suggests momentary relief from an encompassing collar. "Why should anybody want to be released from such a soul-refreshing diversion as this? I've lost all track of time or sense,— I just go on grinning and assenting to everything anybody says to me. I couldn't discuss the simplest subject with any intelligence whatever — I've none left."

"You don't need any. Decent manners and the grin will do. Had anything to eat yet?"

"What's got to be eaten?" Burns demanded, unhappily.

"Punch, and ices — and little cakes, I believe. Cheer up, man, you don't have to eat 'em, if you don't want to."

"Thanks for that. I'll remember it of you when greater favours have been forgotten. Martha has her eye on me — I must go. I'll get even with Martha for this, some time." And the guest of honour, stuffing his handkerchief out of sight and thrusting his coppery, thick locks back from his martyred brow, obeyed the summons.

The next time Macauley caught sight of him, he was assiduously supplying a row of elderly ladies with ices and little cakes, and smiling at them most engagingly. They were looking up at him with that grateful expression which many elderly ladies unconsciously assume when a handsome and robust young man devotes himself to them. Burns found this task least trying of all his duties during that long evening, for one of the row reminded him of his own mother, to whom he was a devoted son, and for her sake he would give all aging women of his best. Something about this little group of un-attended guests, all living more or less lonely lives, as he well knew them in their homes, touched his warm heart, and he lingered with them to the neglect of younger and fairer faces, until his host, again at his elbow, in a strenuous whisper admon-ished him:

"For heaven's sake, Red, don't waste any more of that rare sweetness on the desert air. Go and lavish your Beau Brummel gallantry on the wives of our leading citizens. Those new Winterbournes have sackfuls of money — and a chronic invalid or two always in the family, I'm told. A little atten-tion there ——"

"Clear out," Burns retorted shortly, and deliber-ately sat down beside the little, white-haired old lady who reminded him of his mother. As he had been standing before, this small act was significant, and Macauley, with a comprehending chuckle, moved away again.

"Might have known that wouldn't work," he assured himself. He strolled over to Ellen, and when, after some time, he succeeded in getting her for a moment to himself, he put an interested question.

"What do you think of your husband as a society man? A howling success, eh? He's been sitting for one quarter of an hour by the side of old Mrs. Gillis. And a whole roomful of devoted patients, past and future, looking daggers at him because he ignores them. How's that for business policy, eh? Can't you bring him to his senses?"

"Are you sure they're looking daggers? I passed Mrs. Gillis and Red just now, and thought they made a delightful pair. As for business policy, Jim,— a man who would be good to an old lady would be good to a young one. Isn't that the natural inference, — if you must think about business at all at such an affair. I prefer not to think about it at all."

"You may not be thinking about it, but you're capturing friends, right and left. I've been watching you, and knew by the expression on the faces of those you were talking to that you were gathering them in and nailing them fast. How does a woman like you do it? — that's what I'd like to know!"

"Go and do your duty like a man, Jimmy. Flattering the members of your own family is not a part of it." Dismissing him with a smile which made him more than ever eager for her company, she turned away, to devote herself, as her husband was doing, to the least attractive of the guests.

The evening wore away at last, and at a reasonably early hour the hosts were free. The last fellow citizen had barely delivered his parting speech and taken himself off when Red Pepper Burns turned a handspring in the middle of the deserted room, and came up grinning like a fiend.

"Good-bye — good-bye — 'tis a word I love to speak," he warbled, and seizing his wife kissed her ardently on either cheek.

"Hear — hear!" applauded James Macauley, returning from the hall in time to see this expression of joy. "May we all follow your excellent example?"

"You may not." Red Pepper frowned fiercely at Mr. Macauley, approaching with mischievous intent. "Keep off!"

"She's my sister-in-law," defended Macauley, continuing to draw near, and smiling broadly.

"All the more reason for you to treat her with respect." Burns's arm barred the way.

Macauley stopped short with an unbelieving chuckle. Arthur Chester, Winifred, his wife, and Martha Macauley, coming in from the dining-room together, gazed with interest at the scene before them. Ellen, herself smiling, looked at her husband rather as if she saw something in him she had never seen before. For it was impossible not to perceive that he was not joking as he prevented Macauley from reaching his wife.

"Great snakes! he's in earnest!" howled Macauley, stopping short. "He won't let me kiss his wife, when I'm the husband of her sister. Go 'way, man, and cool that red head of yours. Anybody'd think I was going to elope with her!"

"Think what you like," Burns retorted, coolly, "so long as you keep your distance with your foolery. You or any other man."

"Red, you're not serious!" This was Martha. "Can't you trust Ellen to preserve her own —— "

"Dead line? Yes — in my absence. When I'm on the spot I prefer to play picket-duty myself. I may be eccentric. But that's one of my notions, and I've an idea it's one of hers, too."

"Better get her a veil, you Turk."

Macauley walked away with a very red face, at which Burns unexpectedly burst into a laugh, and his good humour came back with a rush.

"Look here, you people. Forget my heroics and come over to our house. I'll give you something to take the taste of those idiotic little cakes out of your hungry mouths. No refusals! I'm your best friend, Jim Macauley, and you know it, so come along and don't act like a small boy who's had his candy taken away from him. You've plenty of candy of your own, you know."

He was his gay self again, and bore them away with him on the wave of his boyish spirits. Across the lawn and into the house they went, the six, and were conducted into the living-room and bidden settle down around the fireplace.

"Start a fire, Jim, and get a bed of cannel going with a roar. You'll find the stuff in that willow basket. Open all the windows, Ches. Then all make yourselves comfortable and await my operations. I promise you a treat — from my point of view."

And he rushed away.

"It's my private opinion," growled Macauley, beginning sulkily to lay the fire, "that that fellow is off his head. He always did seem a trifle cracked, and to-night he's certainly dippy. What's he going to do with a fire, at 11 P. M., on a May evening, I'd like to know?"

"Whatever it is, it will be refreshing." Winifred Chester, reckless of her delicate blue evening gown, curled herself up in a corner of the big davenport and laid her head luxuriously down among the pillows. "Oh, I'm so tired," she sighed. "Seems to me I never heard so many stupid things said, in one evening, in my life."

Arthur Chester, having thrown every window wide

— though he discreetly drew the curtains over those which faced the street — sat down in a great winged chair of comfortable cushioning, and stretched his legs in front of him as far as they would go, his arms clasped behind his head. He also drew a deep sigh of content.

"I don't recall," said he, wearily, "that I have sat down once during the entire evening."

"How ridiculous!" cried Martha Macauley, bristling. "If you didn't, it was your own fault. I took away hardly any chairs, and I arranged several splendid corners just on purpose for those who wished to sit."

"As there were a couple of hundred people, and not over a couple of dozen chairs —— " began Chester, dryly.

But Martha interrupted him. "I never saw such a set. Just as if you hadn't been going to affairs like this one all your lives,— and Ellen, especially, must have been at hundreds of them in Washington, — and now you're all disgusted with having to bear up under just one little informal —— "

"Cheer up, my children," called Burns, reëntering. He was garbed in white, which his guests saw after a moment to be a freshly laundered surgical gown, covering him from head to foot, the sleeves reaching only to his elbows, beneath which his bare arms gleamed sturdily. He bore a wire broiler in one hand, and a platter of something in the other, and his face wore an expression of content.

"Beefsteak, by all that's crazy!" shouted James Macauley, eying the generous expanse of raw meat upon the platter with undisguised delight. He forgot his sulkiness in an instant, and slapped his friend upon the back with a resounding blow. "Bully for Red!" he cried.

"Well, well! Of all the wild ideas!" murmured Arthur Chester. But he sat up in his chair, and his expression grew definitely more cheerful.

Winifred laughed out with anticipation. "Oh, how good that will taste!" she exclaimed, hugging herself in her own pretty arms. "It is just what we want, after wearing ourselves out being agreeable. Who but Red would ever think of such a thing, at this time of night?"

"I believe it will taste good," and Martha Macauley laid her head back at last against the encompassing comfort of the chair she sat in, and for the first time relaxed from the duties of hostess and the succeeding defence of her hospitality.

"Don't you want my help, Red?" his wife asked him, at his elbow.

He turned and looked at the gray gauze gown. "I should say not," said he. "Lie back, all of you, and take your ease, which you have richly earned, while I play *chef*. Nothing will suit me better.

I'm boiling over with restrained emotion, and this will work it off. Lie back, while I imagine that it's one of the male guests who bored me whom I'm grilling now. I'll do him to a turn!"

He proceeded with his operations, working the quick fire of cannel which Macauley had started into a glowing bed of hot coals. He improvised from the andirons a rack for his broiler, and set the steak to cooking. While he heated plates, sliced bread, and brought knives, forks, and napkins, he kept an experienced eye upon his broiler, and saw that it was continually turned and shifted, in order to get the best results. And presently he was laying his finished product upon the hot platter, seasoning it, applying a rich dressing of butter, and, at last, preparing with a flourish of the knife to carve it.

It was at this to-be-expected moment that the office-bell rang. Miss Mathewson summoned her employer, and Burns stayed only to serve his guests, before he left them hungrily consuming his offering and bewailing his departure.

"Only," Martha Macauley said, "we ought to be thankful that for once he got through an evening without being called out."

Ellen had placed her husband's portion where it would keep hot for him, and the others had nearly finished consuming their own, when Burns came in. He made for the fire, amid the greetings and praises of his guests, and served his own plate with the portion remaining on the platter, covering it liberally with the rich gravy. Then he cut and buttered two thick slices of bread and laid them on the plate.

"Sit down, sit down, man!" urged Macauley, as his host rose to his feet. "We're waiting to see you enjoy this magnificent result of your cookery. It's the best steak I've had in a blue moon."

"If you'll excuse me, I'm going to take mine in the office," Burns explained. "Can't leave my patient just yet." And he went away again, carrying his plate, napkin over his arm.

Five minutes later Macauley, putting down his empty plate, got up and strolled out into the hall. A moment afterward he was heard abruptly closing the office door, saying, "Oh, I beg pardon!" Then he returned to the company. He was whistling softly as he came, his hands in his pockets and his eyebrows lifted.

"He *is* dippy," he said, solemnly. "No man in his senses would act like that."

"You eavesdropper, what did you see?" Winifred Chester looked at him expectantly.

"I saw the worst-looking specimen of tramp humanity who has come under my observation for a year, with a bandage over one eye. He is sitting in that big chair with a plate and napkin in his lap, and his ugly mouth is full of beefsteak."

"And isn't Red having any?" cried Martha, with a glance at the empty platter.

"Not a smell.   He's standing up by the chimney-piece, looking the picture of contentment — the idiot.   But he modified his benevolent expression long enough to give me a glare, when he saw me looking in.   That's the second glare I've had from him to-night, and I'm going home.   I can't stand incurring his displeasure a third time in one day. Come, Martha, let's get back to our happy home — what there is left of it after the fray.   We'll send over a plate of little cakes for the master of the house. A couple of dozen of them may fill up that yawning cavity of his.   Of all the foolishness!"

CHAPTER IV

A RED HEAD

"MARRIAGE," said James Macauley, looking thoughtfully into his coffee cup, as he sat opposite his wife, Martha, at the breakfast-table, "is supposed to change a man radically. The influence of a good and lovely woman can hardly be overestimated. But the question is, can the temper of a red-headed explosive ever be rendered uninflammable?"

"What are you talking about?" Martha inquired, with interest. "Ellen and Red? Red *is* changed. I never saw him so dear and tractable."

"Dear and tractable, is he? Have you happened to encounter him in the last twenty-four hours?"

"No. What's the matter? He and Ellen can't possibly have had any — misunderstanding? And if they had, they wouldn't tell you about it."

"Well, they may not have had a misunderstanding, but if Ellen succeeds in understanding him through the present crisis she'll prove herself a remarkable woman. As near as I can make it out, Red is mad, fighting mad, clear through, with somebody or something, and he can no more disguise it than he ever could. I don't suppose it's with anybody at home, of course, but it makes him anything but an angel, there or anywhere else."

"Where did you see him? Hush — Mary's coming!"

Macauley waited obediently till the maid had left the room again. Then he proceeded. He had not begun upon the present subject until the children had gone away, leaving the father and mother alone together.

"I ran into his office last night, after those throat-tablets he gives me, and heard him at the telephone in the private office. Couldn't help hearing him. He was giving the everlasting quietus to somebody, and I thought he'd burn out the transmitter."

"Jim! Red doesn't swear any more. He surely hasn't taken it up again?"

"He didn't do any technical swearing, perhaps, but he might as well. He can put more giant-powder into the English language without actually breaking any commandments than anybody I ever heard. When he came out he had that look of his — you know it of old — so that if I'd been a timid chap I'd have backed out. He gave me my throat-tablets without so much as answering my explanation of how I came to be out of them so soon. Then I got away, I assure you. He had no use for me."

"He's probably all right this morning. Ellen could quiet him down."

"She didn't get the chance. The light in his old room burned all night,— and you know he's not sleeping there now."

"Well, I'm sorry for her." Martha rose, her brow clouded. "But I'd never dare to ask her what the trouble was, and she'll never tell, so there it is."

"It certainly is — right there. Oh, well, he'll get over it, if you give him time. Queer, what a combination of big heart and red head he is."

At the moment of this discussion the red head was still in the ascendency. R. P. Burns, M. D., had come out of his old quarters downstairs that morning with lips set grimly together, heavy gloom upon his brow. He met his wife at the breakfast-table with an effort at a smile in response to her bright look, and kissed her as tenderly as usual, but it was an automatic tenderness, as she was quick to recognize. He replied monosyllabically to her observations concerning matters usually of interest to him, but he evidently had no words to spare, and after a little she gave over all effort to draw him out. Instead, she and Bob held an animated discussion on certain kindergarten matters, while Red Pepper swallowed his breakfast in silence, gulped down two cups of strong coffee, and left the table with only a murmured word of apology.

"Red,—— " His wife's voice followed him.

He turned, without speaking.

"Do you mind if I drive into town with you this morning?"

He nodded, and turned again, striding on into his office and closing the door with a bang. She understood that his nod meant acquiescence with her request, rather than affirmation as to his objecting to her company. She kept close watch over the movements of the Green Imp, suspecting that in his present mood Burns might forget to call her, and when the car came down the driveway she was waiting on the office steps.

It would have been an ill-humoured man indeed, whose eyes could have rested upon her standing there and not have noted the charm of her graceful figure, her face looking out at him from under a modishly attractive hat. Ellen's smile, from under the shadowing brim, was as whole-heartedly sweet as if she were meeting the look of worshipful comradeship which usually fell upon her when she joined her husband on any expedition whatever. Instead, she encountered something like a glower from the hazel eyes, which did, however, as at breakfast, soften for an instant at the moment of meeting hers.

"Jump in! I'm in a hurry," was his quite needless command, for she was ready to take her place the instant the car drew to a standstill, and the delay she made him was hardly appreciable.

In silence they drove to town, and at a pace which took them past everything with which they came up, from lumbering farm-wagon to motor-cars far more powerful and speedy than the Imp. Ellen found herself well blown about by the wind they made, though there was none stirring, and wished she had been dressed for driving instead of for shopping. But the trip, if breezy, was brief, though it did not at once land her at her destination.

Drawing up before a somewhat imposing residence, on the outskirts of the city, Burns announced: "Can't take you in till I've made this call," and stopped his engine with a finality which seemed to indicate that he should be in no haste to start it again.

"It doesn't matter in the least. I shall enjoy sitting here," his wife responded, still outwardly unruffled by his manner. She looked in vain for his customary glance of leave-taking, and watched him stride away up the walk to the house with a sense of wonder that even his back could somehow look so aggressive.

She had not more than settled herself when a handsome roadster appeared rushing rapidly down the road from the direction of the city and came to a stop, facing her, before the house. She recognized in the well-groomed figure which stepped out, case in hand, one of the city surgeons with whom her husband was often closely associated in his hospital work, Dr. Van Horn. He was a decade older than Red, possessed a strikingly impressive personality, and looked, to the last detail, like a man accustomed to be deferred to.

Descending, he caught sight of Ellen, and came across to the Imp, hat in hand, and motoring-glove withdrawn.

"Ah, Mrs. Burns,— accompanying your husband on this matchless morning? He is a fortunate man. You don't mind the waiting? My wife thinks there is nothing so unendurable,— she has no patience with the length of my calls."

"I've not had much experience, as yet," Ellen replied, looking into the handsome, middle-aged face before her, and thinking that the smile under the close-clipped, iron-gray moustache was one which could be cynical more easily than it could be sympathetic. "But, so far, I find the waiting, in such weather, very endurable. I often bring a book, and then it never matters, you know."

"Of course not. You are familiar with Balzac's 'Country Doctor'? There's a tribute to men like your husband, who devote their lives to the humble folk." He glanced toward the house. "I mustn't keep my colleague waiting, even for the pleasure of a chat with you.   He's not — you'll pardon me — so good a waiter as yourself!"

He went away, smiling.   Ellen looked after him with a little frown of displeasure.   From the first moment of meeting him, some months ago, she had not liked Dr. James Van Horn.   He was the city's most fashionable surgeon, she knew, and had a large practice among folk the reverse of "humble." She had seen in his eyes that he liked to look at her, and knew that in the moment he had stood beside her he had lost no detail of her face.   He had also, after some subtle fashion, managed to express his admiration by his own look, though with his smoothly spoken words he had not hesitated to say a thing about her husband which was at once somehow a compliment and a stab.

"I can't imagine Dr. Van Horn taking much pains with 'humble folk,'" Ellen said to herself. "Yet he's evidently consulting with Red at this house, which doesn't seem exactly a 'humble' abode. I wonder if they get on well together.   They're certainly not much alike."

The wait proved to be a long one.   Ellen had studied her surroundings with thoroughness in every direction before the house-door opened at last, and the two men came down the walk together.   They were talking earnestly as they came, and at a point some yards away they ceased to advance, and stood

still, evidently in tense discussion over the case just
left. They spoke in the low tones customary with
men of their profession, and their words did not
reach Ellen's ears. But it was not difficult to recognize, as she watched their faces, that they were differing, and differing radically, on the matter in hand.

They had turned to face each other, and neither
looked her way, so it was possible for Ellen to study
the two without fear of intrusion. They made an
interesting study, certainly. Dr. Van Horn's face
was impassive as to the play of his features, except
that he smiled, from time to time, — a smile which
bore out Ellen's previous feeling concerning its possibilities for cynicism rather than sympathy. His
eyes, however, steely blue and cold in their expression, told more than his face of antagonism to the
man with whom he spoke. But his command of
manner, to the outward observer, who could not
hear his words, was perfect.

As for R. P. Burns, M. D., there was no disguising
the fact that he was intensely angry. That he
strove, and strove hard, to control his manner, if
not his anger, was perfectly evident to his wife, but
that he was succeeding ill at the task was painfully
apparent. His colour was high — it nearly matched
his hair; his eyes burned like consuming fires under
their dark brows; his lips spoke fast and fiercely.
He kept his voice down — Ellen was thankful for

that — and his gestures, though forceful, were controlled; but she feared at every moment that he would break out into open show of temper, and it seemed to her that this she could not bear.

She had never before seen Red Pepper really angry. She had been told, again and again since her first meeting with him, by her sister and her sister's husband, and by the Chesters, that Burns was capable of getting into a red rage in which nobody could influence or calm him, and in which he could or would not control himself. They invariably added that these hot exhibitions of high temper were frequently over as suddenly as they had appeared, and usually did nobody any harm whatever. But they hinted that there had been times in the past when Red had said or done that which could not be forgiven by his victims, and that he had more than once alienated people of standing whose good-will he could not afford to lose.

"He keeps a woodpile back of the house," James Macauley had told her once, laughingly, in the last days before she had married Burns, "where he works off a good deal of high pressure. If you catch a glimpse of him there, at unholy hours, you may know that there's murder in his heart — for the moment. Art Chester vows he's caught him there at midnight, and I don't doubt it in the least. But — a woodpile isn't always handy when a man is mad clear through, and when it isn't, and you happen to be the one who's displeased His Pepperiness, look out! I give you fair warning, smiles and kisses won't always work with him, much as he may like 'em when he's sane!"

"I'm not afraid, thank you, Jim," Ellen had answered, lightly. "Better a red-hot temper than a white-cold one."

She thought of the words now, as she saw her husband suddenly turn away from Dr. Van Horn, and march down the walk, ahead of him. The action was pretty close to rudeness, for it left the elder man in the rear. Evidently, in spite of his irritation, Burns instantly realized this, for he turned again, saying quickly: "I beg your pardon, Doctor, but I've got a lot of work waiting."

"Don't apologize, Doctor," returned the other, with perfect courtesy. "We all know that you are the busiest man among us."

His face, as he spoke, was as pale as Burns's was high-coloured, and Ellen recognized that here were the two sorts of wrath in apposition, the "red" sort and the "white." And looking at Dr. Van Horn's face, it seemed to her that she still preferred the red. But as his eyes met hers he smiled the same suave smile which she had seen before.

"Not tired of waiting yet, Mrs. Burns?" he said,

as he passed her. "You must be a restful companion for a man harassed by many cares."

She smiled and nodded her thanks, with a blithe word of parting,— so completely can her sex disguise their feelings. She was conscious at the moment, without in the least being able to guess at the cause of the friction between the two men, of an intense antipathy to Dr. James Van Horn. And at the same moment she longed to be able to make her husband look as cool and unconcerned as the other man was looking, as he drove away with a backward nod — which Red Pepper did not return!

It was not the time to speak,— she knew that well enough. Besides, though she was not the subject of his resentment, she did not care to incur any more of the results of it than could be helped. She let Burns drop her at a corner near the shopping district without asking him to take her to the precise place she meant to visit first, and left him without making any request that he return for her, — a courtesy he was usually eager to insist upon, even though it took him out of his way.

At night, when he returned, she met him with the hope that he would be able to spend the evening with her,— a thing which had not happened for a week. Her arms were about his neck as she put the question, and he looked down into her face with again a slight softening of his austere expression. She had seen at the first glance that he was not only still unhappy, he was suffering profound fatigue.

"No, I've got to go back to that infernal case." It was the first time he had disclosed even a hint as to what was the matter.

"The one where I stopped with you this morning?"

"Yes. Each time I go I vow I'll not go again. To-night, if I find things as they were two hours ago, I'll discharge myself, and that will end it."

"Red, you're just as tired and worn as you can be. Come in to the big couch, and let me make you comfortable, until dinner. You'll eat the better for it — and you need it."

He yielded, reluctantly,— he who was always so willing to submit to her ministrations. But he threw himself upon the couch with a long sigh, and let her arrange the pillows under his head. She sat down beside him.

"Can't you tell me something about it, dear?" she suggested. "Nothing I ought not to know, of course, but the thing which makes you so miserable. It can't be because the case is going wrong,— that wouldn't affect you just as this is doing."

"You've seen it, I suppose. I thought I'd kept in, before you." Burns shut his eyes, his brows frowning.

She could have smiled, but did not. "You have

— only of course I have seen that something was wearing you — keeping you on a tension. You've not been quite yourself for several days."

"I am myself. I'm the real fellow — only you haven't known him before. The other is just — the devil disguised in a goodly garment, one that doesn't belong to him."

"Oh, no!"

"No question of it. I'm so swearing mad this minute I could kill somebody, — in other words, that foul fiend of a James Van Horn — smooth-tongued hypocrite that he is!"

"Has he injured you?"

"Injured me? Knifed me in the back, every chance he got. Always has — but he never had such a chance as he has now. And plays the part of an angel of light in that house — fools them all. I'm the ill-tempered incompetent, he's the forbearing wise man. The case is mine, but he's played the game till they all have more confidence in him than they have in me. And he's got all the cards in his hand!"

He flung himself off the couch, and began to pace the room. Speech, once unloosed, flowed freely enough now, — he could not keep it back.

"The patient is a man of prominence — the matter of his recovery is a great necessity. If he were able to bear it he ought to be operated upon; but there

isn't one chance in a hundred he'd survive an operation at present. There's at least one chance in
ten he'll get well without one. I'm usually keen
enough to operate, but for once I don't dare risk it.
Van Horn advises operation — unreservedly. And
the deuce of it is that with every hour that goes by he
lets the family understand that he considers the
patient's chances for relief by operation are lessening.
He's fixing it so that however things come out he's
safe, and however things come out I'm in the hole."

"Not if the patient gets well."

"No, but I tell you the chance for that is mighty
slim — only one in ten, at best. So he holds the
cards, except for that one chance of mine. And if
the patient dies in the end it's because I didn't
operate when he advised it — or so he'll let them
see he thinks. Not in so many words, but in the
cleverest innuendo of face and manner; — *that's*
what makes me so mad! If he'd fight in the open!
But not he."

"Would he have liked to operate himself?"

Burns laughed — an ugly laugh, such as she had
never before heard from his lips. "Couldn't have
been hired to, not even in the beginning, when he
first advocated it. And I couldn't have let him,
knowing as well as I know anything in life that the
patient would never have left the table alive. Don't
you see I've had to fight for my patient's very life, —

or rather for his slim chance to live,— knowing all
the while that I was probably digging my own grave.
Easy enough to let Van Horn operate, in the beginning, and kill the patient and prove himself right,—
if he would have done it. Easy enough to pull out
of the case and let them have somebody who would
operate on Van Horn's advice."

"Is the patient going down?"

"No, he's holding his own fairly well, but the
disease isn't one that would take him off overnight.
It'll be a matter of two or three days yet, either way.
How I'm going to get through them, with things
going as they are; — meeting that Judas there at the
bedside, three times a day, and trying to keep my
infernal temper from making me disgrace myself —— "

"Red, dear,—— "

She rose and came to him, putting her hands on
his shoulders and looking straight up into his face.

"That's where Dr. Van Horn is stronger than
you, and in no other way. He can control himself."

"Not inside! Nor outside — if you know him.
He's exactly as mad as I am, only —— "

"He doesn't show it. And so he has the advantage."

"Do you think I don't know that? But I'm
right and he's wrong —— "

"So you are the one who should keep cool.

You've heard the saying of some wise man — '*If you are right you have no need to lose your temper — if you are wrong you can't afford to.*' "

Red Pepper laid hold of the hands upon his shoulders, and looked down into his wife's eyes with fires burning fiercely in his own.

"You can give me all the wise advice you want to, but the fact remains.— I have reason to be angry, and I am angry, and I can't help it, and won't help it!   Great heavens, I'm human!"

"Yes, dear, you're human, and so am I.   You have great provocation, and I think I'm almost as angry, in my small way, with Dr. Van Horn, as you are, now that I know.   But — I want you somehow to keep control of yourself.   You are a gentleman, and he is not, but he is acting like a gentleman — hush — on the outside,   I mean — and — you are not!"

"What!"

"Dear, *are* you?"

"What do you know about it?"

"From the little I saw outside the house this morning."

He grasped her arms so tightly that he hurt her. "Lord!   If you mean that I ought to grin at him, as he does at me, the snake in the grass —— "

"I don't mean that, of course.   But I do think you shouldn't allow yourself to look as if you wanted to knock him down."

"There's nothing in life that would give me greater satisfaction!"

He relaxed his grasp on her arms, and she let them drop from his shoulders. She turned aside, with a little droop of the head, as if she felt it useless to argue with one so stubbornly set on his own destruction.

He looked after her. "A big brute, am I not? Didn't know me before, did you? Thought I was all fine, warm heart and blarneying words. Well, I'm not. When a thing like this gets hold of me I'm — well, I won't shock your pretty ears by putting it into words."

He walked out of the room, leaving her standing looking after him with a strange expression on her face. Before she had moved, however, the door burst open again, and he was striding across the floor to her, to seize her in his arms.

"I *am* a brute, and I know it, but I'm not so far gone as not to realize I'm wreaking my temper on the one I love best in the world. Forget it, darling, and don't worry about me. I've been through this sort of thing times enough before. Best not try to reform me — let me have my fling. I'm no Job nor Moses,— I wasn't built that way."

She lifted her head, and the action was full of spirit. "I don't want you a Job or a Moses, but a man! It's not manly to act as you are acting now."

He threw up his head. "Not manly! That's a new one. According to your code is there no just anger in the world?"

"Just anger, but not sane rage. You have reason to be angry, but there's no reason in the world why you should let it consume you. Red, dear, why not — *bank the fires?*"

He stared down into her upturned face. He had thought he knew her, heart and soul, but he found himself thoroughly astonished by this new attitude. He was so accustomed to a charming compliance in her, he could hardly realize that he was being brought to book in a manner at once so felicitous yet so firm. She gave him back his scrutiny without flinching, and somehow, though she put him in the wrong, he had never loved her better. Here was a comrade who could understand and influence him!

"Bank the fires, eh?" he growled. "Not put them out? I should suppose you would have wanted them drowned out in a flood of tears of repentance for letting them burn."

"No! You are you, and the fires are warming — when they are kept under control. You're fighting the harder for your patient's life because the fight's a hard one. But when you let the Devil fan the flame —— "

He burst into a great, unexpected laugh and caught her to his breast again. "That's what I'm

doing, is it? That ever I should have lived to hear
you use a phrase like that! But it's a true one, I
admit it. I've let his Satanic Majesty have his own
way with me, and bade him welcome, too. I may
again, when I get away from you. But — well —
I know you're right. I — I'll try to bank the fires,
little wife. Only don't expect too much."

"Red," said she,— and it was not at all the sort
of rejoinder he might have expected after his con-
cession,— "why is there no woodpile now behind
the house?"

"Woodpile?" He was clearly puzzled. "Why,
there's plenty of wood in the cellar, you know, if you
want fires. You can't be suffering for them, this
weather?"

"No, but I wish there were a woodpile there.
Did you think you wouldn't need one any more,
after you were married? You should have laid
in a double supply."

"But, what for? Oh!—— " Light dawned
upon him. "Somebody's told you how I used to
whack at it."

"Yes, and I saw you once myself, only I didn't
know what put the energy into your blows. It was
a splendid safety-valve. Red,— send for a load
of wood to-day, please!"

"In July! You hard-hearted little wretch! Do
you want me reduced to a pulp?"

She nodded. "Better that than burning like a bonfire. And better than running the Imp sixty miles an hour. That doesn't help you,— it merely helps your arch enemy fan the flames."

He laughed again, and the sound of his own laughter did him good, according to the laws of Nature. "Bless you, you've put him to rout for the moment at least, and that's more than any other human soul has ever done for mine, before."

He kissed her, tenderly, and understanding what he did. In his heart he adored her for the sweetness and sense which had kept her from taking these days of trial as a personal affront and finding offence in them.

They went out to dinner, and Burns found himself somehow able to forget sufficiently to enjoy the appetizing dishes which were served to him, and to keep his brow clear and his mind upon the table talk. When he went away, afterward, back to the scene of his irritation and anxiety, he bore with him a peculiar sense of having his good genius with him, to help him tend those devastating fires of temperament which when they burned too fiercely could only hinder him in the fight he waged.

It was almost daybreak when he returned. Ellen was not asleep, although she did not expect him to come upstairs, if only for fear of disturbing her at that hour. But presently the cautious opening of her door caused her to raise her head and lift her arms. Her husband came to her, and sat down close beside her.

"I've discharged myself from the case," he said. He spoke quietly, but his voice vibrated with feeling. "It was the only thing to do. No man could keep on with a case where the family were secretly following the consultant's directions, instead of those of the physician in charge. But,— for your sake, little wife, I've done something I never would have believed I'd do."

She sat up, her eyes fixed on the dim outlines of his face. "Tell me!" she urged.

"To begin with, I had it out with them, and let them know I understood the situation perfectly—and had understood it all along. That I couldn't stay with people who had lost faith in me. That if I were out of it they could have the full benefit of Van Horn's orders, and the nurses would be relieved of a mighty difficult situation. I suppose you don't know — few people do — that it's a bad breach of professional ethics for a consultant to conduct himself so that he throws doubt on the ability of the man in charge? In this case it was a piece of outrageous —— " He caught himself up. "I can't get going on that, or — those fires won't stay banked!"

She had his hand in both hers, and she lifted it to her lips. He drew a smothered breath or two, and went on.

"They were glad enough to see me out of it. Van Horn was — also glad! You see, — within the last 'few [hours the patient had lost ground — Van's prognosis was being verified. But, when it came to taking leave of the patient, there was the dickens to pay. His pulse jumped and his temperature went up, and there was trouble for fair. He begged me not to leave him. From the start his faith has been pinned tight to me. The family hadn't reckoned with that. They found themselves obliged to reckon with it. They saw I must be kept, or the game would be up in short order."

"Oh, then you *had* to stay!"

"Yes, I had to stay — but — I couldn't! Van Horn was in charge, and the family wanted him in charge."

"But the patient would die if you didn't stay. You couldn't let professional etiquette ——"

"Couldn't you, though? You've got to observe the rules of the game, Ellen, or you'll be in a worse mess than if you disregard them. After I had resigned the case, unless Van Horn took himself out of it I could have no recognized place in the house. He could have invited me, in the emergency, to share responsibility equally with himself — but would he do that? Never! There was just one thing I could do,— let the patient think I was still in charge, and continue to see him, while Van Horn ran things and so satisfied the family."

"Oh, Red, they couldn't ask you to do that?"

"That was what they did ask. I saw 'red' then, for a minute, I can tell you. You can't understand just what a humiliation that would be,— it's more than you could expect of any man —— "

"But with the patient needing you —— "

"I know,— but it's an anomalous position, just the same — an unbearable one. Not one man in a thousand would consider it for an instant. But it's the one I've accepted — for you!"

He drew her into his arms, and had his reward. He had not known she would be so deeply touched, and his heart grew very warm.

"Bless you!" he murmured. "Do you care so much about seeing those fires banked? They would never burn *you!*"

"Care? Oh, how I care! But, Red, you haven't accepted an 'anomalous position.' It's a clearly defined one,— the position of the man who is big enough to take second place, because it is his duty. And I'm so proud of you — so proud! And prouder yet because you've controlled that fiery temper."

"Don't praise me yet,— it may break out again. The test is coming in the next forty-eight hours."

"You will stand it,— I know you will."

"You would put backbone into a feather-bed," said Red Pepper, with conviction, and they laughed and clung together, in the early dawn.

Two days later Burns came home again as the first light of the morning was breaking over the summer sky. It had been the third consecutive night which he had spent at the bedside of the patient who would not let him go, — the patient who, every time his weary eyes lifted, during the long stretches of the night, wanted to rest them upon a halo of coppery red hair against the low-burning light. The sick man had learned what it meant to feel now and then, in a moment of torture, the pressure of a kind, big hand upon his, and to hear the sound of a quiet, reassuring voice — *"Steady — steady — better in a minute!"*

As he entered his office his eyes were heavy with his vigils, but his heart was very light. He looked at a certain old leather chair, into which he had often sunk when he came in at untimely hours, too weary to take another step toward bed. But now he passed it by and noiselessly crossed the hall into the living-room, where stood the roomy and luxurious couch which Ellen had provided with special thought of hours like these.

He softly opened the windows, to let in the morning breeze and the bird-songs of the early risers outside, then threw himself upon the couch, and almost instantly was sound asleep.

Two hours later, before the household was astir, Ellen came down. She was in flowing, lacy garments, her hair in freshly braided plaits hanging over her shoulders, her eyes clear and bright with the invigoration of the night's rest. As if she had known he would be there, she came straight to her husband's side, and stood looking down at him with her heart in her eyes.

He looked almost like a big boy, lying there with one arm under his head, the heavy lashes marking the line of the closed eyes, the face unbent from the tenser moulding of waking hours, the whole strong body relaxed into an attitude of careless ease. Even as she looked, though she had made scarcely a breath of noise, his eyes unclosed. He was the lightest of sleepers, even when worn out with work. He lay staring up at her for a minute while she smiled down at him, then he held out his arms.

"He's passed the danger point," he exulted, and he took hold of the two long plaits and wound them about her head. Then he sat up and began deliberately to unbraid her hair, while she submitted laughing.

"At two this morning he had a bad turn," said he, his fingers having their way with the dusky locks. "The nurse gave him Van Horn's drugs,— he grew worse. I rose up and took charge." He laughed at the thought. "We had things doing there that would have made Van's hair curl. Everybody's hair curled but mine. Mine stood up straight. I waved my arms like a semaphore. I said '*Do this!*' and they did it. I sent every one of Van's emergency orders to thunder and tried my own. They were radical — but they worked. The patient pulled out,— he'll live now,— I'll warrant him. They got Van there just as the thing was over. He and I looked each other in the eye — and I won. *Ah — h! — it was worth it!*"

He drew her hair all over her face, like a veil; then he gently parted it and kissed her happy lips.

"Oh, but I'm the hungry boy," said he. "Can't we have breakfast — *now?*"

CHAPTER V

MORE THAN ONE OPINION

"I WANT an opinion," said Burns, one night at dinner, "that shall coincide with mine. Where do you suppose I'm going to find it?"

He had been more or less abstracted during the entire dinner. He now offered, in a matter-of-fact tone, this explanation of his abstraction much as he might have observed that he would like a partridge, if it had happened to be in season.

"What's a ''pinion,' Uncle Red?" inquired his small ward, Bob. Bob's six-year-old brain seemed to be always at work in the attempt to solve problems.

"It's what somebody else thinks about a thing when it agrees with what you think. When it doesn't agree it's a prejudice," replied Burns. He forestalled further questioning from Bob by refilling his plate with the things the boy liked best, and by continuing, himself:

"Grayson's idea about a certain case of mine is prejudice — pure prejudice. Van Horn's is bluster. Field's is non-committal. Buller would like to back

me up — good old Buller — but is honestly convinced that I'm making an awful mess of it.   I want
an opinion — a distinguished opinion."

"Why don't you send for it?" his wife asked.

Burns frowned.   "That's the trouble.   The more
distinguished the opinion I get the more my patient
will have to pay for it, and he can't afford to pay
a tin dollar.   At the same time —— By George!
There's Leaver! I heard the other day that Leaver
was at a sanitorium not a hundred miles away,—
there for a rest.   I'll wager he's there with a patient
for a few days — at a good big price a day.
Leaver never rests.   He's made of steel wires.
I believe I'll have him up on the long-distance and
see if I can't get him to run over."

"Is it Dr. John Leaver of Baltimore you speak of?"

"It surely is.   Do you happen to know him?"

"Slightly, and by reputation — a great reputation."

"Great?   I should say so.   Jack's been sawing
wood without resting for ten years.   We were great
chums in college, though he was two classes ahead
of me.   I was with him again for a winter in Germany, when we were both studying there.   If I can
get him over here for a day, I'll have an opinion
worth respecting, whether it happens to agree with
mine or not.   And if it doesn't, I'll not call it
prejudice."

He left the table to put in a long-distance call. Between the salad and the dessert he was summoned to talk with his friend. Presently he returned, chuckling.

"It must be fully ten minutes since I thought of Leaver, and now I have him promised for to-morrow. I'll meet him in the city, give him the history of the case at luncheon at the Everett, take him to the hospital afterward, bring him out here to discuss things, and give him one of your dinners. Then for a fine evening at our fireside. He's agreed to stay overnight. I didn't expect that. He's usually in too much of a hurry to linger long anywhere."

"He has never seemed in a hurry, when I have seen him," Ellen observed. "He has such a quiet manner, and such a cool, calm way of looking at one, I always thought he must have a wonderful command of himself."

"I always envied him that," admitted Red Pepper, stirring his coffee with a thoughtful air. "I used to wish it were contagious, that splendid calm. He never loses his head, as I do. Takes plenty of time to consider everything, and plenty to get ready in. But when he does come to the point of operating,— he's a wonder. Talk about rapidity and brilliancy! And he never turns a hair. I've often wanted to count his pulse at a crisis, when he'd found something unexpected — one of those times that sends mine racing like a dynamo. He's as cool as a fish — outwardly, at any rate. Well, it will be jolly to see him. I could hardly get his voice to sound natural, over the 'phone. It seemed weak and thin. Poor service, I suppose,— though he had no difficulty in hearing me, apparently."

"Shall I put him in the small guest-room or the large, comfortable one? Which will appeal to him most, space or a reading-light over his bed?"

"Put him in the big room and give him all the comforts of home. I doubt if he gets many of the really homelike sort, living alone with servants, in the old family mansion, since his mother died. I've often wondered why he hasn't married."

"As you've only just married yourself I should think you would be quite able to supply a reason," suggested Ellen, with a sparkle of her dark eyes under their heavy lashes.

"He's had plenty of opportunities. Many fair ladies have made it easy for him to propose to them. But he's not the sort that kindles into flame at the sight of a match in the distance. Yet he's by no means a cold-blooded proposition. His heart is as warm as anybody's, under that reserve of his. That's why I know he'll see my patient for the love of science and humanity, and charge him nothing."

Ellen found herself particularly interested, next

day, in making preparations for the reception of her husband's friend, the first bachelor who should spend a night in the house. It was a fortnight since Red Pepper had insisted upon having the telephones extended to the upstairs rooms, and during that period two more rooms had been furnished and put in readiness for the guests whom it was a part of Mrs. Burns's hospitable creed to expect. The larger of these was a charming apartment, in blue and white, and possessed a small fireplace, in front of which stood a low couch, luxurious with many pillows.

"It's rather a feminine looking room for so manly a man as Dr. Leaver," Ellen reflected, as she looked in at it, an hour before his arrival, "but perhaps he's not above enjoying little softnesses of comfort. I believe I'll have a small fire for him, June though it is. It's a cold June, and it looks like rain. It *is* raining." She crossed to the window and looked out. "Why, it's pouring! What a pity! We shall have to stay indoors."

As she stood contemplating the downpour, it quite suddenly increased, and in the course of a minute or two became a deluge. In the midst of it she discovered a white-clad figure running across the lawn, and recognized Miss Mathewson, evidenently caught in the shower as she was returning to Burns's office.

"She must be soaked through and through," thought Ellen, and ran downstairs to meet her, herself clad in dinner dress of the pale lilac which suited her so well, and for which her husband had conceived a special fondness.

"Oh, don't come near me, please, Mrs. Burns," expostulated Miss Mathewson, as she stood, dripping, on the porch outside the office, while Ellen, in the open door, motioned her within. "I'll just stay here until the worst is over, and then run home and change."

"Indeed you'll come in. Nothing can hurt this floor, and it's turned ever so cold, as I can feel. It may rain for an hour. I'll give you everything you need, and be delighted."

There was no resisting Red Pepper's wife; she was accustomed to have her way. Miss Mathewson, reluctant but shivering, came inside, and when her clothing had ceased to drip moisture, followed Ellen upstairs. Presently, dry-clad, she was taken into Ellen's own room and confronted with an invitation which was rather a command.

"You're to stay and have dinner with us. I've laid out a frock which I'm confident will fit you. Please don't say no. It's a special providence, for I've been wishing all the afternoon I had asked somebody to make a fourth at our table, to meet Dr. Leaver. And now I shall have the pleasure of dressing you for the occasion, since you can't possibly go home through this, and wouldn't have time to dress and come back, if you could."

"But, Mrs. Burns,——" Amy Mathewson began, flushing after a fashion she had which made her for the moment almost pretty and certainly attractive, "there's no real reason why you need me, and I —— "

"I do need you. Three is such a stupid number. You will enjoy Dr. Leaver and he will enjoy you. Come, my dear girl, don't spend any more time remonstrating, but do your hair and put on this simple frock, which I'm confident will just suit you. You're a bit taller, I know, but the dress is long for me, and will be quite the right length for you. Sit down here at my dressing-table, and let me help you dry that beautiful hair. I've often longed to see it all unconfined, and now I'm going to have the chance."

As she spoke she slipped on a loose protecting garment above her lilac daintiness, and waved an inviting hand to her guest, smiling so coaxingly that Miss Mathewson yielded without another word of protest. When the hairpins came out, and the mass of fair hair fell upon the shoulders, Ellen exclaimed with hearty admiration:

"I knew it was wonderful hair, but I didn't dream there was such a wealth. My dear, why do you wear it in such a tight fashion, as if you wanted everybody to think there wasn't much of it? Do let me try dressing it for you in a way I know, which it seems to me would just suit your face. Have you always worn it coiled on top of your head, and shall you feel very strange and uncomfortable if I arrange it lower?"

"Do it as you like, Mrs. Burns, since you will be so kind. But don't expect me not to feel strange, wearing your clothes and staying to dinner. Do you realize how far from society I've lived, all these years that I've been nursing for Dr. Burns?"

"I know you are a lady, and that is quite enough. And our simple dinner isn't 'society,' it's home. Now, please keep quite still, and don't distract my mind, while I lay these smooth strands in place. I want every one to lie in just this shining order."

Ellen worked at her self-appointed task with all the interest of the born artist, who has an ever-present dream of things as they ought to look. When the last confining pin was in place she viewed the fair head before her from every point, then clapped her hands delightedly, and presented Miss Mathewson with a hand-mirror.

"You must get the side view, then you'll recognize how these new lines bring out that distinguished profile that's been obscured all this time. Do you see? Do you know yourself, my dear? Won't you always wear it this way, to please me?"

"But I never could do it myself, in the world," pleaded Amy Mathewson, her cheeks again flooding with colour at the strange sight of herself.

"It's perfectly simple, and I'll teach you with pleasure,— only not now, for we must hurry. I'll slip the frock over your head without disturbing a hair, and then we'll go down, for I want a bit of a blaze on the hearth in the living-room, to offset this dull-gray sky."

On went the frock in question, a "simple" one, undoubtedly, but of the sort of simplicity which tells its own story to the initiated. Whether its new wearer recognized or not its perfection of detail, she could but see that it suited her to a nicety, both in hue — a soft apricot shade — and in its absence of elaboration. Its effect was to soften every line of the face above it, and to set off its wearer's delicate colouring as the white uniforms could never do.

"Don't you quite dare to look at her?" questioned the self-appointed lady's maid, merrily, as she led her charge to stand in front of a long mirror, set in a door.

"Hardly." Miss Mathewson raised eyes grown suddenly shy to view her own image in the glass, which gave her back a picture such as she had never dreamed could be made by herself, under any conditions whatever. Over her shoulder her employer's wife smiled at her.

"She looks very charming, to me, however she looks to you. But I won't force her to stare long at such a stranger. It might make it difficult for her to forget the stranger afterward, which is what I want her to do."

Ellen ran away to make herself ready once more, and returning put her arm about her guest's waist, in the friendly way of her own which came still more naturally now that the uniform was gone. Together the two descended the stairs to the living-room, there to await the arrival of Burns and his friend.

This took place about three quarters of an hour after it was to be expected, as Red Pepper's arrivals usually did, whether accompanied or not by invited guests. The two came in laughing together over some reminiscence, and Ellen recognized the tall, distinguished figure she well remembered, with the clean-cut features, the fine eyes rather deep set under heavy brows, the firm yet sensitive mouth. Yet, after a moment, as Dr. John Leaver stood talking with her, she observed a careworn look, a dimming of the fresh, clear colour she had noted on former meetings; altogether in his whole aspect she found more than a suggestion of undue fatigue, and when the smile ceased to light his face, even of sadness quite unwonted.

While he was in his room before dinner, she held a hasty consultation with her husband, as he dressed with the speed of which he was master through long practice.

"Dr. Leaver can't be quite well, Red,— to look like that?"

"I should say not. I haven't asked him a question and he hasn't said a word, but it shows all over him. He's 'not my old friend Jack Leaver, at all, and it upsets me. I'm hoping he'll unload, and tell me what's wrong, though I can guess fairly well for myself. I could see, all through our consultation, that he held himself in hand with an effort. The old keenness was there, but not the old command. He's worn out, for one thing,— though there may be more than that. But, see here,— do you mean to tell me that's Amy Mathewson you've got downstairs? Never! It might be her younger sister — six years younger — but not my staid nurse. Not even you could bring about such a miracle."

"Isn't it wonderful? Yet — it isn't, at all. She's always worn her hair strained back from her face and put up into that tight coil on the top of her head. Dressing it properly has made two thirds of the difference and the apricot frock makes the other third. Isn't it delightful?"

"No doubt of that. She's a mighty good girl, and if she can make shift to be a good-looking one as well, there may be a bit of fun left in life for her yet. She's by no means old, and you've made her young,— bless your generous heart! I don't know how you ever managed to get her consent, though. She thinks that uniform is her shell, and can't be doffed. But I don't think she's likely to get much fun out of Leaver to-night. He's just about fit for bed, or I'm no diagnostician.

"Then let's put him there," said Ellen, promptly.

"Oh, I don't mean that literally. One of your dinners ought to set him up, and Amy Mathewson won't make any exacting demands on his brilliancy."

"Won't she? You can't tell what pretty clothes may do for her. She will surprise you some time, in spite of the fact that you know her so well."

"Wise woman. She will, if you have a hand in the game. You can be trusted to bring out every one's best. Bother this tie — it acts like original sin."

"I won't offer to tie it for you. I can't imagine Redfield Pepper Burns allowing his wife to tie his cravat for him."

"Can't you? That is to say, won't you?" He came close.

She shook her head, and moved away, smiling. "It would destroy a certain ideal. Stop laughing! One of your most powerful charms for me is your independence."

He groaned and continued to struggle with the bow of black silk which eluded his efforts to fasten it securely. "I thought all women delighted in getting their husband's neckwear adjusted according to their own notions. Another dream shattered! — Well, here goes for the last time. If I can't get it right now I'll go in and implore Jack to do it for me. It will open his eyes as to how far hopes may be slain by realities. There! That's a pretty good result, at last. I'll go across now, and see if he wants any of my assistance."

Ten minutes later both men appeared in the living-room. In his evening attire Dr. Leaver looked a tall and sombre figure, and the contrast between him and his friend, as Red Pepper stood beside him on the hearth-rug, the picture of ruddy health, was startling.

"You must be pretty heavy, Red," Leaver said, considering his host. "Not a particle of superfluous fat, but good, solid structure, I should say. One wouldn't want to try to pass you against your will, in a narrow alley, on a dark night."

"It strikes me you could glide by me in the shadow and never attract my attention," Burns replied, his keen eyes on his friend's face. "The difference between us is that every inch of you represents concentrated energy, while my plant spreads all over the landscape without producing half as much power."

Leaver smiled. There was both strength and sweetness in his smile, but there was depression in it also. "That sounds like you," he said. "I suppose many men envy other men the possession of some supposed source of efficiency. Just now I find myself envying you your home — and its occupants. What a delightful room."

He turned to his hostess and her friend. While they talked together Burns regarded Amy Mathewson, his long-time associate, with renewed wonder, and presently found himself addressing her from an entirely new point of view. This fair girl with the graceful head and the glowing blue eyes could not possibly be the sedate young woman who was accustomed to hand him instruments and sutures, ligate arteries, and attend to various minor matters from the other side of his operating-table. He wondered why he had never before noticed how much real individuality she possessed, nor how really attractive she was of face and person. He decided afresh that his wife was the most wonderful woman in the world, to be able to see at a glance that which had escaped his attention for so long, and he congratulated Miss Mathewson, in his mind, on the possibilities he for the first time saw ahead of her. Clearly after all she was a woman, not a machine!

The party went out to dinner, and Burns looked to see his friend enjoy, as he thought he must, the cleverly planned and deliciously cooked meal which came, perfectly served, upon the table. It was such a dinner as he himself delighted in, unostentatious but satisfying, with certain touches, here and there, calculated to tempt the most capricious palate,— such as he shrewdly judged Leaver, in his presumably lowered state of vitality, to possess.

But to his surprise and dismay the guest barely touched most of the dishes, and ate so sparingly of others that Burns felt himself, with his hearty, normal appetite, a gormandizer. Nobody made any comment whatever upon Dr. Leaver's lack of appetite, but all three noted, with growing concern, that there were moments when he seemed to keep up with an effort. Instinctively the others made short work of the later courses, and felt a decided relief when it became possible to leave the table and return to the living-room.

By a bit of clever management Ellen was able to put the guest's tall form into a corner of the big davenport, among the blue pillows, where he could receive more support than was possible in any other place. After a little he seemed less fatigued, and charmed them all with his pleasant discourse. Burns himself was soon summoned to the office. He would not allow Miss Mathewson to take up her duties there, though she followed him to offer eagerly to run home and change her attire.

"Not a bit of it," Burns assured her, in the hall. He regarded her with mischief in his eyes. "Cinderella isn't due at home till the clock strikes twelve," he whispered. "Besides,— the Prince isn't in his usual form to-night.   He may need her services as nurse at any minute, judging by his appearance."

That sent her back into the room, as he knew it would.   It was, for her, a wonderfully interesting hour which followed, for Dr. Leaver and Mrs. Burns fell to discussing life in a certain great city, as both knew it from quite different standpoints, and she herself had only to listen and observe.   She thought the pair upon the davenport made a striking picture, the woman in her rich and still youthful beauty, her smile a thing to wonder at, her voice low music to the ear; the man, though no older than Burns, worn and grave, yet with a strangely winning personality, and eyes which seemed to see far beneath the surface.   In all Amy Mathewson's experience with the men of Burns's profession, she had never met just such a one as John Leaver.   The sense of his personal worth and dignity was strong upon her as she watched him; his evident fatigue and weakness appealed to her sympathies; and she forgot herself more completely than she had imagined she could when first summoned to the unaccustomed part she was this evening playing.

But, quite suddenly, the scene changed.   In the

act of speaking Dr. Leaver suddenly stopped, put one hand to his side, and lay back against the high end of the davenport, breathing short, his face turning pallid, ashen. Ellen rose to her feet in dismay, but Amy Mathewson sprang toward him, drew him with strong arms gently down to a position more nearly recumbent, and with fingers on his pulse said in a low voice, "Call the Doctor, please."

Ellen ran, and in a minute had Burns there, striding in, in his white office jacket, his face tense with sudden anxiety. Leaver was panting for breath as Burns felt his pulse and nodded at Amy, who hurried quietly away. She was back very quickly, handing Burns a tiny instrument ready for use. In a moment more the supporting drug was on its way to lend aid, and Burns was bending over his friend again, laying a gentle hand upon the damp forehead, and saying with quiet assurance:

"All right, old boy. We'll have you comfortable in no time. You were too tired to play society man to-night, and we oughtn't to have allowed it."

It was not very long before Leaver was breathing more easily, and a trace of colour had come back to his face. He moved his head and tried to speak naturally:

"I am — rather — ashamed of myself —— "

"You've no business to be. When a fellow is played out Nature takes her innings — and she takes all that's coming to her. You're going up to bed in a few minutes, and you're going to stay there till the rest has had a chance to get in some work. Miss Mathewson will stay with you for a bit. She's a famous nurse."

Leaver's head moved in surprised protest, and Miss Mathewson spoke:

"He doesn't know, Dr. Burns, that that is my profession."

Burns laughed. "Oh, I see. That was a bit startling, for a fact. But she is, Leaver, the most accomplished of her guild, and my right-hand man. She can make you more comfortable in an hour than I can in a week."

Upstairs, while she released Amy from the apricot frock, that something more in keeping with the duties of a nurse might be donned, Ellen questioned anxiously:

"The Doctor must think him really ill, to speak of keeping him in bed. Do you know what is the matter?"

"His heart action is weak. I don't know the cause, of course. He seems worn out; that showed plainly all the evening. I'm going to run home, Mrs. Burns; my wet things must be quite dry, now. There'll be time, I'm sure. The Doctor won't bring him upstairs for a little yet."

She hurried away, and was back within the half

hour. Although she no longer looked the part of
the fine lady, the old rôle seemed hardly hers. The
new fashion of her hair had changed her appearance
very completely, and the youthful look it had
restored to her remained, to Ellen's no little pleasure.
Her cheeks were still flushed with the evening's
excitement, and her eyes were charmingly bright
and happy.

When everything was in readiness, Burns, in spite
of all remonstrance from his friend, lifted him in his
powerful arms and carried him upstairs. The
exertion made him breathe a little heavily for a
moment, but that was all. Leaver was not a
light burden, in spite of his thinness, for his frame
was that of a man who should carry many pounds
more than he now bore.

"You strong man, how I envy you," Leaver
said, sadly, as Burns laid him upon the bed.

"Your envy of me can't be a circumstance to
that I've felt, many a time, when I've watched you.
But you've been working like a slave too long.
Rest is all you need, man."

But Leaver slowly shook his head. He did not
reply to this confident statement, and Burns knew
better than to try to argue it out with him just then.
Instead, with a warm grip of the hand, he turned
his new case over to the care of his nurse, and went
away, his heart heavy at sight of a strong man prone.

CHAPTER VI

BROKEN STEEL WIRES

"BUT I can't stay here," John Leaver protested, a few days afterward. He was still in bed, much against his will, but not, as he was forced to admit, against his judgment, when he allowed it consideration. "I can't impose on Mrs. Burns's and your kindness like this. I shall soon be fit for travel, and then ——"

"Would you mind listening to me?" R. P. Burns, M. D., sat comfortably back in a large willow chair, by the bedside, and crossed one leg over the other in a fashion indicative of an intention to settle down to it and have it out. "Just let me state the case to you, and try to look at it from the outside. Of course that's a difficult thing to do, when it happens to be your own case, but you have a judicial mind, and you can do the trick, if anybody can."

Leaver was silent. He lay staring out of the open window beside which his bed had been drawn, his thin cheek showing gaunt hollows, his eyes heavy with unrest. All the scents and sounds of June were pouring in at the three windows of the room; a tangle of rose vines looked in at him from this nearest one. Just before Amy Mathewson had left him, a few minutes ago, for her afternoon rest, she had brought him one wonderful bloom, the queen, it seemed, of all the roses of that June. It lay upon the window-sill, now, within reach of his hand.

Burns began to speak. His tone was matter-of-fact, yet it held inflections of tenderness. His friend's case appealed to him powerfully; his sympathy with Leaver's state of mind, as he was confident he understood it, was intense. "If it were I!" he had said to himself — and to Ellen — and had groaned in spirit at the thought. If it had been his own case, it seemed to him he could not have endured it.

"You were at that sanitorium," Burns began. "Sanitoriums are useful institutions, some of them get splendid results. But they have their disadvantages. It's pretty difficult to eliminate the atmosphere of illness. And, for a man whose training and instincts lead him to see behind every face he meets in such a place, it's not an ideal spot at all. What you need is a home, and that's what we're offering you, for as long as you need it."

"And I appreciate it more than any words can express," Leaver said gratefully. He turned his head now, and looked at his host. "Just to know

that I have such friends does me good. And I
know that you mean all you say. If I were a subject
for a cure I might almost be tempted to take you
at your word."

"You are a subject for a cure."

Leaver shook his head, turning it away again.
"Only to a certain point," he said, quietly. "Of
course I know that rest and quiet will put my heart
right, because there's no organic lesion. Probably
I shall build up and get the better of my depression
of mind — to a certain extent. But, there's one
thing I'm facing I haven't owned to you. You
may as well know it. I shall never be able to operate
again. . . . Perhaps you can guess what that
means to me," he added. His voice was even, but
his breathing was slightly quickened.

Burns was silent for a time, his own heart heavy
with sympathy for Leaver. Guess what a conviction like that must mean to a man of Leaver's
early eminence in the world of distinguished operative
surgery? He surely could. It had been his almost
certain knowledge that this was his friend's real
trouble which had made him say to himself with a
groan, "If it were I!" So he did not answer hastily
to persist in assurance that all would yet be well. He
knew Leaver understood that sort of professional
hypnosis too thoroughly to be affected by it.

Burns got up and took a turn or two up and down

the room, thinking things out. His face was graver than patients usually saw it; there was in it, however, a look of determination which grew, moment by moment, as he walked. Presently he came back to the bedside and sat down again.

"Suppose you tell me all about it, Jack," said he. "You haven't done me that honour, yet, you know. Will it be too hard on you? Just to make a clean breast of every thought and every experience which has led you to this point? I know I'm rather forcing myself upon you as your physician. If you prefer, I'll withdraw from the case, in favour of any better man you may choose, and send for him to-day."

Leaver's head turned back again. "I know no better man," he said, and their eyes met.

"There are plenty of better men," Burns went on, "but I confess I want this case, and am ready to take advantage of having it in my house, for the present, at least. Well, then,— if you can trust me, why not do as I suggest?"

Leaver shivered a little, in the warm June light, and put one hand for a moment over his eyes.

"You don't know what you ask, Red," he said, slowly.

"Don't I? Perhaps not. Yet — I have a notion that I do. It would be a trifle easier to face the rack and thumbscrew, eh? Well, let's get it over.

Possibly telling will ease you a bit, after all. It works that way sometimes."

By and by, persisting, gently questioning, helping by his quick understanding of a situation almost before Leaver had unwillingly pictured it, he had the whole story. It was almost precisely the story he had guessed,— an old story, repeated by many such sufferers from overwork and heavy responsibility, but new to each in its entirety of torture, even to this man, who, still in his youthful prime, had himself heard many such a tale from the unhappy lips of his patients, yet to whom his own case seemed unique in its suffering and hopelessness.

The recital culminated in an incident so painful to the subject of it that he could recount it only in the barest outlines. His listener, however, by the power of his experience and his sympathy, could fill in every detail. A day had come, some six weeks before, when Leaver, though thoroughly worn out by severe and long continued strain, had attempted to operate. The case was an important one, the issue doubtful. Friends of the patient had insisted that no one else should take the eminent young surgeon's place, and, although he had had more than one inner warning, in recent operations, that his nerve was not what it had been, his pride had bid him see the thing through. He had given himself an energizing hypodermic,— he had never done that before,— and had gone into it. There had come a terrible moment. . . . Leaver's lips grew white as he tried to tell it.

He felt his friend's warm, firm hand upon his own as he faltered. "Steady, old fellow," said Burns's quiet voice. "We've got this nearly over. You'll be better afterward."

After a little Leaver went on.

He had come upon an unexpected complication — one undreamed of by himself or the consulting surgeons. "You know——" said Leaver. Burns nodded, emphatically. "You bet I know," said he, and his hand came again upon Leaver's, and stayed there. Leaver went on again, slowly.

Instant decision had been necessary, instant action. It was such a moment as he had faced hundreds of times before, and his quick wit, his surgeon's power of resource, his iron nerve, had always come to the support of his skill, and together these attributes had won the day for him. Fear, at such crises, had never possessed him, however much, afterward, reviewing the experience, he had wondered that it had not. But this time, fear — fear — a throttling, life-destroying fear had sprung upon him and gripped him by the throat. Standing there, entirely himself, except for that horrible consciousness that he could not proceed, he had had to beckon to the most experienced of the surgeons present who surrounded him as onlookers, and say to him: "Get ready — and take this case. I can't go on."

There had been no apparent physical collapse on his part, no fainting nor attack of vertigo, nothing to help him out in the eyes of that wondering, startled company of observers. He had been able to direct his assistants how to hold the operation in suspension until the astonished, unwilling colleague could make ready to step into the breach, cursing under his breath that such an undesired honour should have been thrust upon him. Then Leaver had walked out of the room, quite without assistance, only replying wanly to those who questioned, "There's nothing to say. I couldn't go on with it. Yes, I am perfectly well."

It had not got into the papers. They had been kind enough to see to that, those pitying professional colleagues who had witnessed his dispossession. The patient had lived. If he had died the thing must have come out. But he had lived. The situation could not have been as desperate a one as it had seemed. The other man had handled it,— and he was by no means a man eminent in his profession. There had been no excuse, then, for such a seizure,— no excuse. It meant — the end.

Well, it was certainly the end of recounting it, for when he had reached this point Leaver's power to endure the thought of it all failed him, and he lay back upon his pillows, his brow damp and his breath short.

Burns silently ministered to him, pain in his eyes, his lips drawn tight together. His sympathy for his friend was intense.

It seemed to him incredible that this shaken spirit before him could be John Leaver — Leaver, whom, as he had told his wife, he had often envied his perfect self-command, his supposed steadiness of pulse, his whole strong, cool personality, unaffected by issues such as always keyed Burns himself up to a tremendous tension, making him pale with the strain. "Leaver's made of steel wires," had been his description of his friend to Ellen. Well, the steel wires were stretched and broken, now, no doubt of that. The question was whether they could ever be mended and restrung.

When Leaver was comfortable again,— comfortable as far as an evenly beating heart and a return of blood to the parts which needed it could make him,— Burns spoke to him once more.

"We won't talk about this any more to-day, Jack," he said. "You've had enough for now, and I have what I needed,— the facts to work upon. Just let me say this much. I'm not discouraged by anything I've heard to-day. I'll not try any bluffs or jollyings with you, because I know they wouldn't work, but I do say this, honestly: I'm not discouraged. And I'm interested — interested to the bottom of my heart. I'm going to put the best there is in me into this problem. I never tackled anything in my life that appealed to me more powerfully. If that's any comfort just now, I offer it. If you were my brother I couldn't be more anxious to pull you out of this ditch. Now, trust me, and try to go to sleep."

Leaver did not look up at the kind, almost boyishly tender face above him, but he pressed the hand which grasped his own, and Burns saw a tear creep out from under the closed lids of the eyes under which the black shadows lay so deeply. The well man took himself away from the sick one as quickly as he could after that,— he couldn't bear the sight of that tear! It was more eloquent of Leaver's weakness than all his difficult words.

When he met Miss Mathewson, an hour afterward, in the hall, on her way back to her patient, he delayed her.

"I want you to do more than nurse this case, Amy," he said, fixing her with a certain steady look of his with which he always gave commands. "I want you to put all your powers, as a woman, into it. Forget that you are nursing Dr. Leaver, try to think of him as a friend. You can make one of him, if you try, for you have in you qualities which will appeal to him — if you will let him see

them. You have hardly let even me see them,"
— he smiled as he said it,— "but my eyes have been
opened at last. I'm inclined to believe that you can
do more for our patient than even my wife or I,—
if you will. Suppose," — he spoke with a touch of
the dangerously persuasive manner he could assume
when he willed, and which most people found it
hard to resist,— "you just let yourself go, and try
— deliberately try — to make Dr. Leaver like you!"

She coloured furiously under the suggestion.
"Dr. Burns! Do you realize what you're saying?"

"Quite thoroughly. I'm asking you not to hesi-
tate to make of yourself a woman of interest and
charm for him, for the sake of taking him out of
himself. Isn't that a perfectly legitimate part for
a nurse to play when that happens to be the medicine
needed? You have those powers,— how better
could you use them? Suppose you are able, through
your effect of sweetness and light, to minister to
a mind diseased; — isn't that quite as worthy an
occupation as counting out drops of aconite, or
applying mustard plasters?"

Amy Mathewson shook her head. "Do you
realize, Dr. Burns, that a man like — your guest —
is so far beyond me in mind and — tastes — in
every way, that I could never — interest him in
the way you speak of — even if I were willing
to try?"

She spoke with difficulty. As Burns studied her downbent face, the profile his wife had brought out by her skill at hair-dressing showing like a fine cameo against the dark background of the wall, he was thinking that unless Leaver were blind he must find her rather satisfying to the eye, at least. He answered her with confidence.

"He's a man of education, it's true. But what are you? Come,— haven't I found all sorts of evidences, about my office, that you are a woman of education? It doesn't matter whether you got that education in a college or from the books I know you have read,— you have it. I'll trust your ability to discuss six out of a dozen subjects Leaver may bring up — or, if you can't discuss them all, you can do what is better — let him instruct you. Don't tell me you can't handle those cards every fascinating woman understands so well. If there's anything a man likes to do it's to teach an interested woman the things she cleverly professes she wants to know — and the best of it is that no matter how often you play that game on us we're always caught by it. Leaver will be caught by it, just as if he hadn't had it tried on him a thousand times. And while he's playing it with you, he'll forget himself, which is the first step on the road I want him to travel."

She looked up. "Do you mean that I am to

keep on attending him after he is able to leave his room? Is he going to stay with you after that? He told me only to-day that he intends to go as soon as he is able to travel."

"We shall keep him as long as we can possibly persuade him to stay. Meanwhile, my plan is to have you settle down and stay with us, as a member of the family. We'll have some one else attend to the office. You can go with me, as usual, when I operate, but I shall put you on no case but Dr. Leaver's, and the greater part of your time will be his."

"But what will he think? Doesn't he know that I'm your office nurse?"

"How should he know it — unless you have taken pains to tell him?"

She shook her head. "He only knows that I am your assistant at operations. The other point hasn't come up."

"Good. Then he will accept whatever situation he finds, and never think of questioning it. The way is clear enough. And it's the only way I know of to insure his having what he needs — the close companionship of a sympathetic — yet not too sympathetic — woman — with a face like yours," he added, slyly.

The quick colour answered this, as he knew it would. "Dr. Burns! You know I'm not even good looking! Please don't say such things."

"I only said 'a face like yours.' That may imply a face as plain as you think Amy Mathewson's is — and as my wife and I know it is not. It's time you waked up, girl, to your own attractions. You ought to have faith in them when I'm asking the use of them for this patient of mine. I'd give about all I own to put him on his feet again."

"I hope you can — indeed I do. And of course — anything I can do —— "

He nodded. "I'll leave that to you. Consult — not your head alone, but — your heart!"

And he let her go, smiling at her evident confusion of mind. But when left alone he sighed again.

"He needs a woman like my Ellen,— *that* would be a drug of a higher potency. But — he can't have that — he can't have that! I must do the next best thing."

And he went on his way, studying it out.

That evening he took his wife into his confidence. He did not tell her the whole story,— it was not his to tell. But he made her acquainted with the fact that Leaver had had a severe nervous shock and that the thing to be overcome was his own distrust of himself, the thing to be recovered was his entire self-command.

"I have insisted on his staying as long as he can be content," Burns explained. "I had your consent to that, I know?"

"Of course, Red.   You knew that."

"In my enthusiasm I went a step further, without realizing that I had not consulted you.   I asked Amy Mathewson to stay with us too, as a member of the family.   I asked her coöperation as a woman, as well as a nurse, and to have that it seemed to me necessary to have her here, even after he is up and able to look after his own wants.   How will you feel about that?"

He looked straight into her eyes.   They were sitting upon a small side porch, in the late June evening.   He had come in from a visit to a near-by patient, and, finding her upon the porch, had thrown himself upon the cushion at her feet, his head against her knee.   Now, he turned and looked up at her, and she could see his expression clearly in the moonlight.

"I don't believe I quite understand yet," she said.   "What is it that you want Amy to do for him, 'as a woman'?   Read to him, and walk with him, and be a sort of comrade?"

"Precisely that — and a bit more."

"Can you prescribe that sort of thing, and make sure that it will work out?   He may not care for it."

"I want him to have a woman's companionship; it's what he needs, I firmly believe.   It must be a certain sort of woman — the kind who will be good for his nerves, gently stimulating, not exacting.   One of the brilliant society women he knows wouldn't do at all. The ideal kind would be — your own kind. But he can't have that." He spoke so decidedly that she smiled, though he did not see it. "It seems to me that Amy, if she puts her heart into it, can give him just what he needs. Remember he's a sick man, and will continue to be a sick man for some time after he's walking about our streets and climbing our hills."

"Yes, I'm afraid he will be. And you think he will accept Amy's companionship, after he is walking about, as a part of his medicine? Shall you insist on her being with him, or is she to wait to be invited to read to him and walk with him?"

His brows knit in a frown. "You think I'm prescribing something I can't administer? But I think that he will grow so used to having her with him, while he actually needs her as a nurse, that, when he gets about and finds her still here, he will quite naturally fall into the way of seeking her company."

"Perhaps he will. At any rate, she is very welcome to stay, as long as you want her for the experiment."

"You are an angel! I realize that I shouldn't have made such an arrangement without asking your permission. To tell the truth, I'm so used to —— "

He stopped short, with a little ejaculation of dismay.

"I understand, dear," she said quickly. "You are so used to being master of the house that you forgot the new conditions. It's all right — you are still master — particularly in everything that has to do with your profession. And if you can find a cure for poor Dr. Leaver's broken spirit I shall be as happy as you."

"It's going to make you a lot of trouble,— two guests in the house, for an indefinite period. You see, I'm just waking up to what I'm asking of you. It's precisely like my impetuosity to create a situation I can't retreat from, and then wonder at my own nerve. Will it bother you very much?"

"It's what we're here for, isn't it?" She smiled at him as he turned and put both arms around her, kneeling beside her in the shadow of the vines. "It's certainly what you are here for, and I am your partner, or I'm not much of a wife."

"Bless you, you darling; you surely are. And such a partner! If Leaver had one like you — he wouldn't be where he is. But he can't have you," he repeated, and held her closer. "I couldn't see you reading to him and walking with him, and being a friend to him,— I couldn't see it, that's all, no matter how much good you might do him. Queer — I didn't know that was in me — that feeling. Macauley calls me a Turk. I guess that's what I am. It's a primitive sort of instinct, scoffed at in these days when half the married women are playing with fire in the shape of other women's husbands. But I hate that sort of thing — have always hated it. I'm a Turk, all right. Do you mind?"

"No, I don't think I mind," she answered softly. "But I want your perfect trust, Red."

"You have it, oh, you have it, love. No possible question of that. And I don't mean that I'm not willing to have Leaver get what he can of your dearness, as he's bound to feel it, in our home. But this comrade business, which I feel he's so much in need of,— that's what he can't have from you. And if he stayed on, and there was no other woman about, why, quite naturally —— "

He stopped. Then, as she was silent, "You won't misunderstand me, little wife?" he begged. "I've seen so much of the other thing, you know. Can I be — enough for you?"

"Quite enough, Red."

After a minute he went back to the thing which absorbed him. "I can see you haven't much confidence in my plan for Amy's helping him?"

She hesitated. "You spoke just now of playing with fire. You don't feel that in throwing two people so closely together you are risking something?"

He considered it. "My idea is that Amy will administer her comradeship as she would her medicines. She is the most conscientious girl alive; she won't give him a drop too much."

"Not a drop too much for his good, perhaps. But what about hers, dear? When he is himself Dr. Leaver can be a wonderfully interesting and compelling man, you know. It would be a pity for her to grow to care for him, if — I don't suppose it is at all possible to expect him to care seriously for her, — do you?"

"Well, I shouldn't have said so a month ago. But I'm just beginning to realize a new side to Amy Mathewson. I don't suppose I ever saw her — to look at her — out of her uniform, before that night when you dressed her up. By George, along with the clothes she seemed to put on a new skin!"

"Uniforms are disguising things," Ellen admitted, "and Amy is a lady, born and bred, in her uniform and out of it. But it's not much use speculating on what will happen, when the arrangements are already made. We must just do our best for Dr. Leaver, and hope that no harm will come to either of them."

"None will — under your roof," her husband asserted confidently.

CHAPTER VII

POINTS OF VIEW

A LADY downstairs to see you, Mrs. Burns."
Cynthia presented a card.

It was early morning. Ellen had just seen her
husband off in the Green Imp, and was busy at
various housewifely tasks. She took the card in
some surprise, for morning calls were not much in
vogue in this small town. But when she read the
name —"Miss Ruston" — she gave a little cry of
delight, and ran downstairs as one goes to welcome a
long absent friend.

A graceful figure, radiant with health and good
looks, dressed in the trimmest and simplest of
travelling attire, yet with a gay and saucy air about
her somewhere, quite difficult to locate, rose as
Ellen came in. Dark eyes flashed, lips smiled
happily, and a pair of arms opened wide. Ellen
found herself caught and held in a warm embrace,
which she returned with a corresponding ardour.

"Why, Charlotte, dear!" she cried. "Where
did you come from? And why didn't you let me
know?"

"Straight from home, Len, darling. And I didn't let you know because I didn't know myself till I was here. Oh, do let me look at you! How dear, how dear you are! I had almost forgotten anybody could be so lovely."

"That sounds like you, you enthusiastic person. How glad I am to see you — it seems so long. I hope you have come to make me a visit, now you are here."

"Just a wee one, for a day, while I make plans at express speed, and fly back again to grandmother. I left her in Baltimore."

"Really? Did you bring her 'way up from Charleston? Then she must be pretty well?"

"Very well, if, like a piece of old china, I keep her quiet on the top shelf. Baltimore is the bottom shelf, for her, even though she's with the Priedieus, who will take the kindest care of her. Hence my haste. Oh, I can't wait a minute till I tell you my plans. Let me splash my dusty face and I'll plunge in. I want your advice, your interest, and your — coöperation!"

"You shall have them all, my dearest girl. Come upstairs," and Ellen led the way, Miss Ruston following with a small travelling bag of which she would not give her hostess possession.

"What a dear house!" The guest was throwing rapid glances all about her as she mounted the stairs. "I should have known that living-room was yours if I hadn't had your Aunt Lucy's famous old desk to give me a clue. O, Len, the very back of you is enchanting!"

Ellen turned to laugh at Charlotte Ruston's characteristic fervour of expression. "I remember you are always admiring people's backs," she observed.

"Yes, they're often so much more interesting than their faces. But yours — merely gives promise of what the face fulfills! Forgive me, Len,— you know when I haven't seen you for ages I have to tell you what I think of you. In here? Oh, what an adorable room!"

It was Ellen's own. She was thinking rapidly. Dr. John Leaver occupied one of her two guest-rooms, Amy Mathewson the other. She should have to turn Bob out of the bachelor's room, and send him down to stay with Cynthia. But Miss Ruston put an end to her planning at once by adding:

"I can't even sleep under your roof, Len, for I've engaged my berth on the sleeper to-night. I'm always in such anxiety about Granny when I get her away from her quiet corner. Now let me make myself clean with all haste, that I may not lose a minute of this happy day with you."

She was as good as her word, and in five minutes was looking as fresh as the fortunate possessor of much rich and youthful bloom can be at a touch of soap and water. She gave her hostess a second embrace, laying a cheek like a June rose against Ellen's more delicately tinted cheek, and murmuring:

"I never can tell you how I have missed you since that all-conquering husband of yours brought you off up North. By the way, is that his photograph?"

She was looking over Ellen's shoulder at a picture in an ivory-and-silver frame upon the dressing-table. She answered her own question.

"Of course it is. I'd know by the look of him that he must be Red Pepper Burns." She went over and examined the pictured face closely. "I could make a better picture of him than that,— I know it without seeing him in the flesh. What a splendid pair of eyes! Do they look right down into your inmost thoughts — or do they see only as far as your liver? Fine head, good mouth, straight nose, chin like a stone wall! Goodness! do you never meet up with that chin?"

She looked around at Ellen with mischief in her bright brown eyes.

"Of course I do! Would you have a man chinless?"

"Luckily, you have a determined little round chin of your own," Miss Ruston observed. "And you're happy with him? Yes, I can see it in your face. Well, now, shall we talk about me? Because I

have so little time, you know, and so much has to
be settled before night."

"Tell me all about it at once, dear." And Ellen
established her guest in a high-backed, cushioned
wicker chair by the window, and sat down close by.
The two looked at each other, smiling.

"Well, Len, I never could lead up to a thing;
I have to tell it in one burst, and trust to Providence
to sustain the hearer. What would you say — to
— my coming to this place for a year, renting a
cottage, putting in a skylight, and — practising my
profession of photography in your midst?"

"Charlotte Ruston!"

"My middle name is Chase," observed Miss
Ruston, laying her head back against the chair, and
smiling out at Mrs. Burns through half-closed lids.
"Charlotte Chase Ruston forms a quite imposing
signature to imprint upon the distinguished portraits
she is to make. Portraits of the aristocracy who
can afford to pay ever so many dollars a dozen for
likenesses of themselves in exquisite, informal poses,
with wonderful shadows just where they will hide
the most defects, and splendid high lights where they
will bring out all the charm the subjects didn't know
they possessed."

"Charlotte! Have you been studying in secret?
I know you do delightful amateur work, but — a
studio! Do you dare?"

"I've worked a year in the developing room of
the Misses Kendall, and have been allowed to make
trial studies of subjects, when they were busy.
I have their friendship, also that of Brant —
Eugene Brant — who does the cleverest profession-
ally amateur studio work in the world, according
to my humble opinion. And the Kendalls do the
finest garden and outdoor studies, as you know.
Could I have better training? Mr. Brant thinks
me fit to start a city studio — a modest one — but
the Misses Kendall advise a year in a small town,
just working for experience and perfection. Then
when I do begin in a bigger place I'll be ready to do
work of real distinction. Come, tell me, isn't it a
beautiful plan?"

"Any plan, which brings you to live near me,
is a beautiful plan. And you've really chosen this
little town? How did you come to do it?"

"Tales of the beauty of the region, and the re-
flection that, since one small town in it was probably
as good as another, there was no reason why I
shouldn't be near one of my dearest friends, and
have, frankly, the help of her patronage. Shall
you mind giving it to me?"

"I'll bring you a dozen subjects the first day.
I suppose you haven't looked about at all as yet
for the place?"

"I shall not need to, if you won't object to having

me close by, even so near as across the road. As I stood on your doorstep I saw my future studio spring, full-fledged, into view, with a *'To rent'* notice already up. Could I have a plainer sign that my good fairy is attending my footsteps?"

Miss Ruston leaned forward to the window as she spoke, drew aside the thin curtain which swayed there in the summer breeze, and pointed across the street. "Isn't there a little old cottage, back in there somewhere, in a tangle of old-fashioned flowers? It doesn't show from here, I see, but from below I caught just a glimpse of its unimposing dimensions. The sign is on the gate, in the hedge. It's simply perfect that the place should have a hedge!"

"Evidently you didn't inspect it very closely, Charlotte dear. It's a most forlorn little old place, and much run down. Two old ladies have lived there all their lives, and have died there within the year. They would never sell, although, as you see, the neighbourhood all about is built up with modern houses — all except our own. This house is quite old, I believe, too."

"Two old ladies lived and died there, did they?" mused Charlotte Ruston. "Their gentle ghosts won't trouble us, and Granny will delight in that garden. What a background for an outdoor studio! Do let's go over and explore the place, will you?"

As they crossed the street the newcomer was using her eyes with eager observation. "It's a fine old street," she said, "with all these beautiful trees. What a pity it is mostly so modern in the matter of architecture! I wonder if the people in those houses will think me out of my head, to begin with, because I choose this quaint little dwelling-place. I shall choose it, Len, if I can get it, I warn you."

With some difficulty they opened the gate in the hedge, and proceeded up the path of moss-grown stones to the house, set so far back from the street that it was nearly concealed by the growth of untrimmed shrubbery, old rose-bushes heavy with pink and white roses, lilac trees, and barberry-bushes.

"Of all the dear, queer, little front porches!" Miss Ruston cried, setting her exploring foot on a porch floor which promptly sagged beneath her weight. She threw a quizzical glance at her companion. "Even though the roof falls in on my head, and the walls sway as I pass by, I must have this house — if it is dry! Of course I can't bring Granny to a damp house. Putting in my skylight and shingling the rest of the roof will take care of dampness from above, but I must look after the floors and foundations. Who owns it, and how can we get in?"

An hour later the key had been obtained from the

astonished owner, an inhabitant of one of the modern houses near by and a nephew of the former occupants, and the place had been thoroughly gone over. It was examined by a future tenant who made light of all the real drawbacks to the place—as the owner secretly considered them — but who demanded absolutely water-tight conditions as the price of her rent. As she was willing to pay what seemed to the land-lord an extraordinary rent — though he carefully concealed his feelings on this point — he somewhat grudgingly agreed to put in the skylight and shingle the roof.

"But when it comes to paint and paper and plumbing, the house isn't worth it, and I can't agree to do it," he declared positively. "Not for any one year rental."

"I don't want paint, paper, or plumbing," she replied, and he set her down as eccentric indeed. "But I do want that fireplace unsealed, and if you will put that and the chimney in order, so I can have fires there, I won't ask for any modern conveniences. When can you have it ready for me? By the middle of July?"

He did not think this possible, but his new tenant convinced him that it was, and went away smiling, her hands full of June roses, and her spirits high. It was with her vivid personality at its best that she presently took her place at the luncheon table, meeting there, however, at first, only Miss Mathewson.

"My patient has fallen asleep after his walk," Amy explained to Mrs. Burns, as she came in. "I thought he had better not be wakened."

"You were quite right, I am sure," Ellen agreed. Then she made the two young women known to each other, and the three sat down. R. P. Burns, M. D., rushing in the midst of the meal, found them laughing merrily together over a tale the guest had been telling.

As Burns came forward Miss Ruston rose to meet him. The two regarded each other with undisguised interest as they shook hands.

"Yes, I can make a much better photograph of you than the one on your wife's dressing-table," said she, judicially, and laughed at his astonished expression.

"Can you, indeed?" he inquired. "Have you a snapshot camera concealed anywhere about you? If so, I'll consider going back to town for my luncheon."

"You are safe for to-day," Ellen assured him, and he sat down.

He was told the tale of the morning, the subject introduced by his wife, and amplified by their guest. He expressed his interest.

"You have a good courage, Miss Ruston," said

he. "And we'll agree to stand by you. Any time, in the middle of the night, that we hear the crash and fall of decayed old timbers, we'll come to the rescue and pull you out. We don't have much excitement here. The wreck will have the advantage of advertising you thoroughly. Then you can build a tight little bungalow on the spot and settle down to real business."

Miss Ruston shook her shapely head. "No tight little bungalows for me," she averred. "Those vine-clad old walls will make wonderful backgrounds for my outdoor subjects — they and the garden. Then, indoors — the fireplace, the queer old doors —— "

Red Pepper looked at his wife. "Has the village a passion for quaintness?" he asked her. "Will our leading citizens want to be photographed in their old hoopskirts, with roses behind their ears?"

"Oh, you don't understand!" cried Miss Ruston. "Ellen — will you excuse me while I run up and bring down an example or two of my work?"

She was back in a minute, several prints in her hand. She came around behind Burns's chair and laid one before him, another before Amy Mathewson. Ellen, who had already seen the prints, watched her husband's face as he examined the photograph.

"You don't intend me to understand," said he,

after a minute's steady scrutiny, "that this is a photograph of actual children?"

Miss Ruston nodded. Her face glowed with enthusiasm over her work. "Indeed it is. Flesh and blood children — Rupert and Rodney Trumbull. And it's really the night before Christmas, too. They were not acting the part — it was the real thing."

Burns continued to study the picture — of two small boys in their night-clothes, standing before a chimney-piece, looking up at their stockings, at that last wondering, enchanted moment before they should lay hands upon the mysteries before them. The glow of the firelight was upon them, the shadows behind held the small sturdy figures in an exquisitely soft embrace. It was such a photograph as combines the workings of the most delicate art with the unconscious posing of absolute realism.

Burns looked from the picture to his wife's face. "We must have one of Bobby like that," said he.

Ellen agreed, her eyes meeting her friend's over his head. The guest laid another print before him. "Since you like fireplace effects," she explained. Then she gave the Christmas-eve picture to Miss Mathewson, smiling as Amy, returning the print she had been studying, said softly, "It is wonderful work, Miss Ruston. I shall want one of my mother like this."

"You shall have it," Miss Ruston promised.

Burns exclaimed with pleasure over the present-
ment of a little old lady, knitting before a fire, a
faint smile on her face, as if she were thinking of
lovely things as she worked. As in the other
picture the shadows were soft and hazy, only the
surfaces touched by the fireglow showing with
distinctness, the whole effect almost illusive, yet
giving more of the human touch than any clear and
distinct details could possibly have done.

"That is Granny," said Miss Ruston, a gentle
note in her eager voice. "My little piece of priceless porcelain which I guard with all the defences
at my command. Tell me, Dr. Burns, I shall not
be bringing her into any danger if I put her in the
little old house, when it is made right?"

"If you are thinking of bringing *this* old lady here,"
said he, emphatically, his eyes on the picture again,
"you must let me look the place over thoroughly
for you first."

"But I've engaged it!" cried his wife's friend, in
dismay.

"That doesn't matter. You will call it all off
again, if I don't find the place can be made fit,"
said he. "Old ladies like this shall not be risked in
doubtful places, no matter how quaint and artistic
the background, not while I am on hand to prevent."

Miss Ruston looked at Mrs. Burns. "Is this

what he is like?" said she, in dismay. "I didn't reckon with him!"

"You will have to reckon with me now," said Red Pepper Burns, with coolness.

"But the owner says it can be made perfectly tight. And I have to go back to-night!"

"The owner of a sieve would say it could be made perfectly tight — if it was wanted for a dishpan. And you are at liberty to go back to-night — much as we shall dislike to lose you. I will take time to go over, right now, and make sure of this thing for you."

He rose as he spoke.

"Well, of all the positive gentlemen! Will you stay to look at one more? It may soften that austere mood."

Miss Ruston gave him a third print. It was of a very beautiful woman standing beside a window, the attitude apparently unstudied, the lighting unusual and picturesque, the whole effect challenging all conventional laws of photography.

"It's very nice — very nice," said Burns, indifferently. "But it's not in it with the old lady by the fire. I'll run across and make sure of her quarters, if you please."

"That will be wonderfully good of you," and the guest looked after her host, dubiously, as he went out.

"Does one have to do everything he says, in these parts?" she inquired, glancing from Mrs. Burns to Miss Mathewson, both of whom were smiling. Her own expression was an odd mixture of interest and rebellion.

Miss Mathewson spoke first. "I have been his surgical assistant for more than nine years," said she. "When I have ventured to depart from the line he laid out for me I have — been very sorry, afterward."

"Did you ever venture to depart very far?"

"Do I look so meek?"

"You don't look meek at all, but you do look— conscientious." Miss Ruston gave her a daring look.

Amy spoke with more spirit than the others had expected. "If I were not conscientious I couldn't work for Dr. Burns."

"He doesn't look conscientious, to me," declared Miss Ruston. "He looks adventurous, audacious, unexpected."

"Perhaps he is. But he doesn't expect his assistant nurse to be adventurous, audacious, or unexpected!"

"Good for you!" Miss Ruston was laughing, and looking with newly roused interest at this young woman, whom she had perhaps taken to be of a more commonplace type than her words now indicated. "As for my friend, Mrs. Burns — he is her husband, and she must have known what he was like, since I, in one short hour, have already discovered two or three of his characteristics! Well, here's hoping he's on my side, when he comes back. If he's not —— "

But when he came back he was on her side, reluctantly convinced by a painstaking examination of the possibilities in the old cottage, and by a man-to-man talk with its owner as to his good faith in promising to carry out the lessee's requirements.

"Though what in the name of time possesses a stunning girl like that to come here and shut herself up in Aunt Selina's old rookery, I can't make out," the landlord, Burns's neighbour, had confessed.

"Possibly she won't shut herself up," Burns had suggested, though he himself had been unable to discover the mysterious attraction of the little old house. The garden promised better, he thought. He could understand her being caught by the forsaken though powerful charm of that. Doubtless it would furnish backgrounds for her outdoor photography, which would put to blush any painted screens such as the village photographers were accustomed to use.

He returned to give Miss Ruston his sanction of her project, and to receive her half-mocking, wholly grateful acknowledgment.

"And I hope, Dr. Burns," said she, as he took leave of her, his watch in his left hand as he shook hands with his right, "that you will let me make that photograph of you, at the very beginning of my stay here."

"With a clump of hollyhocks behind me, or a 'queer old door'?" he inquired.

"With nothing behind you except darkness and mystery," said she.

"I thought those were the things one looked toward, not out of?"

"Your patients looking toward 'the black unknown,' and seeing your face, must find their future lighted with hope!"

He turned and looked at his wife, a sparkle in his eye. "She's from the big town," said he. "Here in the country we don't know how to give fine, fascinating blarney like that, eh? Good-bye, Miss Ruston, and good luck. Bring the little grandmother carefully wrapped in jeweller's cotton — nothing is too good for her!"

When luncheon was over Mrs. Burns and her guest went off for a long drive, Miss Ruston being anxious to explore the region of which she had heard as offering a field for her camera. The drive, taken in the Macauley car, by Martha's invitation, and in the company of Martha herself, Winifred Chester, and several children, prevented much confidential

talk between the two friends, and it was not until
a few minutes before train time, at five o'clock, that
the two were for a brief space again alone together.

"I'm so sorry you are not to be here at dinner,"
Ellen said, as Miss Ruston repacked her small
travelling bag, while the car waited outside to take
her to the station. "I should have liked you to
meet our guest, Dr. Leaver. He is an old friend
of my husband's, who has been ill and is here
convalescing. He over-tired himself in taking a
walk this morning, and has been resting in his room
all the afternoon."

Charlotte Ruston, adjusting a smart little veil
before Ellen's mirror, her back to her friend, asked,
after a moment's pause:

"Dr. Leaver? Not Dr. John Leaver, of Baltimore?"

"Yes, indeed. Do you know him?"

"I have met him. Is he ill? I hadn't heard
of that."

"He has worked very hard, and is worn out,"
explained Ellen, choosing her terms carefully. Her
husband had warned her against allowing any
definite news concerning Leaver to get back to his
home city. "He is improving, and we are keeping
him here because it is a place where he can be out
of the world, for a time, and not be called upon to
go back before he should. So please don't mention

to your Baltimore friends that he is here. I am ever so sorry, if you know him, that he wasn't down to-day. It might have done him good to see the face of an acquaintance."

"It might be too stimulating for him," suggested Miss Ruston. She seemed difficult to satisfy in the matter of the veil's adjustment. Though she had had it fastened, she now took it off and began again to arrange it.

"Can't I help you?" Ellen offered, coming close.

"Thank you, I can manage it. I had it too tight. I suppose your guest will be gone before I come back?"

"I don't know. He needs a long rest, and we shall keep him just as long as he can be contented. Not that he is contented to be idle, but it is what he needs. He is going to need diversion, too, and perhaps you can help supply it, when you come back. Do you know him well enough to know what an interesting man he is?"

"I have heard people talk about him who do," said Miss Ruston. "But I hope he will be quite recovered and away before I come back — for his own sake. There, I believe this veil's on, at last. What a terrible colour it gives one to drive in the sun all afternoon! I must put on plenty of cold cream to-night, or I shall be a fright to-morrow."

"Why, you *are* burned! I hadn't noticed it before. And the top was up, all the time, too. But it's very becoming, Charlotte, since it seems to have confined itself to your cheeks. One's nose is usually the worst sufferer."

"That will probably show later. I must be off. Thank you, dear — dearest — for all you have done for me to-day. It's been such a happy day, I can't tell you how I feel about it."

Charlotte Chase Ruston laid her burning, rose-hued cheek against her friend's — cool and quite unburned by the drive — embraced her, and hurried down the stairs. She seemed in haste to be off, but it was like her to be eager to do whatever was to be done. Ellen looked after her as the Macauley car bore her away.

"Dear Charlotte!" she said to herself. "It's like having a warm, invigorating wind sweep over one to have her company, even for a day. How I shall enjoy her, when she comes! Of all the young women I know she seems to me the most alive. I wish Dr. Leaver had been down to-day. He would surely have liked to see her; I never knew a man who didn't. If he has ever met her, he must remember her. But perhaps he will want to run away, if he knows any one who knows him has found him out. Perhaps it will be better not to tell him — just yet."

CHAPTER VIII

UNDER THE APPLE TREE

A WALK, Miss Mathewson? Yes, I'll take a walk — or a pill — or whatever is due. Did you ever have a more obedient patient?"

John Leaver rose slowly from the steamer-chair in a corner of the porch where he had been lying, staring idly at the vines which sheltered him from the village street, or out at the strip of lawn upon which the early evening light was falling. His tall figure straightened itself; evidently it cost him an effort to force his shoulders into their naturally erect carriage. But as he walked down the path by Miss Mathewson's side there was not much look of the invalid about him. His face, though still rather thin, showed a healthy colour, the result of constant exposure to the sun and air. His days were spent wholly out of doors.

"Which way, this time?" Amy asked, as they reached the street.

"Away from things rather than toward them, please. I shall be very glad when I can tramp off into the open country."

Amy glanced across the street. "Don't you want to approach a visit to the country by exploring the old garden, over there? I hear that it has all sorts of treasures of old-fashioned flowers in it. Do you care for old gardens?"

"Very much, though it is a long time since I've been in one."

"Have you heard that the old house over here is to have a new tenant?"

"No, I haven't heard."

Leaver opened the gate in the hedge for his companion, looking as if the least interesting thing in the world to him were the matter of tenants for the little old cottage before him. But his tone was, as always, courteously interested.

"I was so sorry, the other day, that it happened you didn't meet Mrs. Burns's friend, such an interesting young woman. She is coming here to open a photographic studio in this old house — as an experiment."

"A professional photographer?"

"I believe not — as yet. She would still call herself an amateur, but from the pictures she showed us she would seem an expert. I never saw anything like them. Dr. Burns — he had never met her — was very much taken with them, especially with one of the little old lady, her grandmother, whom she is to bring here."

They strolled along the moss-grown path, past the house, aside into the garden, its tangle of flowers and shrubbery rich with neglected bloom and sweet with all manner of scents — sweet-william, larkspur, clove-pink. Leaver, stooping, picked a spicy-smelling, fringe-bordered pink, and sniffed its sun-warmed fragrance.

"It takes me back to my boyhood," he said, "when I used to think a visit at my grandfather's old country place the greatest thing that could happen to me. There was a big bed of these flowers under my window. When the sun was hot upon them they rivalled the spices of Araby."

Miss Mathewson stood looking back at the house. From the garden, which lay at the side and behind it, it showed all of its forlornness and few of its possibilities.

"What will she make of living there, even for the year she means to stay?" she wondered, aloud. "Now, if it were I, it wouldn't seem strange; I am used to living in a little old house. But such a girl as Miss Ruston — I can hardly imagine her here. She thinks the house and the old garden will make fine backgrounds for her work. I suppose they will."

"Miss Ruston?" Dr. Leaver repeated. "Was that the name?"

"Miss Charlotte Ruston, of South Carolina, I believe. I never heard the name before, have you?"

"It is an unusual one. I have known only one person of that name." Leaver walked slowly over to a decayed and tumbling bench beneath an apple-tree, whose boughs had been so long untrimmed that they spread almost to the earth. He sat down upon it, rather heavily, and lifted the clove-pink to his nostrils again. His dark brows contracted slightly. He looked at the house. "It will have to have a good deal done to it before it is fit for any one," he observed. "You said there was an old lady to come, too?"

"A most beautiful little old lady, whom Miss Ruston seemed to be very anxious over, lest she suffer any harm. Dr. Burns, when he heard of it, insisted on coming over here to make sure the house could be made perfectly dry and comfortable for her."

"He was right. Little old ladies must be taken care of, and young women are apt to think any place that is picturesque is safe."

Miss Mathewson, seeing him apparently more interested in the subject than he was apt to be in the topics she brought up to amuse him, except as he assumed interest for her sake, went on with this one, and told him all she knew about Miss Ruston's plans, ending with a description of the photographs she had shown.

"But I should like to see one of herself,"

she added. "She has such a — brilliant face.
I can't think of any other word to describe it!
When she looks at you she looks as if she — cared
so much to see what you were like!" She laughed
at her own attempt to make her description clear.
"Not as if she were curious, you know, but as if
she were interested — attracted. Can you imagine
the expression?"

Leaver leaned his head back against the apple-
tree trunk, and closed his eyes. The spice-pink,
still held at his nostrils, shielded his lips. He looked
rather white, his nurse noticed, but she had become
accustomed to seeing these moments come upon
him — they passed away again, and Dr. Burns had
said that no notice need be taken of them unless they
were long in passing. In spite of his pallor, he
spoke naturally enough.

"Yes, I have seen such a face. But many women
— Southern women, especially — have that look
of being absorbed in what one is saying; it is a pretty
trick of theirs. Won't you sit down, too, on this
old bench? It is so warm yet, we may as well rest
a little and walk when it is dusk and cooler."

She sat down beside him, a pleasant picture to
look at in her white lawn in which, at Ellen's suggestion, she now made of herself, in the afternoons,
a figure less severe than in her uniform. She had
even added a touch of turquoise to the chaste white-

ness of the dress, a colour which brought out the beauty of her deep blue eyes and fair cheeks and even lent warmth to the pale hues of her hair.

"If you want to sit here, Dr. Leaver, I might run across and bring the book we are reading. Would you like to hear a chapter?"

"Thank you, not to-night. It's a great book, and stirs the blood with its attempt to tell the story of a war whose real story can never be told by any one, no matter what skill the historian brings to the telling. But I'm not in the mood for it to-night. I wonder if, instead, you won't tell me a bit about yourself. You've never said a word about the work you do with my friend, Dr. Burns. Do you like it?"

She hesitated. Was this a safe subject, she wondered, for a surgeon who, she understood, had broken down from overwork? But the question had been asked.

"Very much," she answered, quietly. "One could hardly help liking work under Dr. Burns."

"Why? Do you think him a fine operator?"

"Very fine. He is considered the best in the city, now, I believe, even though his office is out here in the village. Of course it is not a great city, but his reputation extends out into the towns around."

"He is an enthusiast in his profession, I know. And you are one in yours, I see."

"Do you see it, Dr. Leaver? I thought I spoke quite moderately."

"So moderately that I recognized the restraint. You assist Dr. Burns whenever he operates?"

"Yes — if I am free."

"He can't have been doing much lately, then."

She glanced at him. He was still leaning back against the apple-tree trunk, but his eyes were open and regarding her rather closely. They were eyes whose powers of discernment, as Burns had said, one could not hope easily to elude.

"He is so interested in your recovery, Dr. Leaver, that he is willing, anxious, to spare me. There are other capable assistants, plenty of them."

"But none trained to his hand, as you are trained."

In spite of herself, the quick colour rose in a wave and bathed her face in its tell-tale glow.   He smiled.

"I see. It's worth everything to an operator to have a right-hand man — or woman — like that. One doesn't often find a woman capable of taking the part, but, when one is, she is like a second brain to the operator. Well, I'll soon release you. I don't need to be coddled now, though it's very pleasant. I shall remember these walks and talks and hours with books. If one must be disabled, it's much to be looked after by one who seems a friend."

"But — Dr Leaver!—— " She spoke in some alarm. "You mustn't talk of dismissing me

like this — unless you are dissatisfied with me.
I know Dr. Burns is taking great satisfaction in
having me give my time to you. If I am helping
you at all —— "

"You are. But — I must help myself. . . .
Never mind." He closed his eyes again. "Tell
me about yourself — as Dr. Burns's assistant. Do
you enjoy making things ready for him?"

She saw that he would have it, so she answered.
"Yes, I suppose I take pride in having everything
as he will want it. I know quite well what he wants,
by this time."

"Yes. And he can depend on you. When the
time comes for the start, you have yourself well
in hand? No quick pulse — short breath?"

"Why, it would not be possible, I suppose, to be
so self-controlled as that. Even Dr. Burns is
not. He has told me, more than once, that his heart
is pounding like an engine when he goes into an
operation, or when he faces an unexpected emergency, in the course of it."

"Ah! . . . But it doesn't affect his work —
or yours — this racing of the engine?"

"One forgets it, I think, when one is once at
work. Dr. Leaver, look at that squirrel! Out on
the roof of the house — at the back. Do you see
him peering over at us? Inquisitive little creature!"

"Like myself. Yes, I see his small majesty.

Well, tell me, please, why you like the work so much? You wouldn't give it up?"

She drew a quick breath. "Oh, no!"

"And the reason why you like it — am I too curious? Do you mind telling me?"

"Why, not at all. I can — hardly tell you, though, what it is that makes me like it. Of course, I'm happy to have a hand, even though it's only an assistant's hand, in saving life. But — the life isn't always saved. I suppose, the real secret of it is one likes to be doing the thing one can do best."

"That's it!" He drew a heavy breath. "The thing one can do best. And when that thing is the setting poor, disabled human machinery straight — making it run smoothly again! One can hardly imagine turning one's hand to — book-binding, making things in brass, dressing dolls, to take up one's time, occupy one's mind, keep one's hands busy, after having known the practice of a profession like that!"

He got up from the bench and strode a few paces with a quick, impatient step, such as she had never seen him take. Then, wheeling suddenly, he came back to the bench and dropped upon it, breathing short. She had instantly to his support a small bottle of strong salts which she always carried, but for a moment she feared that this might not be stimulant enough to a heart still inclined to be erratic upon small provocation. She laid anxious fingers upon his pulse, but found it already steadying.

"This will be over in a minute," she said quietly. "Soon, you will have got above such bothersome minutes. I shouldn't have let you talk about a thing which means so much to you."

"No, I can't even talk about it," he said. "I'm as much of an infernal hypochondriac as that. I beg your pardon —— " and he set his lips.

They sat in silence for a little. Then, suddenly a voice hailed them — a cheerful, familiar voice.

"'Under the spreading chestnut-tree?' Or is it an apple? May I join the party?"

Redfield Pepper Burns appeared, looking like a schoolboy lately released from imprisonment. But his face sobered somewhat as his eye fell upon his friend. It was not that John Leaver had not looked up with a smile, as Burns approached, nor was it that he now showed physical distress of any significant sort. A certain hard expression of the deep-set eye told the story to one who could read signs.

"There's a caller for you at the house, Miss Mathewson," said Burns.

As she went away he dropped down upon the grass near Leaver. "It's at least five degrees cooler under this tree," said he, "than in any outdoor spot I've found yet."

"Work must have been trying to-day."

"Rather. But so much worse for my patients that I haven't thought much about it for myself. At two places I had the satisfaction of personally seeing to the moving of the invalid from a little six-by-nine inferno of a bedroom to a big and airy sitting-room. It gave me the keenest pleasure to see it hurt the tidy housewife, who didn't want her best room mussed up." He chuckled. "In one case I made her take down the stuffy lace window-curtains and open things up in great shape. She came near having a convulsion on the spot. Curious how a certain type of mind regards any little innovation like that. That woman would have let her unlucky husband smother to death in that oven before it would have occurred to her to move him out of it.'

"I rather wonder at your continuing to practise in a village like this, with that sort of people, when you have so much city work, and could do a large business with a city office."

Burns stretched out an arm, thrusting his hand deep into the long grass. "That sort — narrow-minded people — aren't all found in the country, though — not by a long shot. I've sometimes thought I'd take an office in town, but, when it comes to making the move, I can't bring myself to it. You see, I happen to like it out here, and I like the village work. This way I get both sorts. I don't know why one's ambition should be all for city work. The people out here need me just as much as those where the streets are paved. There's a heap more fresh air and sunshine and liberty here than in town. And, as for being busy, there are only twenty-four hours in the day, anywhere."

"And you fill the most of those full. So you do. Yet, I should think your love for surgery would lead you to take up an exclusive surgical practice. You could make a name. You have a good-sized reputation already, with your ability you could make it a great one."

Burns looked at Leaver. The two men regarded each other with a sudden fresh interest, a sudden wonder as to the operation of each other's minds. The man on the bench, broken down by just such a life as he recommended to his friend, looked at the man on the grass, unworn and vigorous, and questioned whether, with all his virtues, Burns were really possessed of the proper ambition. The man on the grass, aware of large interests in his busy life, looked at the man on the bench, whose interests were at present wholly concerned with recovering his health, and wondered what insanity it was which bound his fellow mortal's brain that he could not see things in their right values. There was a long minute's silence. Then Burns, lying at full length upon

his side in the warm grass, his head propped upon
his elbow, began, in a thoughtful tone:

"Ever since a period early in our acquaintance my wife and I have had a vision before us.
It was one that, curiously enough, we both had
separately first, and then discovered, by accident,
that it was mutual. The time has come when we
are to carry it out. My wife has bought an old
place, in the real country, three miles out on a road
that turns off from the main road to the city. She
is going to fit it up for a hospital for crippled children,
curables, mostly, though her heart may lead her
into keeping a few of the other sort, if there is no
other home for them to go to. I'm to have the
distinguished honour of being surgeon to the place."

He made this final announcement in the tone in
which he might have made it if it had been that of
an appointment to the greatest position the country
could have given him.

"Well," said Leaver, after a moment, his weary
eyes still studying Burns's face, "that is a fine thing
for you two to do. I can see that such an interest
might well hold a man away from an ordinary city
practice. There is no children's hospital near here,
then?"

"None at all. Children's wards, of course, but
nothing like what ought to be. Of course we can't
take care of the surplus. It will be only special

cases, here and there, that we shall try to handle. But I'm meeting with those every day — cases where the country air and the country fare are almost as much a part of the cure as the surgical interference. My word! but it will be a satisfaction to bundle the poor little chaps off to our farm!"

His eyes were very bright. He lay smiling to himself for a minute, then he sat up.

"In a month," said he, "we shall be ready for business. I have four little patients waiting now for the place. On three of them I'm going to operate at once. On the fourth — *you* are."

Again the two pairs of eyes met — hazel eyes confident and determined, brown eyes startled, stabbed with sudden pain. Burns held up his hand.

"Don't say a word," he commanded. "I'm merely making an assertion. I'm willing to back it up by argument, if you like, though I'd rather not. In fact, I'd much rather not. I prefer simply to make the assertion, and let it sink in."

But Leaver would speak. "You forget," he said, bitterly, "that I've put all that behind me. I told you I should never operate again. I meant it."

"Yes, you meant it," said Burns comfortably. "A man means it when he swears he'll never do again something that has become second nature to him to do. He'll do it — he's made that way.

You will do this thing, and do it with all your old grip and skill. But I'm not going to discuss it with you. Some day, if you are good, I'll describe the case to you. It's one you can handle better than I, and it's going to be up to you."

He got to his feet, ignoring the slow shaking of Leaver's downbent head. "By the way," he said, with a glance at the cottage, now a mere blur in the oncoming twilight, "have you heard of the young photographer who is to sweep down upon us and make wonderful, dream-like images of us all, for good hard cash and fame? A friend of my wife's: a girl who looks twenty-five, but is a bit more, I am told. A remarkably good-looking, not to say fascinating, person with a grandmother still more fascinating — at least to me. They are to come as soon as this rookery can be made habitable."

"Miss Mathewson spoke of it. It will be an interesting event to the village, I should suppose. But I shall not be among the victims of the lady's art. I may as well tell you, Red — I must get away next week."

Burns wheeled upon him. "What's that you say?"

The other proceeded with evident effort, laying his head back against the tree-trunk again. "I am as grateful to you and Mrs. Burns as a man can possibly be, so grateful that I can't put it into words —— "

"Don't try. Go on to something more important."

"I have trespassed on your hospitality ——"

"Don't use hackneyed phrases like that. Say something original."

—" as long as I can be willing to do it. I am as much improved as I can expect to be — for a long time. I can't hang on, a useless invalid on your hands —— "

"Cut it, old man! You're not an invalid, and you're not useless. You're giving me one of the most interesting studies I've engaged in in a long time. I'm liable to write a book on you, when I get sufficient data."

Leaver smiled faintly. "Nevertheless, I can't do it, Red. You wouldn't do it in my place. Be honest — would you?"

"Probably not. I'd be just pig-headed fool enough to argue the case to myself precisely as you are doing. Well, Jack, I've expected this hour. It's a pity there isn't more faith and trust in friendship in the world. We're all deadly afraid of trying our friends too far, so after just about so long we strike out for ourselves. But since it is as it is, and you're growing restless, I'll agree that you leave us, if you'll stay for a while where you'll be under my observation. I've set my heart on making a complete cure in this case — or, rather, you understand, assisting

Nature to do so. If you go off somewhere I shall lose track of you. Suppose you stay in the village here for a while longer. I know a splendid place for you, just round the corner. Quiet, pleasant home, middle-aged widow and her young son — a lady, and a sensible, cheerful one — she'll never bore you by talk unless you feel like it — and then the talk will be worth while. What do you say? You know perfectly well that you're not yet quite fit to shift for yourself. Be rational, and let me manage things for you a while longer."

Leaver stood up; in the dim light Burns could not see his face. But he heard his voice — one which showed tension.

"You don't know what you're asking, old friend. There are reasons why I feel like getting away, entirely apart from any conditions under your control. Yet since you ask it of me, and I owe you so much, and since — I suppose it doesn't really make much difference where I am — I'll stay for the present."

"Good! I'm much obliged, Jack."

Burns got up, also, and the two strolled away together, in the pleasant summer dusk.

CHAPTER IX

A PRACTICAL ARTIST

HERE I am! And the goods are here too. Isn't it a miracle? It could never have been done if I hadn't found a kind friend among the railroad men, who sent my things by fast freight. Now to settle in a whirlwind of a hurry and fly back for Granny."

These were Miss Charlotte Ruston's words of greeting as she shook hands with the occupants of the Macauley car, which had met her at the station on the last day of July. She looked as fresh and eager to carry out her plans as if she were not just at the end of a journey.

"I suppose you'll stop for luncheon first," Martha Macauley suggested. She noted, with the approval of the suburbanite who cares much to be well dressed, the quietly smart attire of the arriving traveller.

"Indeed I will. Fuel first, fire afterward. But I'm fairly burning to begin, July weather though it is. How are my hollyhocks? A splendid row? I've dreamed of those hollyhocks!"

"They are all there — as well as one can see them

above the weeds. We would have had the grass cut for you, but didn't venture to touch so much as a spear, lest we destroy some picturesque effect," Ellen said, giving her friend's hand an affectionate grasp as Charlotte took her place beside her.

"I do want to see to it all for myself. I've had the greatest difficulty in waiting these four weeks, or should have had if I hadn't been so busy. But now that I'm here I'll show you how to make a home out of four chairs, three rugs, a table, a mirror, and an adorable copper bowl. Talk of the simple life — you're going to see it lived just across the street, you matrons with innumerable things to dust!"

"We shall be delighted to watch you do it," Ellen assured her, and Martha gave an incredulous assent.

It was but a few hours before they saw the prophecy coming true. Miss Ruston barely took time for luncheon, and by the time the dray containing her modest supply of household goods was at her door she was ready for work. A blue painter's blouse slipped over her travelling dress, her sleeves rolled well up her shapely arms, she had plunged into the labour of settling. She had for an assistant a woman whom Ellen had engaged for her, and a tall youth who was the woman's son, and these two she managed with a generalship little short of genius.

The floors had been cleaned and stained with a

simple dull-brown stain a week before, and Miss
Ruston eyed them with satisfaction, uneven though
they were. She set the lad at work oiling them,
demonstrating to him with her own hands, carefully
gloved, the way to do it. Every window she flung
wide, and Mrs. Kelsey was presently scrubbing
away at the dim, small panes, trying her best to
make them shine to please the young lady who
from time to time stopped as she flew by to comment
on her work.

"That's it, Mrs. Kelsey, you know how, don't
you? I haven't much in the way of hangings for
them, so we must have them bright as mirrors.
Hard to get into the corners? Yes, I know. But
it's somehow the corners that show most. Try
this hairpin under your cloth," — she slipped one
out from her heavy locks — "you can get into the
corners with that, I'm sure. Tom, there's a spot
as big as a plate you haven't hit. You can't see it
in that light; bend over this way a minute, and
you'll find it. That's it! It would have been a
pity to leave it, wouldn't it! Don't miss any more
places, Tom. I haven't many rugs, and the floors
will show a good deal."

"I didn't know artists were ever such practical
people," confessed Mrs. Red Pepper Burns, sitting
on the edge of a straight-backed old chair in the
small kitchen. The house boasted but four rooms,

two below and two above, with a small enclosure off the kitchen which had been used for a bedroom in the benighted days when people knew no better, and which Charlotte had promptly set aside for a dark room.

"Practical? I'm not an artist, as you use the word, but I assure you real artists are the most practical people in the world. Not one of them but can make a whistle out of a pig's tail, or a queen's robe out of a sheet and a blue scarf! What do you think of my light-housekeeping outfit?"

She held up an aluminum skillet which she had just taken from the box she was unpacking. "Here's everything we can need in the way of cooking utensils, packed into a foot square, and light as a feather, the whole thing. My purse was rather light when I had bought it, too." She made a funny little grimace, then laughed. "But my most trying purchase was my tin bath! You can't imagine what a hunt I had for it. But I found it at last in an Englishman's little out-of-the-way shop, and a big tin ewer to go with it. I'm proud of them now, and emptying the tub once a day is going to be fine for my muscles."

"You have splendid courage, dear, and I can see you're not afraid of hard work. I want you to promise me this, though, Charlotte. When you are specially tired, and there's luncheon or dinner to get, run over and let us give you a trayful of things. Cynthia always cooks more than we eat, and then has to contrive to use it in other ways."

Charlotte nodded. "Thank you. Luckily, though I'm poor I'm not proud. By the way, you haven't an unused kitchen chair, have you? To tell the truth I forgot several things, and one of them is a chair for the kitchen. I probably shall not sit down myself, and shall always serve our little meals in the living-room, but I foresee that I shall have guests here in the kitchen, and I'd like to be able to offer them a chair. That one you're sitting in is my very best old split-bottomed, high-backed photographer's treasure, which must go in the front room by the fireplace."

"When you are through explaining I will assure you that two kitchen chairs will arrive as soon as I go home," promised Ellen.

"Bless you! I foresee that you will make a splendid neighbour. Do you want to climb upstairs and see the nest I'm going to feather for Granny?"

She turned to the narrow little staircase between the walls, and gayly led the way. But Ellen exclaimed in dismay over the steepness of the stairs.

"Charlotte! Do you think dear little old Madam Chase can climb these? They are the steepest I ever saw!"

"She won't need to. Private lift, always ready."

"What do you mean?   Surely not —— "

Charlotte extended two round, supple arms.
"Why not? Granny weighs just eighty pounds —
if she is wearing plenty of clothes. In her little
nightie and lavender kimono considerably less.
And I'm strong as strong."

"But even then she's more than you ought to
carry up and down this ladder."

Charlotte turned at the top of the stairs, and
laughed back at her friend. "Granny's a sports-
woman," said she. "She will — whisper it! —
thoroughly enjoy sliding down these stairs, and, as
for my carrying her up them, haven't you yet found
out that a weight you love devotedly is just no weight
at all?   Now, look here!   Aren't these bits of
rooms fascinating?   Hot, just now, I admit——"
She ran to the windows, wrenched them open and
propped them up. "Too hot in July, certainly;
we'll camp downstairs while this weather lasts.
But fine and warm and sunny through the winter.
A bit of an oilstove will make Granny as snug as
a kitten, and her maid Charlotte will see that she's
never left alone with it burning."

"I see you're quite invincible in your determination to make the best of everything. I can hardly
believe you are the same girl I used to know, brought
up to be waited on and petted by everybody.
You've developed splendidly, and I'm proud of you."

"Thank you, Len. No, I'm not the same girl at all. I've been having to depend upon my own management for four years now — long enough to learn a good many makeshifts. It's been rather a pull, but I've had Granny through it all, and as long as she's left to me I won't complain. I used to be an extravagant person, but you've no idea how I've learned to make money last. Don't stay up here, it's too hot for you. But I'll get the place in order, for it may be cooler by the time I bring Granny, so we can sleep here."

"I'll help. What comes first?"

"Nothing — for you. I'll run up and down with rugs and curtains, — really, they're about all there are to go up here, except Granny's dressing-table. I've saved that for her, and a little old single bed she likes. I'll have Tom bring them up."

But Ellen insisted on helping, and when the bed was in place made it up with the fine old linen Charlotte produced, exclaiming over its handsome monograms, of an antique pattern much admired in these days.

"But where is your bed, Charlotte? I want to get that ready, too," she urged, when various small tasks were completed.

"Oh, never mind about mine. I'll see to that later." Charlotte was rubbing away at an old brass candlestick upon the dressing-table.

"I didn't see another bed.   Surely you can't both sleep in this?"

"Hardly — poor Granny!   No; mine is a folding cot, the nicest thing!"

"And you've no furniture at all for your room?"

"Don't want it.   Granny will let me peep in her mirror.   Don't look so shocked, Len.   We're just camping out for a year, you know, and I brought all we needed.   What's the use of being encumbered with household goods?"

"But you have them, somewhere?   Let me send for them, dear, please.   If you are to stay all winter you must be comfortable."

"We shall be.   And — I haven't any more things, if you must have it.   When the estate was sold I bought in all I could afford, but have sold some since.   You may as well know it, but I want you to understand that I don't consider it a hardship at all to live as I intend to live this year.   I shall be making money hand over fist, presently, and by the time I have had my city studio a year or two shall be affording Eastern rugs and hand-carved furniture.   Wait and see!"

She stopped polishing and stood looking at her friend with the peculiar, radiant look which was her greatest charm, her dark eyes glowing, her lips in proud, sweet lines of resolution, her round chin held high.   Then she laughed, throwing her head higher yet, with a gay spirit; came forward and caught Ellen Burns by the shoulders and bending kissed her.

"I told you I wasn't proud," she said, "but I am! *Too proud to be proud!* I never believed in the pride which covers up, but in that which frankly owns its poverty, and laughs at it. I laugh!"

"You splendid girl! Where did you get it?"

"Picked it up. But I really think I shall have the happiest year out of this I've known yet."

"I believe you will. And I shall delight in having you so near."

The two descended. By the time Mrs. Kelsey's work-day was over the front room was in order, and Charlotte, bidding good-night to her servitors, gave them hearty praise and bade them come back early in the morning. Ellen had gone home, bidding Charlotte follow her at convenience.

"I must run out and pick some flowers for my copper bowl," Charlotte had said. "Then the room will be ready to show your husband this evening. I'm anxious to have it make a good impression on him, and I've discovered that men always notice posies."

So, out in the tangled garden she chose a great bunch of delphinium, in mingled shadings from pale blues and lavenders to deepest sapphire tones, and bringing it in exultingly filled the copper bowl

and set it on the old spindle-legged table opposite
the fireplace. Woven rag rugs in dull blues lay
on the floor; one great winged chair, Granny's chair,
stood by the window. Besides this were the splint-
bottomed, high-backed chair, two Sheraton chairs,
and a Chippendale mirror,— all relics of a luxurious
old home. Two small portraits in oil hung upon the
wall, painted by some master hand, portraits of
Charlotte's parents. This was all the furnishing the
room contained, but somehow, in the warm light of
the late July afternoon, it looked anything but bare.

The Chesters, the Macauleys and the Burnses, all
came across the street in the early July evening,
to view the work which had been done. Charlotte
had slipped on a thin white gown and pinned a
bunch of old-fashioned crimson-and-pink "bleeding-
hearts" at her waist, to do the occasion honour.
She looked, somehow, already as if she belonged
with the place. She sat upon the doorstone and
hemmed small muslin curtains which were to go
in the bedrooms upstairs, and Martha, Winifred,
and Ellen, seeing this, sent for their sewing materials
and helped her, while the daylight lasted.

Burns, looking on, hands in pockets, suddenly
observed, "We fellows ought to be doing something
for her. What do you say to every man going for
a scythe and cutting the grass? No lawn mower
can tackle a tangle like this."

Macauley groaned. "Why begin to be neighbourly at such a pace? Cutting this grass is going to be no easy task."

But Chester and Burns had already started across the street, and Macauley was obliged to follow. By the time darkness fell the front yard had been cropped into at least a semblance of tidiness, and Charlotte was offering her thanks to three warm gentlemen, and regretting that she had not been keeping house long enough to have any refreshment to offer them.

"Come over when we are settled, and Granny and I will have some sparkling Southern beverages for you," she promised.

"You are coming over to sleep, child," Ellen said, as the time for departure arrived, and Charlotte showed signs of closing up her small domain.

"Not at all. I mean to have the fun of spending my first night in my new home," Miss Ruston declared, and held to her decision, in spite of the arguments and entreaties of the women and the assertions of the men that she would be afraid.

"Well, then, beat on a dishpan if anything disturbs you, and we'll rush across in a body and rescue you," promised Macauley.

Left alone, Charlotte went inside, lighted a genial looking lamp, and sat down alone in her little living-room. Chin in her palms, she leaned her elbows upon the spindle-legged table, looking up at the portrait of her mother, its fine colourings glowing in the mellow light from the lamp. She sat for a long time in this posture, her eyes losing their sparkle and growing dreamy, and — at last — a trifle misty. When this stage occurred she suddenly jumped up, carried the lamp into the kitchen, searched until she found a candle and lighted it, then, extinguishing the lamp, she went slowly upstairs to the cot bed.

By the following evening her preparations were so far complete that she could take the evening train for Baltimore, announcing that the two future occupants of the little house would return within forty-eight hours. During her absence the three women who were her friends put their heads together, ordered extra baking and brewing done in their own kitchens, and ended by stocking her small shelves with a great array of good things.

Before the forty-eight hours had quite gone by Miss Ruston was leading a tiny figure, with shoulders held almost as straight as her own, in at the hedge gate. It was twilight of the August evening. The cottage door was open and the rays from the lamp lately lighted by her neighbours streamed down the path.

Charlotte stooped — she had to stoop a long way

— and put her lips close to the small ear under the white hair which lay softly over it. "Doesn't it look like home, Granny?" she said, in a peculiar, clear tone, a little raised.

"What say, dear?" responded a low and quite toneless voice — the voice of the very deaf.

"Home, Granny?" repeated the younger voice. The strong arm of the taller figure came about the little shoulders in the small gray travelling coat.

"Warm? Not so warm as it was on the train. I shall be quite comfortable once I am sitting quietly in my chair."

Doctor and Mrs. Burns, following the travellers with certain pieces of hand luggage, looked at one another.

"Bless her small heart, is she as deaf as that?" queried Red Pepper, in a whisper. "I shall have difficulty in getting my adoration over to her!"

"She has grown much deafer since I knew her, several years ago," Ellen explained. "But as her eyes seem bright as ever I imagine you will have no difficulty in making her understand your adoration. She is used to it."

"I should think she might be. She is the prettiest old lady I ever saw, and looks one of the keenest. We shall understand each other, if we have to write on slates."

Charlotte led Madam Chase — Mrs. Rodney

Rutherford Chase was the name on the visiting cards she still used with scrupulous care for the observances of etiquette — in at the cottage door and placed her in the winged chair. She untied and removed a microscopic bonnet, drew off the gray coat, and laid an inquiring finger on her charge's wrist.

"Let me attend to that," begged R. P. Burns, looming in the small doorway. "I'll find out how tired she is. I doubt if she would admit it by word of mouth."

He went down on one knee beside the chair, a procedure which brought his smiling face beside the old lady's questioning one. His fingers clasped her wrist, and held it after he had found out what it told him.

"Tired?" he said, very distinctly, his lips forming the word for her to see.

Madam Chase shook her head decidedly. "Not at all, Doctor. But the train was very warm and very dusty. I shall be glad to feel a cool linen pillow under my head instead of a hot cotton one."

He nodded. "Could you eat a bit, and drink a cup of tea?"

"What say, Doctor? Tea? Yes, I should be glad of tea. I never like the decoction they serve upon trains and call tea."

"I'll have it for her in a minute," and Ellen went out into the kitchen.

Burns looked up at Miss Ruston. "As soon as she has had her tea she must go to bed. She has stood the journey well, but she needs a long rest after it." Then he looked again at Mrs. Rodney Rutherford Chase. "I can see you are a very plucky small person," said he, and her nod and smile in answer showed that at least she caught the indications of a compliment.

Presently, when she had had her tea, had patted Ellen's hand for bringing it, and had looked about her a little with observant eyes which showed pleasure when they rested on certain familiar objects, she laid her white curls back against the chair and looked up at her granddaughter like a child who asks to be put to sleep.

Burns advanced again. "May I have the honour?" he asked, stooping over the tiny figure with outstretched arms.

"You'll find me pretty heavy, Doctor," said she, but she put up her arms and clasped his neck as he lifted her, quite as if it were a matter of course with her to have stalwart men offer their services on all occasions. Burns strode up the steep and narrow staircase with her as if she had been a child, Charlotte preceding him with a pair of candles. In her own room he laid the little old lady on her bed, then stooped once more.

"May I have a reward for that?" he asked, and

without waiting for permission kissed the delicate cheek, as soft and smooth as velvet beneath his lips.

"You are a very good young man," said the old lady. "I think I shall have to adopt you as a grandson."

Burns laid his hand on his heart and made her a deeply respectful bow, at which she laughed and waved him away.

"Adorable," said he to Charlotte, on his way down, "is not a word which men use over every small object, as you women do, therefore it should have the more force when they do make use of it. No other word fits little Madam Chase so well. Consider me yours to command in her service, at any hour of day or night."

"Thank you," Charlotte called softly after him. "I assure you she will command you herself, and delight in doing it. She never fails to recognize homage when she receives it, or to demand it when she does not. But she will give you quite as much as she takes from you."

"I'm confident of it," and Burns descended to his wife. "You have a rival," he told her solemnly.

CHAPTER X

A·RUNAWAY ROAD

CAMERA hung by a strap over her shoulder, small tripod tucked under her arm, Charlotte Chase Ruston, photographer, turned aside from the country road along which she was walking, to follow a winding lane leading into a deep wood. The luring entrance to this lane had been beyond her power to resist, although the sun had climbed nearly to the zenith, warning her that it was time to turn her steps toward home. In her search for picturesque bits of landscape to turn to account in her work, her enthusiasm was likely at any time to lead her far afield.

Just as the lane promised to debouch into an open meadow and release its victim from any special sense of curiosity, it suddenly swerved to one side, forced its way under a pair of bars, and ran curving away into deep shadows, fringed with ferns, and overhung with the dense foliage of oak and walnut. A distant glimpse of brilliant scarlet flowers, standing like sentinels in uniform against the dark green of the undergrowth, beckoned like a hand. With a laugh

Charlotte set her foot upon the bottom rail. "I'm coming," she called blithely to the scarlet flowers. "You needn't shout so loud at me."

Hurrying, because of the hour, she pulled her blue linen skirts over the fence, and dropped lightly upon the other side. She ran along the lane to the flowers, stopped to admire, but refused to pick them, telling them they were better where they were, and would droop before she could get them home. Then she went swiftly on around a bend in the cart-path, catching the faint sound of falling water, and impelled to seek its source, just as is every one at hearing that suggestive sound. And, of course, the water was farther away than it sounded.

A trifle short of breath, from her haste, she ran it down at last, and came upon it — a series of small waterfalls down which a small stream tumbled recklessly along a vagrant watercourse, seeming to care little when it reached its destination, so that it contrived to have plenty of fun and exercise by the way. And on the bank, stretched recumbent, hands clasped under head, lay a long figure in gray flannels, a straw hat and a book at its side.

Charlotte stopped short. The figure turned its head, sat up, and got rather quickly to its feet, pushing back a heavy, dark lock of hair which had fallen across a tanned forehead. Dr. John Leaver came forward.

"I'm so sorry I disturbed you," said Charlotte Ruston, finding words at last, after having been surprised out of speech by the sudden apparition. "I hope I didn't wake you from a nap."

"You haven't disturbed me, and I was not asleep. I'm only waiting for Dr. Burns, who may come now at any minute. This is a pleasant place to meet in, isn't it?"

Their hands met, each looked with swift, straight scrutiny into the face of the other, and then hands and eyes parted abruptly. When they regarded each other after that, it was as two casual acquaintances may exchange glances, in the course of conversation, when other things are of more interest than the personal relation.

"Indeed it is pleasant — charming! The path lured me on and on, I couldn't stop. I ought to be at home this minute. Did you walk so far? Mrs. Burns told me you were here, and that you had been ill. I was very sorry, and I'm now so glad to see you looking so well."

"Thank you. I am much myself again, but not yet quite equal to a walk of this distance. Dr. Burns and his car are just a few rods away, on the other side of this bit of woods. He has a patient in a little shack over there, and brought me along to see this spot. It was worth coming for."

"You must enjoy Dr. Burns very much."

"We are old friends, and being together again, after a nine-years' separation, is a thing to make the most of."

"I should think so. He seems so alive, so full of interest in every living thing. He must be a fine comrade."

"The finest in the world. To me there is nobody like him, and most people who know him, I've noticed, feel in the same way. He has a beautiful wife. She is a friend of yours, she tells me."

"Also an old friend, and almost the dearest I have. I'm very happy to be near her. Dr. Leaver, will you tell me what time it is, please? I have a dreadful suspicion that I shall be very late."

As he drew out his watch a voice was heard from the other side of a clump of undergrowth, calling crisply:

"All right, Jack, we're off. One more call before luncheon, and it's blamed late, so get busy."

"In a minute," Leaver called back, smiling, as he showed Charlotte his watch's dial.

Red Pepper Burns looked over the bushes, discerning in his friend's tone an intention of delay, and inclined to be still more peremptory with him about it. Discovering now what looked like an interesting situation, he came forward, bareheaded, his frown of impatience turning to a smile of greeting.

"What luck, to find a dryad in the woods!"

he cried. "Did this gentleman invade your domain?"

"Not at all. I invaded his most unexpectedly. I was following a lane, intending to turn back at any moment, when it ran away under a fence and treacherously led me into trouble."

"Call it trouble, do you, meeting your friends in the woods? That's always the way! Call a woman luck, and she calls you trouble! Let me tell you, Miss Charlotte, it's luck for you, meeting us, for we can give you a lift of a mile down the road. We have to turn off there, but you'll be less late for a luncheon that's probably already cold than you would be after walking the whole distance. You won't refuse? You mustn't, for I expect it's my only chance to get John Stone Leaver of Baltimore started. Otherwise he'll stand here till mid-afternoon, showing you his watch and pointing out to you the beauties of this noisy brook."

"Thank you, Dr. Burns, but you can't very well take me in a car built for two."

"Can't I? The car has frequently carried half a dozen, judiciously distributed over the running-boards, to the imminent peril of the tires and springs. We'll put Dr. Leaver on the running-board. It will hurt neither his clothes nor his dignity, and if it does he can get off and walk."

He led the way. If she could have done so

Charlotte would gladly have turned and run away.
But there are people from whom one cannot easily
run away, and Red Pepper Burns was one of them.
With all his powers of discernment, he had no
possible notion that the two who followed him were
not eager to accept this arrangement. They looked
well together, too, he had observed as he neared
them — exceedingly well. He was sure he was doing
them a favour in keeping them together as long as
possible.

In point of actual distance he certainly succeeded
literally in keeping them extremely near together,
during the few minutes it took to get out of a winding
wood-road to the main highway, and to drive at
a stimulating pace a mile down that road. When
Leaver took his place upon the running-board he was
unavoidably close to Charlotte's knee, and his head
was within reach of her hand. His hand, grasping
the only available hold with which to keep himself
in place, as Burns let the car go at high speed, was
close under her eyes.

Keeping his eyes upon the road, Burns, in a gay
mood now, kept up a running fire of talk, to which
Charlotte, as became necessary, responded. Leaver,
straw hat in hand, also stared straight ahead, and
Charlotte, unobserved by either companion, looked
at the head below her, its heavy, dark-brown hair
ruffled by the wind of their progress, noted — not

for the first time — the fine line of the partial profile, the shoulder in its gray flannel, the well-knit hand, tanned, like its owner's face, with much exposure. And, as she made these furtive observations, something within her breast, which she had thought well under control, became suddenly unmanageable.

"I'm sorry to desert you here, so ungallantly," Burns declared, bringing the car to a standstill at a cross-road. "If my friend here were quite fit I'd put him down, too, and give him the pleasure of walking in with you. In a week or two more I'll turn him loose. Looks pretty healthy, doesn't he?"

"I'm entirely able to walk in with Miss Ruston now," said Leaver, standing, hat in hand, in the road, as Charlotte adjusted her belongings and prepared to walk rapidly away.

"That's my affair, for a bit longer," and Burns put out a peremptory hand. "Be good and jump in. The lady will excuse you, and I won't, so there you are. Forgive me, Miss Ruston, and don't bring on heart failure by walking too fast in this August sun."

"I won't. Good-bye, and thank you both," and Charlotte set briskly off toward home, while the car swept round the turn and disappeared into a hollow of the road.

"That's what I call a particularly worth-while

girl," commented Burns, as the Imp carried them away. "Beauty, and sense, and spirit, not to mention originality and a few other attributes. You don't often get them all combined. Good old family, according to my wife, but all gone now, and this girl left to make her way on her own resources. But perhaps you know all this already, since you've met her before?"

"I know the main facts — yes," Leaver responded. His lips had taken on a curiously tight set, since the car had left the corner. His eyes, under their strongly marked brows, narrowed a little, as he looked out across a field of corn yellowing in the sunlight. "She has visited more or less in Baltimore, where she has been very much admired."

"Why 'has been'?" queried Burns. "She doesn't look like a 'has-been' to me. More like very much of a " now-and-here "— eh?"

"I mean only that since she has been thrown upon her own resources she has applied herself closely to the study of photography, and has been little seen in society."

"I imagine when she was seen she kept a few fellows guessing. She looks to me as if she might have refused her full share of men."

"I have no doubt of it."

That which Burns would have enjoyed saying next he refrained from. But to himself he made the observation: "By the signs I haven't much doubt you were one of them, old man." Aloud he questioned innocently:

"You know her rather well?"

"Quite well."

"Your manner says 'Drop it,'" observed Burns, with a keen glance at a side-face clean-cut against the landscape. "I've encountered that manner before, and I'll take warning accordingly. This is a fine day, and it's rather an interesting case I'm going to see, up this road. If you care to come in I'll be glad of your opinion, but I won't insist on it."

"Unless you really wish it, I'll stay out, thank you."

Burns left his companion in the car, open book in hand. It was a book Red Pepper had strongly recommended, with the motive of stirring up his friend to interested resentment,— a particularly unfair and prejudiced discussion of a subject just then being torn to pieces by all manner of disputants, with the issue still very much in doubt. He knew precisely the place Leaver had reached in his reading, and noted, as he got out of the car, the page at which he was about to begin. The page was one easily recognizable, for it was one upon whose margin he himself had drawn, in a moment of intense irritation with the argument advanced thereon, a rough outline of a donkey's head with impossibly long and obstinate ears.

He left Leaver with eyes bent upon the page, not the semblance of a smile touching his grave mouth at sight of the really striking and effective cartoon which so ably expressed a former reader's sentiments. Burns went into the house making with himself a wager as to how far Leaver's perusal of the chapter would have progressed in the ten minutes which would suffice for the visit, and was divided whether to stake a page against a half-chapter, or to risk his friend's being aware of his observation and leaping through the chapter to its end.

When he came out the book was closed and lying upon Leaver's knee. Burns took his place and drove off, malice sparkling in his eye.

"What did you think of that chapter?" he inquired.

"Interesting argument, but weak in spots."

"Hm — m. Which spots?"

Leaver indicated them. There could be no doubt that he had read the chapter carefully to the end. Burns put him through a severe cross-examination, but he stood the test, much to his examiner's disgust. In detective work it is usually irritating to have one's theories disproved. But he still doubted the evidence of his ears. Either John Leaver was a colder blooded deceiver than he thought him, or his powers of concentration were more than ordi-

narily great, that he could turn from the contempla-
tion of a subject like the one left at the cross-roads
corner, a subject which Burns was pretty sure
vitally concerned him, to a mere abstract discussion
of a modern sociological problem, bare of practical
illustration, and dealing purely with one man's notions
not yet worked out to any constructive conclusion.

"Well," said Leaver, turning suddenly to look at
Burns with a smile, "are you satisfied that I have
read the chapter?"

Burns also turned, met his companion's eye, and
broke into a laugh. "I shall have to admit you
have," said he.

"Why should you have doubted it?"

"I haven't been gone long enough for you to have
read and digested it."

Leaver looked at his watch. "You were gone
seventeen minutes. That's long enough to take in
the argument pretty thoroughly. As to digesting
it — it's indigestible. Why try?"

"No use at all. But having given my mental
machinery a lot of friction I enjoyed trying to stir
yours up also to irritation and discontent. But
I haven't done it. You've remained calm where
I grew hot. Also you've proved your ability to
change the subject of your thinking as you would
switch off one electric current and switch on another.
It shows you're a well man."

"I must warn you, as I have done at various times in our association: 'Don't jump to conclusions.' Your first one, that I hadn't read the chapter, was wrong. I had read it. Your second one, that, after all, I had read the chapter while you were in the house, was also wrong. I had read it by the side of the brook, an hour ago."

Burns's laughter spoke his enjoyment as heartily as if he were not the one cornered. But his amusement ended in triumph, after all, though to this he discreetly did not give voice. Since he had met Miss Charlotte Ruston in the woods Dr. John Leaver had not given himself to the study of any other man's ideas.

CHAPTER XI

AFTER DINNER

"CHARLOTTE CHASE RUSTON, I want you to come over to a little dinner to-night. Just a few people, and as informal as dinners on hot August evenings should be. Afterward we'll spend the time on the porch."

"Thank you, Len. Whom are you going to have? I want to prepare my mind for what is likely to happen."

Mrs. Burns mentioned her guests. "I've arranged them with special reference to Dr. Leaver," she explained. "I think it will do him good, just now, to have to exert himself a little bit. He seems well enough, but absolutely uninterested in things or people, — except the children. He spends hours with them. I'm going to put you next him, if I may."

"Please don't. I particularly want the chance to talk with Mr. Arthur Chester about something I've found he can tell me. We never can get time for it, and this will be just the chance. Give Miss Mathewson to Dr. Leaver, and put some pretty girl on his other side."

"I will, if you prefer, of course," Ellen agreed promptly. She had observed that, although she had taken pains to have them meet, Dr. Leaver and Miss Ruston seemed to be in the habit of quietly avoiding each other. But she was not the woman to ask her friend's confidence, since it was not voluntarily given. She could only wonder why two people from the same world, apparently so well suited to each other, should be so averse to spending even a few moments together.

An hour later Charlotte, having dispatched considerable business, bundling it out of the way as if it had suddenly become of no account, was delving in a trunk for a frock.

"It's the one and only possible thing I have that will do for one of Len's 'little dinners,'" she was saying to herself. "I know just how she'll be looking, and I must live up to her. I wonder if I can mend it to be fit — I wonder."

She carried it downstairs. Madam Chase, sitting by the window with her knitting, looked up.

"Mending lace, dearie?" she asked. "Can't I do it for you?"

"I'm afraid it's beyond even you, Granny," she said, ruefully. To the deaf ears her gesture told more than her words.

"Let me see," commanded the old lady. When

the gauzy gown was spread before her she examined it carefully.

"If it need not be washed —— " she began.

"It must be. Look at the bottom." Charlotte's expressive hands demonstrated as she talked. " I've danced in it and sat out dances in all sorts of places in it. But I can wash it, if you can mend it. I'll wash it with the tips of my fingers."

"I will try," said her grandmother.

That afternoon Charlotte carefully laundered the mended gown, dried it in the sun and ironed it, partly with her fingers, partly with a tiny iron. Finished, it was a work of art, a frock of rare lace of exquisite design, several times made over, and now, in its last stage, prettier than in its first.

"If it will hold together," Charlotte said laughing, as she put it on, and, kneeling before Granny, waited while the delicate old fingers slowly fastened each eyelet. When she rose she was a figure at which the old lady who loved her looked with pleased eyes.

"You are beautiful, dearie," she said. "And nobody will guess that your dress is mended."

"Not a bit, thanks to your clever fingers. Now I'll go find some flowers to wear, and then I'm off. I'll come back to put you to bed, and you'll send Bob over if you want the least thing, won't you, even the least?"

Charlotte went out into her garden, holding her

skirts carefully away from possible touch of bush
or briar. Late August flowers were many, but
among them were none that pleased her. She
came away therefore without a touch of colour
upon her white attire, yet seeming to need none,
the bloom upon her cheek was so clear, the dusk of
her hair so rich.

"Isn't she fascinating?" said Winifred Chester
in the ear of John Leaver, as Charlotte came in.
"I never saw a girl who seemed so radiantly well
and happy, with so little to make her so. I think
she and Madam Chase must be very poor, all the
nice things they have seem so old, and the new
things so very simple. Ellen says the family was
a very fine one."

"Very fine," he agreed. His eyes were upon
Charlotte as she greeted her hosts. He answered
Winifred's further comments absently. He bowed
gravely in response to Charlotte's recognition of
him, then turned and talked with the pretty girl
whom Ellen had asked him to take in to dinner.

At the table Miss Ruston and Dr. Leaver found
themselves nearly opposite. Leaver talked con-
scientiously with his companion, then devoted
himself to Winifred Chester, upon his other side.
Returning to do his duty by Miss Everett, he found
her eager to discuss those opposite.

"They say Miss Ruston does the most wonderful

photographs," she observed. "One would know she was devoted to some art, wouldn't one? The way that frock is cut about her shoulders — only an artist would venture to wear it like that, without a single touch of colour. Every other woman I know would have put on a string of gold beads or pearls or at least a pendant of some sort."

For a moment Leaver forgot to answer. He had not looked at Charlotte since he had first taken his seat. Now, with Miss Everett calling his attention to her, and everybody else, including the subject of their interest, absorbed in their own affairs, he let his eyes rest lingeringly upon her. He had had only brief glimpses of her since she had come to town, and had seen her at such times always in the summer street-or-garden attire which she constantly wore. Now he saw her under conditions which vividly brought back to him other scenes. The white lace gown she wore, with its peculiar cut, like the spreading of flower petals about the beautifully modeled shoulders — it struck him as familiar. Had she worn any jewels upon that white neck when he had seen her? He thought not. He had never known her to wear ornament of any sort, he was sure. She needed none, he was equally sure of that. As she sat, with her head turned toward Arthur Chester, who was expounding with great elaboration something which called for maps upon the tablecloth drawn with a rapidly moving finger, she was showing to the observers across the table a face and head in profile, an outline which had been burned into the memory of the man who now regarded it and forgot to make answer.

Miss Everett glanced at him curiously. Then she murmured: "Don't you think the leaving off of all ornaments is sometimes just as much a coquetry as the wearing of them would be? It certainly challenges notice even more, doesn't it?"

"It depends on whether one happens to possess them, I should say," Leaver returned.

"About their drawing attention, or their absence drawing it? I suppose so. But when you don't know which it is, but judge by the richness of the gown that the wearer can afford them —— "

"I'm no judge of the richness of a gown."

"I am, then. That is the most wonderful lace — anybody can see — at least any woman."

"Tell me, Miss Everett," — Leaver made a determined effort to get away from the personal aspect of the subject,— "why does a woman love jewels? For their own sake, or because of their power to adorn her — if they do adorn her?"

The young woman plunged animatedly into a discussion of the topic as he presented it. She was wearing certain striking ornaments of pearl and turquoise, which undoubtedly became her fair

colouring whether they enhanced her beauty or not.
It was while this discussion was in progress, Leaver
forcing himself to attend sufficiently to make intelli-
gent replies, that Charlotte Ruston suddenly turned
and looked at him. He looked straight back at
her, a peculiar intentness growing in his deep-set
eyes.

He did not withdraw his gaze until she had turned
away again, and the encounter had been but for
the briefest space, yet when it was over John Leaver's
colour had changed a little. For the moment it was
as if nobody else had been in the room — he was
only dully conscious that upon his other side Winifred Chester was addressing him, and that he must
make reply.

When the company which had spent the sultry
August evening upon the porch in the semi-darkness
was near to breaking up, Leaver came to Charlotte
and took his place beside her. When she left the
house he was with her, and the two crossed the
street and went in at the hedge gate together.

"May I stay a very little while?" he asked.
And when she assented he added, "Shall we find
the bench in your garden?"

"Do you know that bench?" she questioned,
surprised.

"I spent many hours upon it before you came,
and during the days when I was not getting about

much. I listened to the reading of two books, lounging there. So it seems like a familiar spot to me."

"It is my favourite resting place. I am sorry you were driven away by my coming. You and Miss Mathewson would have been very welcome there, all the rest of the summer, if I had known."

"Thank you. But I have passed the invalid stage and am not being treated as a patient. I read for myself, at present, and tramp the country, instead of sitting on benches, anywhere. It's a great improvement."

"I am very glad."

Charlotte let him lead the way to the retreat under the apple-tree, and he proved his knowledge of it by stopping now and then to hold aside hindering branches of shrubbery, and to lift for her a certain heavily leafed bough which drooped across the path, but which would hardly have been discerned in the summer starlight by one not familiar with its position.

"It would be a pity to tear that gown," he remarked, as the last barrier was passed. "It occurred to me, as I looked at you to-night, that it was one I had seen you wear in Baltimore, last winter. Am I right?"

"Last winter, and the winter before, and even the winter before that, if you had known me so

long," she answered, with a gay little laugh. "I am
so fond of it I shall not discard it until it can no
longer be mended."

"You are wise. I believe it is hardly the attitude
of the modern woman toward dress of any sort,
but it might well be. We never tire of Nature,
though she wears the same costume season after
season."

"Her frocks don't fray at the edges — or when
they do she turns them such gorgeous colours that
we don't notice they are getting worn."

"Aren't there some rough edges on this bench?
Please take this end; I think I recall that it is
smoother than the other."

"Thank you. One good tear, and even Granny's
needle couldn't make me whole again."

He bent over to pick up a scarf of silver gauze
which had slipped from her shoulders. He laid it
about them, and as he did so she shivered suddenly,
though the air was warm, without a hint of dampness. But she covered the involuntary movement
with a shrug, saying lightly, "A man I know says
he thoroughly believes a woman is colder rather
than warmer in a scarf like this, on the theory that
anything with so many holes in it must create an
infinite number of small draughts."

"He may be right. But I confess, as a physician,
I like to cover up exposed surfaces from the open

night air — to a certain extent — even with an excuse for a protection like this."

He sat down beside her. The bench was not a long one, and he was nearer to her than he had yet been to-night. She sat quietly, one hand lying motionless in her lap. The other hand, down at her side, laid hold of the edge of the bench and gripped it rather tightly. She began to talk about the old garden, as it lay before them, its straggling paths and beds of flowers mere patches of shadow, dark and light. He answered, now and then, in an absent sort of way, as if his mind were upon something else, and he only partly heard. She spoke of "Sunny Farm" — the children's hospital in the country — of Burns and Ellen and Bob — and then, suddenly, with a sense of the uselessness of trying all by herself to make small talk under conditions of growing constraint, she fell silent. He let the silence endure for a little space, then broke it bluntly.

"I'm glad," he said, in the deep, quiet voice she remembered well, "that you will give me a chance. What is the use of pretending that I have brought you here to talk of other people? I have something to say to you, and you know it. I can't lead up to it by any art, for it has become merely a fact which it is your right to know. You should have known it long ago."

He stopped for a minute. She was absolutely still beside him, except for the hand that gripped the edge of the bench. That took a fresh hold.

When he spoke again, his voice, though still quiet, showed tension.

"Before I saw you the last time, last spring, I meant to ask you to marry me. When I did see you, something had happened to make that impossible. It had not only made it impossible, but it made me unable even to explain. I shall never forget that strange hour I spent with you. You knew that something was the matter. But I couldn't tell you. I thought then I never could. Seeing you, as I have to-night, I realized that I couldn't wait another hour to tell you. But, even now, I don't feel that I can explain. There's only one thing I am sure of — that I must say this much: All my seeking of you, last winter, meant the full intent and purpose to win you, if I could. And — you can never know what it meant to me to give it up."

The last words were almost below his breath, but she heard them, heard the uncontrollable, passionate ache of them. Plainer than the words themselves this quality in them spoke for him.

For a moment there was silence between them again. Then he went on: "I can't ask — I don't ask — a word from you in answer. Neither can I let myself say more than I am saying. It wouldn't be fair to you, however you might feel. And I want you to believe this — that not to say more takes every bit of manhood I have."

Silence again. Then, from the woman beside him, in the clearest, low voice, with an inflection of deep sweetness:

"Thank you, Dr. Leaver."

Suddenly he turned upon the bench — he had been staring straight before him. He bent close, looked into her shadowy face for a moment, then found her hand, where it lay in her lap, lifted it in both his own, and pressed it, for a long, tense moment, against his lips. She felt the contact burn against the cool flesh, and it made intelligible all that he would not allow himself to say, in terms which no woman could mistake.

Then he sprang up from the bench.

"Will you walk as far as the house with me?" he asked, gently. "Or shall I leave you here? It is late: I don't quite like to leave you here alone."

"I will go with you," she answered, and, rising, drew her skirts about her. He stood beside her for a moment, looking down at her white figure, outlined against the darkness behind them. She heard him take one deep, slow inspiration, like a swimmer who fills his lungs before plunging into the water; she heard the quick release of the breath, followed by his voice, saying, with an effort at naturalness:

"If I had such a place as this, where I'm staying, I should be tempted to bring out a blanket and sleep in it to-night."

"One might do worse," she answered. "These branches have been so long untrimmed that it takes a heavy shower to dampen the ground beneath."

They made their way back along the straggling paths, and came to the cottage, from whose windows streamed the lamplight that waited for Charlotte. As it fell upon her Leaver looked at her, and stood still. Pausing, she glanced up at him, and away again. She knew that he was silently regarding her. Quite without seeing she knew how his face looked, the fine face with the eyes which seemed to see so much, the firm yet sensitive mouth, the whole virile personality held in a powerful restraint.

Then he opened the door for her, and she passed him. She looked back at him from the threshold.

"Good-night," she said, and smiled.

"Good-night," he answered, and gave back the smile. Then he went quickly down the path and away.

Ten minutes afterward she put out the light in the front room, and stole out of the door, leaving it open behind her. Still in the white gown of the evening, but with a long, dark cloak flung over it,

she went swiftly back over the paths to the garden
bench.   Arrived there she sat down upon it, where
she had sat before, but not as she had been.   Instead,
she turned and laid her arm along the low back of
the bench, and her head upon it, and remained
motionless in that position for a long time.   Her
eyes were wide, in the darkness, and her lips were
pressed tight together, and once, just once, a
smothered, struggling breath escaped her.   But,
finally, she sat up, threw up her head, lifted both
arms above it, the hands clenched tight.

"Charlotte Ruston," she whispered fiercely, "you
have to be strong — and strong — and stronger
yet!   You have to be!   *You have to be!*"

Then she rose quickly to her feet, with a motion
not unlike that with which John Leaver had sprung
to his an hour before.   It was a movement which
meant that emotion must yield to action.   She
went swiftly back to the house, in at the door, up the
straight, high stairs to her room.

As she lighted her candle a voice spoke from
Madam Chase's room, its door open into her own.

"Charlotte?"

"Yes, Granny?"

The girl went in, taking the candle, which she
set upon the dressing-table.   She bent over the bed,
putting her lips close to the old lady's ear.

"Can't you sleep, dear?" she asked.

"Not until you are in, child. Why are you so late?"

"It's not late, Granny. You know I went to Dr. Burns's to dinner."

"It's very late," repeated the delicate old voice, slightly querulous, because of its owner's failure to hear the explanation. "Much too late for a girl like you. You should have had your beauty sleep long ago."

Charlotte smiled, feeling as if her twenty-six years had added another ten to themselves since morning. She patted the soft cheek on the pillow, and tenderly adjusted the gossamer nightcap which, after the fashion of its wearer's youth, kept the white locks snugly in order during the sleeping hours.

"I'm here now, Granny. Please go to sleep right away. Or — would you like a glass of milk first?"

"What say?"

"Milk, dear,— hot milk?"

"Yes, yes, it will put me to sleep. Quite hot, not lukewarm."

Charlotte went down the steep stairs again, heated the milk, and brought it back. When it had been taken she kissed the small face, drew the linen sheet smooth again, and went away with the candle. In her own room she presently lay down upon her cot, rejoicing that the old lady could not hear its creaking.

Toward morning she fell asleep.

CHAPTER XII

A CHALLENGE

"MISS RUSTON!"

"Yes?" The answer came through the door of the dark-room. "I can't come out for four minutes. Can you give me the message through a closed door?"

"Certainly," responded Amy Mathewson, standing outside. She was dressed for motor travel and her eyes were full of anticipation. "Mr. Macauley is taking some of us out to meet Dr. Burns at Sunny Farm. The Doctor has telephoned from there that he would be very glad if you could come with us, bring your camera, and take some photographs of a patient for him."

"Delighted — if I can arrange for Granny," Charlotte called back.

"Mrs. Burns's Cynthia will stay with her."

"How soon must we start?"

"As soon as you can be ready."

"Give me ten minutes, and I'll be there."

The big brown car was waiting outside the hedge gate when, nearly as good as her word, Charlotte ran down the path. She had pulled a long linen coat over her blue morning dress, and a veil floated over her arm

"Dear me, you all look so correct in your bonnets and caps! Must I tie up my head, or may I leave off the veil until my hair gets to looking wild?"

"It never looked wild yet that I can recall, so jump in and go as you please. It's too hot for caps, and I'll keep you company," responded Macauley, from the front seat. His wife, Martha, sat beside him, swathed in brown from head to foot. Martha had acquired a motoring costume which she considered matched the car and was particularly smart besides, and she seldom left off any detail, no matter how warm the day. Martha looked around as Charlotte took her place beside Miss Mathewson on the broad rear seat. The two swinging seats which equipped the car to carry seven passengers were occupied by Bobby Burns and young Tom Macauley.

"People who have hair like Miss Ruston can go bareheaded where the rest of us have to tie ourselves together to keep from blowing away," observed Martha.

Her husband laughed. "I never heard you own quite so frankly before that parts of you were detachable," said he.

"They're not!" cried Martha, indignantly. "But

Miss Ruston's hair is that crisp, half curly sort that stays just where you put it, and mine is so straight and fine that it gets stringy. It makes all the difference in the world."

The car moved off. After a minute it turned a corner and came to a standstill before a house. Macauley sounded a penetrating horn, and after a minute the door opened and John Leaver came out.

"Come on, Doctor," called Macauley. "R. P. has been telephoning in, in the usual fever of haste, to have us get out there. It seems the place is in order and two patients have arrived. He wants a doctor, nurse, and photographer on the job at once. Find a place on the back seat, there?"

Leaver came quickly down the walk. He looked like a well man now, whether he felt like a well one or not. He had gained in weight, his face had lost its worn look, his eyes were no longer encompassed by shadows. The sun was in his eyes as he opened the rear door and prepared to take the one seat left in the car, that beside Charlotte Ruston, who had moved to one side as she saw what was about to happen. Her shoulder pressed close against that of Miss Mathewson, she left so large a space for the newcomer.

After the first exchange of small talk, it was a silent drive. Macauley was making haste to obey the summons he had received, and the rush of air

past those in the car with him was not conducive
to frequent speech. Soon after they were off
Charlotte drew her big white veil over her head and
face, and was lost to view beneath its protecting
expanse. One of the veil's fluttering ends persisted
in blowing across Leaver's breast, quite unnoticed
by its owner, whose head did not often turn that
way. The man did not put it aside, but after a
time he took hold of it and kept it in his hand,
secure from the domineering breeze.

"Here we are! Behold Sunny Farm, the dream
of Doctor and Mrs. Red Pepper, given tangible
shape. Not a bad-looking old rambling place,
is it?"

Macauley brought his car to rest beside the long
green roadster already there. Its occupants jumped
out and strolled up the slope toward the white
farmhouse, across whose front and wing stretched
long porches, on one of which stood a steamer chair
and a white iron bed, each holding a small form.
Upon the step sat Ellen Burns and a nurse in a white
uniform; by the bed stood Burns himself.

Miss Mathewson's observant eyes were taking
veiled note of her recent charge as he went up the
steps and approached the bed. The little patient
upon it had not lifted his head, as had the child in
the chair, to see who was at hand.

"Oh, the little pitiful face!" breathed Charlotte

Ruston in Amy's ear, as she looked down into a pair of great black eyes, set in hollows so deep that they seemed the chiseling of merciless pain.

"This is Jamie Ferguson," said Burns, with his hand on the boy's head. "He is very happy to be here in the sunshine, so you are not to pity him. Come here, Bob, and tell Jamie you will play with him when he is stronger. He knows wonderful things, does Jamie. And this is Patsy Kelly, in the chair."

There was a pleasant little scene now enacted upon the porch, in which Bob and Tom were introduced to the small patients, and everybody looked on while shy advances were made by the well children, to be received with timid gravity by the sick ones. Through it all Red Pepper Burns was furtively observing the demeanour of Dr. John Leaver.

He had hardly taken his eyes from Jamie Ferguson. Into his face had come a look his friend had not seen there since he had been with him, the look of the expert professional man who sees before him a case which interests him. He stood and studied the child without speaking while Bob and Tom remained, and when the small boys, too full of activity to stay contentedly with other boys who could not play, were off to explore the place, Leaver drew up a chair and sat down beside the bed.

Burns glanced at his wife, and gave a significant

nod of his head toward the interior of the house. Ellen rose.

"Come Martha, and Charlotte," said she, "and let me show you over the rooms. I'm so proud of the progress we have made in the fortnight since the house was vacated for us."

She led them inside. Amy Mathewson went over to the chair and Patsy Kelly, turning her back upon the pair by the bed.

"When did you come, Patsy?" she asked.

"We come the morn," said Patsy, a pale little fellow of nine, with a shock of hair so red that beside it that of Red Pepper Burns would have looked a subdued chestnut. "In the ambilunce we come. I liked the ride, but Jamie didn't. He was scared of bein' moved."

"Jamie is not so well as you. How fine it is that you can lie in this chair and have your head up. You can see all about. Isn't it beautiful here?"

"It is. I'm glad I come. He said I'd be glad, but I didn't believe him. I didn't know," said Patsy Kelly, with a sigh of satisfaction. "I had mate and pitaty for breakfast the morn," he added, and rapture shone out of his eyes.

By the side of Jamie Ferguson Dr. John Leaver was telling a story. He was apparently telling it to Dr. Burns, who listened with great interest, but at the same time shy Jamie Ferguson was listening

"The narrator turned to the boy in the bed and inquired, smiling: 'Could you do that, Jamie?'"

too. There were curious points in the story when
the narrator turned to the boy in the bed and
inquired, smiling: "Could you do that, Jamie?"
to which questions Jamie usually replied in the
negative. They were mostly questions concerning
backs and legs and hips, and the boy in the story
seemed to find difficulty in using his, too, which made
Jamie feel a strong interest in him. Altogether it
was a fascinating tale. When it was over the two
men walked away together down the slope, and
between them passed other questions and answers,
of a sort which Jamie could not have understood.

Down by the gate Leaver came to a pause, nodding
his head in a thoughtful way. "You are quite right,
I believe, both in your conclusions and in your plan
for operation. I should go ahead without further
delay than is necessary to get him into a bit better
condition."

"I thought you would agree with me," Burns
replied. "I'm gratified that you do. But I'm
not going to operate. I've got a better man:
Leaver, of Baltimore."

The other turned quickly. A strange look swept
over his face.

"I told you my decision about that," he said.

"I know you did. But I told you some time
ago about this case, and warned you that it was
your case. I haven't changed my mind."

Leaver shook his head. "I haven't changed mine, either. But I didn't know this was the case you meant. If I had I shouldn't have gone to examining it without an invitation."

"You had an invitation. That was what I got you out here this morning for. I didn't bring you myself because I didn't want you steeling yourself against looking into it, as you would if I had told you about it on the way out. My plan worked all right. The minute you saw the child your instincts and training got the better of your caution. That's what they'll continue to do if you give them a chance. See here, you don't mean to quit your profession and take to carpentry, do you?"

"I expect to practise medicine," Leaver said, and there was a queer setting of his lips as he said it.

"Medicine! You? Jack, you couldn't do it."

"Couldn't I? I don't know that I could." He drew a half shuddering breath. "But I can try, somewhere, if not in Baltimore."

"I'd like to thrash you!" cried Red Pepper Burns, and he looked it. "Standing there the picture of a healthy man and telling me you're going to take to doling out pills and writing prescriptions. . . . See here. We've put in a little surgery up there in the north wing, it's a peach of a place. Come and see it."

He led the way rapidly back up to the house, in

at the door and up the stairs. At the end of a long corridor he threw open the door of a small room, whose whole northern side was of glass. Its equipment was as complete as could be asked by the most exacting of operating surgeons.

"Good!" Leaver cried, quite forgetting himself for the moment. "I had no idea you meant to carry things so far as this. Fine!"

"Isn't it? Could you have a better place to try your hand again? Nobody looking on but Amy Mathewson, Miss Dodge — whom you met downstairs — and Dr. Buller — for the anæsthetic. Buller's the best anæsthetizer in the state and a splendid fellow besides. Also my humble self, ready to be your right-hand man. I promise you this,— if the least thing goes wrong — *and you ask it* — I'll take your place without a word. Jack, the case is one that needs you. I've never done this operation: you have. You've written a monograph on it. It's up to you, John Leaver. I don't dare you to do it, *I dare you not to do it!*"

For the first time, in response to his arguments on this subject, Burns got no answer but silence. But his friend's face was slowly flushing a deep, angry red. At this sight Burns rejoiced. His theory had been that if he could wake something in Leaver besides deep depression and sad negation he had a chance to influence him. He believed thoroughly that if he could force the distinguished young surgeon through one successful operation confidence would return like an incoming tide. He had hoped that the pathetic sight of the little malformed body of Jamie Ferguson would arouse the passion for salvage which lies in the breast of every man who practises the great profession; he saw that thus far his plan had succeeded. Now to accomplish the rest.

"Suppose," said Leaver, turning slowly toward the other man, "I agree to stand beside you and direct the operation?"

It was Burns's turn to colour angrily, his quick temper leaping to fire in an instant.

"Not *much!* Let every tub stand on its own bottom! Either I do the job or I don't do it; but I don't take the part of an apprentice. I'll agree to play second fiddle to you, with you playing first. But I'll be — condemned — if I'll play first, with a coach at my elbow. Take that and be hanged to you!"

He walked over to the open window, threw back the screen and put his head out, as if he needed air to breathe. Leaver was at his side in an instant.

"I beg your pardon, my dear fellow, I do sincerely. It was an unworthy suggestion, and I don't blame you for resenting it. Nobody needs help less than you. You could do the operation brilliantly. That's why there's no need in the world to force me into the situation — no need —— "

Burns wheeled. "There *is* need! There's need for you — to save your soul alive. You've been no coward so far — your overworked nerves played you a trick and you've had to recover. But you have recovered, you are fit to work again. *If you don't do this thing you'll be a coward forever!*"

It bit deep, as he had known it would. If he had struck a knife into his friend's heart he could not have caused so sharp a hurt. Leaver turned white under this surgery of speech, and for an instant he looked as if he would have sprung at Burns's throat. There followed sixty silent seconds while both men stood like statues. But the merciless judgment had turned the scale. With a control of himself which struck Burns, as he recalled it afterward, as marvellous, Leaver answered evenly: "You shall not have the chance to say that again. I will operate when you think best."

"Thank God!" said Red Pepper Burns, under his breath.

The two walked out of the little white room, with its austere and absolute cleanliness, without another word concerning that which was to come. Burns took his friend over the house, and Leaver looked into room after room, approving, commending, even suggesting, quite as if nothing had happened. And

yet, after all, not quite as if nothing had happened. He was not the same man who had come
out to Sunny Farm an hour before. Burns knew,
as well as if he could have seen into Leaver's mind,
the conflict that was going on there. The thing
was settled, he would not retreat, yet there was
still a fight to be fought — the biggest fight of his
life. On its issue was to depend the success or failure
of the coming test. Burns's warm heart would have
led him to speak sympathetically and encouragingly
of the issue to be met; his understanding of the
crisis it precipitated kept him mute. Whatever
help he was now to give his friend must be given,
not through speech but through silence, and by that
subtler means of communication between spirit and
spirit which cannot be analyzed or understood, but
which may be more real than anything in life.

They went downstairs, presently, and rejoined
the party. Miss Ruston and Miss Mathewson,
Mr. James Macauley and his son Tom, with Bobby
Burns, were engaged in a spirited game of "puss
in a corner," for the benefit of Patsy Kelly, who lay
looking on from his chair with sparkling, excited
eyes. Beside Jamie Ferguson, who could not see,
Mrs. Burns sat, describing to him the game and
interpreting the shouts of laughter which reached
his ears as he lay, too flat upon his back to see what
was happening twenty feet away.

Ellen looked up, as her husband approached, and something in his face made her regard him intently. He smiled at her, his hazel eyes dark as they often were when something had stirred him deeply, and she guessed enough of the meaning of this aspect to keep her from looking at Dr. Leaver until he had been for some time upon the porch.

When she did observe him, he was standing, leaning against a pillar and looking at the wan little face below her, from a point at which Jamie could not know of his scrutiny. His back was turned upon the game upon the grass, though the others were watching it. When it ended Burns called Charlotte Ruston to the taking of the photographs he wanted — snapshots of the two little patients carried into the full sunlight. This being quickly accomplished, he announced his own immediate departure.

"Will you go back with me in the Imp, or at your leisure with the crowd in the car?" Burns asked Leaver, in an undertone. "My wife will be glad to go in either car; she suggested your taking your choice."

"If the Macauleys will not misunderstand, I should prefer to go with you," Leaver replied.

"They won't. Two medicine-men are supposed always to wish for a chance to hobnob, and we'll put it on that score. I really want to consult you about Patsy's case."

"Not going with us? Willing to forsake three fair ladies for one red-headed fiend, just because you know he's going to give us his dust? I like that!" cried Macauley, who could be trusted never to make things easy for his friends.

"Abuse him as you like. He's off with me at my request," called Burns, pulling out into the road and turning with a sweep.

Martha Macauley looked after the Green Imp's rapidly lessening shape through the dust-cloud which it left behind. "I never thought till to-day that Dr. Leaver seemed the least bit like a noted surgeon," said she, as they waited for Macauley to get his car under way. "I could never imagine his acting like Red, and rushing enthusiastically from bedside to operating-room, pushing everything out of his way to make time to cut somebody to pieces and sew him up again, for his ultimate good. But to-day somehow, he seemed more — what would you call it — professional?"

"That's the word," her husband agreed. "It's the word they juggle with. If a thing's 'professional,' it's all right. If it's not, it may as well be condemned to outer darkness at once."

CHAPTER XIII

A CRISIS

L ITTLE wife?"

"Yes, Redfield Pepper ——"

"I'm as nervous as a cat up a tree with a couple of dogs at the foot!"

"Why, Red, I never heard you talk of being nervous! What does it mean?"

"An operation to-morrow."

"But you never are 'nervous,' dear."

"I am now."

"Is it such a critical one?"

"The most critical I ever faced."

Ellen looked at her husband, or tried to look, for they were moving slowly along the street, at a late hour, Burns having suggested a short walk before bedtime. It was quite dark, and Ellen could judge only by her husband's voice that he spoke with entire soberness.

"Can you tell me anything about it?" she suggested, knowing that relief from tension sometimes comes with speech. Any confession of nervousness from Red Pepper Burns seemed to her most extraordinary. She knew that he often worked under tremendous tension, but he had never before admitted shakiness of nerve.

"Not much, if anything at all. It's a particularly private affair, for the present. It's a queer operation, too. I may not handle a knife, tie an artery, or stitch up a wound — may do less than I ever did in my life on such an occasion, yet — I'll be hanged if I'm not feeling as owly about it as if it were the first time I ever expected to see blood."

Ellen put her hand on his arm, slipped it into the curve, and kept it there, while he held it pressed close against him. "Red, have you been working too hard lately?" she asked.

"Not a bit. I'm fit as a fiddler. Don't worry, love. I've no business to talk riddles to you, of all people. But for a peculiar reason I'm horribly anxious about the outcome of to-morrow's experiment, and had to work it off somehow. Just promise me that when you say your prayers to-night you'll ask the good God not to let me be mistaken in forcing a situation I may not be able to control."

"I will," Ellen promised, with all her heart, for she saw that, whatever the crisis might be, it was one to which her usually daring husband was looking forward with most uncharacteristic dread.

She was conscious that Burns spent a restless night. At daybreak he was up and out of the house.

Before he went, however, he bent over her and kissed her with great tenderness, murmuring, "A prayer or two more, darling, won't hurt anything, when you are awake enough. I've particular faith in your petitions."

She held him with both arms.

"Don't worry, Red. It isn't like you. You will succeed, if it is to be."

"It's got to be," he said between his teeth, as he left her.

He swallowed a cup of Cynthia's hot coffee — bespoken the night before, as on many similar occasions — and ran out to his car just as the slow September sunrise broke into the eastern sky. In two minutes more he was off in the Imp, flying out the road to Sunny Farm.

Arrived there he astonished Miss Dodge, the nurse in charge, who was not accustomed to Dr. Burns's ways. He had left the small patient, Jamie Ferguson, the night before, entirely satisfied with his condition for undergoing the operation set for nine o'clock this morning. He now went once more painstakingly over every detail of the preparation he had ordered, making sure for himself that nothing had been omitted.

Then he called for Miss Mathewson, who had spent the night at the Farm. She was to assist Leaver as she was accustomed to assist Burns.

He took her off by herself and addressed her solemnly, more solemnly than he had ever done.

"Amy, if you ever had your wits on call, have them this morning. In all my life I never cared more how things went at a time like this. I care so much I'd give about all I own to know this minute that the thing would go through."

"Why, Dr. Burns," said she, in astonishment, "it should go through. It is a critical operation, of course, but the boy seems in very fair shape for it, and Dr. Leaver has done it before. Dr. Leaver is quite well now —— "

"I know, I know. Feel of that!"

He touched her hand with his own, which was icy cold. She started, and looked anxiously at him.

"Doctor, you can't be well! This isn't you — to be so — nervous! Why, think of all the operations you've done, and never a sign of minding. And this isn't even your responsibility — it's Dr. Leaver's."

"That's right, scold me," said he, trying to laugh. "It's what I need. I'm showing the white feather, a hatful of them. But you're mistaken about one thing. It *is* my responsibility, every detail of it. Don't forget that. If the case goes wrong, it's my fault, not Dr. Leaver's."

Then he walked away, leaving Miss Mathewson utterly dumbfounded. She understood perfectly that Dr. John Leaver had suffered a severe break-down from overwork, and that this was his first test since his recovery. But she knew nothing of the peculiar circumstances of his last appearance in an operating-room, and could therefore have no possible notion of the crisis this morning's work was to be to him. She did know enough, however, to be deeply interested in the outcome, and she watched the Green Imp flying down the road toward home with the sense that when it returned it would bear two surgeons for whom she must do the best work of support in her life.

"Ready, Jack?"

"Ready."

John Leaver took the seat beside Burns, giving the outstretched hand a strong grip. He carried no hand-bag, there was no sign of his profession about him. He had sent to Baltimore for his own instruments, but they were waiting for him in the little operating-room at Sunny Farm, having been through every rite practised by modern surgery.

The car set off.

"It's a magnificent morning," said Red Pepper Burns.

"Ideal."

"September's the best month in the year, to my fancy."

"A crisp October rivals it, to my notion."

"Not bad. There's a touch of frost in the air this morning."

"Quite a touch."

The car sped on. The men were silent. His one glance at his friend's face had showed Burns that Leaver had, apparently, his old quiet command of himself. But this, though reassuring, he knew could not be trusted as an absolute indication of control within. For himself, he had never been so profoundly excited in his life. He found himself wondering how he was going to stand and look on, unemployed, yet ready, at a sign, to take the helm. He felt as if that moment, if it should come, would find him as unnerved as the man he must help. Yet, with all his heart and will, he was silently assuring himself that all would go well — must go well. He must not even fear failure, think failure, imagine failure. Strong confidence on his own part, he fully believed, would be definite, if intangible, assistance to his friend. . . .

Rounding a curve in the road, the white outlines of Sunny Farm house stood out clearly against the background of near green fields, and distant purple hills.

"House gets the sun in great shape mornings," observed Burns.

"The location couldn't be better," responded Leaver's quiet voice.

The car swung into the yard. The two men got out, crossed the sward, and stood upon the porch. Miss Mathewson met them at the door, her face bright, her eyes clear, only a little flush on either cheek betraying to Burns that she shared his tension.

"Jamie seems in the best of condition," said she.

"That's good — that's good," Burns answered, as if he had not made sure of the fact for himself within the hour.

"I will go in and see him a minute," Leaver said, and disappeared into Jamie Ferguson's room.

Outside Burns walked up and down the corridor, waiting, in a restlessness upon which he suddenly laid a stern decree. He stopped short and forced himself to stand still.

"You idiot," he savagely addressed himself, "you act like a fool medical student detailed to give an anæsthetic at a noted surgeon's clinic for the first time. Cut it, and behave yourself."

After which he was guilty of no more outward perturbation, and, naturally, of somewhat less inner turmoil.

"Satisfied?" he asked of Leaver, as the other came out of Jamie's room.

Leaver nodded. "Rather better than I had hoped. He's a plucky little chap."

"You're right, he is."

The two went up to the dressing-room. Half

an hour later, clad in white from head to foot, arms bare and gleaming, hands gloved, allowing assistants to open and close doors for them lest the slightest contamination affect their rigid cleanliness, they came into the operating-room. For the moment they were left alone there, while the nurses went to summon the bearer of the little patient. It was the moment Burns had dreaded, the stillness before action which most tries the spirit at any crisis.

He could not help giving one quick glance at his friend before he turned away to look out of the window with eyes which saw nothing outside it. In that instant's glance he thought the old Leaver stood before him, cool, collected, armed to the teeth, as it were, for the fight, and looking forward to it with eagerness. There had been possibly a slight pallor upon his face, as Miss Dodge had adjusted his mask of gauze, but, as Burns recalled it, this was a common matter with many surgeons, and it might easily have been characteristic of Leaver himself, even though Burns had not remembered it. His own heart was thumping heavily in his breast, as it had never thumped when he had been the chief actor in the coming scene.

"Lord, make him go through all right," he was praying, almost unconsciously, while he eyed the September landscape unseeingly, and listened for the sound of the stretcher bearers. . . .

As they came in at the door Burns turned, and saw, or thought he saw, Leaver draw one deep, long breath. Then, in a minute or so, the fight was on. He remembered, of old, that there was never much delay after the distinguished surgeon saw his patient before him, had assured himself that all was well with the working of the anæsthetic, and had taken up his first instrument. . . .

Swift and sure moved Leaver's hands, obeying the swift, sure working of his brain. There was not a moment's indecision. More than one moment of deliberation there was, but Burns, watching, knew as well as if his friend had been a part of himself that the brief pauses in his work were a part of the work itself, and meant that as his task unfolded before him he stopped to weigh feasible courses, choosing with unerring judgment the better of two possible alternatives, and proceeding with the confidence essential to the unfaltering touch. As Burns beheld the process pass the point of greatest danger and approach conclusion, he felt somewhat as a man may who, unable to help, watches a swimmer breasting tremendous seas, and sees him win past the last smother of breakers and make his way into calmer waters. He was conscious that he himself had been breathing shallowly as he watched, and now drew several deep inspirations of relief.

"By George, that was the gamest thing I ever saw," thought Burns, exultingly. "He hasn't shown the slightest sign of flinching. And Amy Mathewson — she's played up to every move like a little second brain of his."

He looked at the small clock on a shelf of the surgery, and his head swam. "He's outdone himself," he nearly cried aloud. "This will stand beside anything he's ever done. If he'd been slower than usual it would have been only natural, after this interval, but he's been faster. Oh, but I'm glad — glad!"

The event was over. Both Leaver and Burns, no longer under the necessity of avoiding contact with things unsterilized, felt the small patient's pulse and nodded at each other. The assistants bore Jamie Ferguson's little inert body away, Miss Dodge attending.

Dr. Leaver turned to Miss Mathewson. He drew off the masking gauze from his head, showing a flushed, moist face and eyes a little bloodshot. But his voice was as quiet as ever as he said:

"I've never had finer assistance from any one, Miss Mathewson. If you had been trained to work opposite me you couldn't have done better."

"You work much like Dr. Burns," she said, modestly. "That made it easy."

Burns burst into a smothered laugh. "That's

the biggest compliment I've had for a good while," said he.

As they dressed, neither man said much. But when coats were on, and the two were ready to go to Jamie's room, they turned each to the other.

"Well, old man?" Burns was smiling like the sunshine itself into his friend's eyes. "I think I never was so happy in my life."

"I know you're happy," said the other man. "I don't believe I'll trust myself yet to tell you what I am."

"Don't try. We won't talk it over just yet. But I've got to say this, Jack: You never did a more masterly job in your life."

Leaver smiled — and shivered. "I'm glad it's over," said he.

They went down to Jamie's room, and there, on either side of the high hospital cot, watched consciousness returning. With consciousness presently came pain.

"I'm going to stay with him," Leaver announced, by and by. Jamie's little, wasted hand was fast in his, Jamie's eyes, when they rested anywhere with intelligence, rested on his face—a face tender and pitiful.

"Good for you. I shall feel easier about him if you do," and Burns went away with the feeling that this course would be as good for the surgeon as for the patient.

He stopped in the lower hall to telephone Ellen.

"All safely over, dear," he said. "The patient doing well so far, and no reason why he shouldn't continue, as far as we can see."

"Oh, I'm so glad, Red," came back the joyous reply, and Burns responded:

"That goes without saying, partner. I'll tell you a lot more about it, now, when I get back."

The Green Imp went back at a furious pace. Half-way home, however, as it neared a figure walking by the roadside, it suddenly slowed down.

"Will you ride home, Miss Photographer?" Burns called. "Or do you prefer trudging all the way back with that camera and tripod?"

"I'm delighted to ride, Dr. Burns," replied Charlotte Ruston. "Captivating roadside views enticed me much farther than I intended, and the camera weighs twice what it did when I started."

"Jump in, then, and let me give you a piece of good news I'm bursting with," and Burns held out his hand for the camera. "You're getting a beautiful sunburn on that right cheek," he commented.

"I'll burn the left to match it, if you won't drive too fast. You'll have to go a little slower while you talk. I've noticed you're always silent when you're scorching along the road."

"So I am, I believe. Well, I'm not going to be

silent now. I've just come from seeing Jamie Ferguson put on the road to future health and happiness, the good Lord willing — and I've a notion He is."

"Jamie — the little cripple who lies on his back?"

"The same. He'll lie on his back some time longer and then, I think, he'll get up."

"You operated on him to-day? How glad I am!"

"No, I didn't operate. It took a better man than I. I've never done this particular stunt, and Jamie was not a patient for experiment. Jack Leaver did the trick, and a finished trick it was, too. I'm so full of enthusiasm over his performance that I'm bursting with it, as I warned you."

Charlotte Ruston had turned suddenly to face him. As he looked at her, with this announcement, he had a view of lovely, startled eyes.

"What's the matter?" he asked, wondering. He had to look ahead at the road, but he cut down on the Imp's speed, so that he could spare a glance at his companion again. "You look as if I'd given you bad news instead of good."

"Oh, no! — oh, no!" she said, in odd, short breaths. "It's great — wonderful! Poor little fellow! I'm very glad. You said — Dr. Leaver did it? I was simply — surprised."

"Did it brilliantly. But there's no occasion for surprise about that. Having been in Baltimore as much as you have, you must know his position there. There's nobody with a bigger reputation."

"But I thought he had been — ill?"

"Tired out. Small wonder, at the pace he was going — the working pace, I mean. He never let up on himself. I got him here to rest up. He would have been off long ago if I would have given him leave, but I had his promise to keep away from work till he was thoroughly fit for it, so I've made the most of my chance. I shall never get another. If I know him he'll be back in his office before the week ends. Once give a chap like him a taste of work after idleness, and there's no use trying to hold him."

"You think him fully fit, now?"

"Never so fit in his life, if I'm any judge. I've seen him at work many a time, and I never saw finer methods than his to-day, his own or any man's — and I've watched some pretty smooth things. By the way, I understand you had met Dr. Leaver before you met him here?"

"Yes, I had met him."

Burns was not possessed of more than the ordinary amount of curiosity concerning other people's affairs, but he was accustomed to observe human nature and note its signs, and it struck him now rather suddenly that both John Leaver and Charlotte Ruston had seemed rather more than necessarily non-committal concerning an acquaintance which both admitted. He saw no reason why he should not ask a question or two. Asking questions was a part of his profession.

"I hope you've managed to coax him before your camera. He's looking so well now, I'd like a picture of him before he goes back and works himself down again."

"You might suggest it to him," said Miss Ruston. She was looking straight ahead. She wore a hat of white linen, of a picturesque shape, such as are in vogue in the country in warm weather, and it drooped more or less about her face. Burns could not see her eyes when she looked forward, but he could see her mouth. It was an expressive mouth, and it looked particularly expressive just now. The trouble was that he could not tell just what it expressed.

"I'll do it, this afternoon, and keep it as a reminder of a patient of whom I think a heap. No, I can't do it this afternoon, either, for he won't leave Jamie till he can leave him comfortably over the first stage. But by to-morrow afternoon, perhaps. We'll have to catch him on the fly, for I'm confident he'll be off the minute the youngster is out of danger. Well, I hope you know my friend well enough to appreciate that he's about the finest there is anywhere?"

"I'm beginning to know *you* well enough, **Dr.** Burns, to see that you care more to have your friends appreciated than to win praise yourself."

"No, no — oh, Cæsar, no! I've not reached such a sublime height of altruism as that. To tell you the honest truth — which is supposed to be good for the soul — I'm horribly envious of Jack Leaver for having done that stunt this morning."

"Envious? Of course you are. At the same time would you have taken it away from him and have done it yourself, if you had had the chance?"

"Trust a woman to confront a man with the unthinkable, and then expect him to take credit for not having been guilty of it! Would I have snatched a juicy bone away from a starving lion? That's what Leaver has been all these months. It's what any man gets to be when his job is taken away from him and he doesn't know when he will get another. No — at the same time that I'm envious I'm genuinely happy that the lion got his bone. He needed it. It's going to make a well lion of him; he is one now. You're glad, too, aren't you?"

He gave her one of his quick, discerning glances.

"Of course I am." She spoke quite heartily enough to satisfy him.

"Good! Then, if I can wheedle him before the camera, you'll be interested in making a picture

of him that Ellen and I shall want to frame and look
at every day?"

"I will give you my amateur's best, certainly,
Dr. Burns."

"Prunes and prisms!" he exclaimed, and broke
into a laugh. "I didn't expect that, from a girl
like you. I should have expected you to — well,
never mind. I was on the verge of being im-
pertinent, I'm afraid. Forgive me, will you, for
what I might have said? I'll bring him over at the
first opportunity."

CHAPTER XIV

BEFORE THE LENS

RED, this is certainly the unkindest cut of all!
I haven't minded your other prescriptions,
but to insist on giving a well man the worst dose
of his experience to take —— "

"Stuff and nonsense! A bad prescription — to
go across the street and let the prettiest photographer in the United States take a sun picture of
you before you leave town? Besides, you owe it to
us. I haven't the smallest kind of a likeness of you.
I want a nice big one, to use in my advertisements.
I only wish I had a picture of you 'as you were,' to
put beside the 'as you are.' It would be telling.
'The great Burns's greatest cure. The celebrated
Leaver of Baltimore as he was when Burns finished
with him.' I'll send you a dozen copies of the
paper."

"Please, Dr. Leaver." Mrs. Red Pepper Burns
added her plea. "Red really wants it very much,
and so do I. You admit you have no photograph
to send us, and we know quite well you won't go
and have one made by Mr. Brant, as you should.

So please let Miss Ruston try her art. We think you owe it to us."

Leaver looked at her, and his determined lips relaxed into a smile. "I admit that argument tells, Mrs. Burns," he said. "I suppose it is ungracious of me, but, to tell the truth, I've always preferred to be able to say I had no portraits of myself."

"Oh, I see," Burns broke in. "We're not considering, Ellen, the urgent demands for a popular bachelor surgeon's photograph. It's precisely like Jack not to hand them out to the ladies, or to the newspaper men. All right, old chap. Give us what we want and we'll have the plate smashed. Now will you be good? Come, let's go over. If you really mean to leave to-night this is our last chance."

The two men crossed the street, in the mellow September sunshine. Burns preceded Leaver and knocked at the door.

"Will you take a shot at my friend before he goes?" Burns asked Charlotte. "He hates standing up to be shot at, but I have him primed for the ordeal."

"Must it be a shot, or may I make a portrait?" asked the photographer, in her professional manner.

"I want a portrait," replied Burns, promptly. "Your best indoor work — Brant and the Misses Kendall put on their mettle to rival it."

While Charlotte was absent, making ready her

plates, her visitors waited in the little living-room
and looked about it. Its walls were now possessed
of many interesting photographs of people in the
village, among them several of Burns himself, at
which he gazed with a quizzical expression.

"She certainly succeeds in making a hero of me,
doesn't she?" he observed. "Red hair turns dusky
before the camera, luckily for me. I look as if there
wasn't much of anything I couldn't do, including
playing leading man in a melodrama — eh?"

"She has caught the personality, cleverly enough,"
Leaver commented, looking over Burns's shoulder.

"I rather think, though," mused Burns, "that
I don't look so much as if there wasn't anything I
couldn't do as that I thought there wasn't. There's
a difference, Jack, — eh? Do I really seem as ready
to bounce out of my chair and tackle somebody as
that picture makes me look? If I do I need to have
a tourniquet applied somewhere about my neck to
stop the flow of blood to my bumptious head."

Smiling, Leaver studied the photograph in question. "It's the best I ever saw of you. It's
precisely that air of being all there and ready for
action which is your most endearing characteristic.
It is the quality which made me willing to put
myself in your hands last April."

"Much obliged. But you didn't put yourself
in my hands. I laid hands on you and tied you

down. I couldn't do it now, though," and Burns turned to survey his friend with satisfaction. "You are in elegant trim, if I do say it who shouldn't, and that's why I want a picture of my handiwork — and Nature's. It's just possible that Nature deserves some credit, not to mention Amy Mathewson. By the way, she's another who must have this portrait of you, my boy."

"She certainly shall, if she cares for it," admitted Leaver, gravely. "I'm very willing to remind her how much I owe her, in that and better ways."

Charlotte appeared. As she set about her work Bob came racing over the lawn and in at the open door.

"Uncle Red, somebody wants you right away quick!" he announced.

"Just my luck! I wanted to help pose the picture," grumbled Burns, but went off, the boy on his shoulder shouting with delight.

The photographer, in the plain dress of dull blue, which, artist-wise, she had chosen as her professional garb, and in which she herself made a picture to be observed with enjoyment, moved deftly about the room arranging her lights and shadows. This done, she turned to her sitter. When she came in he had been standing before a set of prints upon the wall, studying them critically, but from the moment of her entrance he had been watching her, though he held a photograph in his hand with which he might have seemed to be engaged.

"Ready?" she asked, smiling. "Or, rather, as ready as you ever will be?"

"Does my reluctance show as plainly as that? But I am quite ready now to do your bidding."

"Sit down in that chair, please. But first — I really can't wait longer to ask you — how is Jamie Ferguson?"

"Doing finely." His face lighted with pleasure at the thought.

"Will he have the full use of his poor little legs?"

"It is too soon to say positively. We hope quite confidently for that result. He shows better powers of recuperation than we dared expect."

"Yesterday," said Charlotte, her hand on a certain bulb out of sight, "Miss Mathewson told me something Jamie had said. It was the most extraordinary thing —— "

She related the incident, in which the lad had shyly praised both Leaver and Burns as seeming to him like big brothers. She told it with animation, her watchful eyes on her sitter's face. At a certain point, just before the climax of the story, she gave the bulb a long, slow pressure; then, ending, she remarked:

"Now, if you are ready, Dr. Leaver."

His face immediately grew grave, lost its expres-

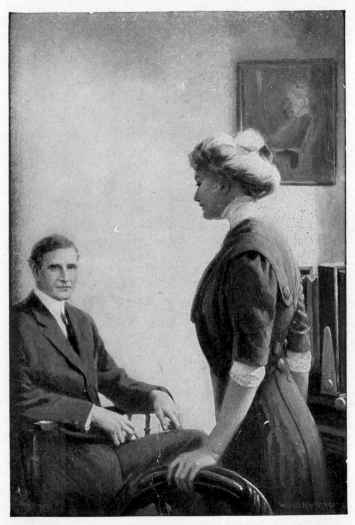

"She told it with animation, her watchful eyes on her
sitter's face"

sion of interested attention, and set in lines of resignation. She went through a number of motions and announced that the sitting was over.

"It wasn't so bad, was it?" she questioned, gayly, as she removed the plate she had used. "I'm not even going to try again. I've discovered that it's not always best to repeat an attempt, and when you are pretty sure you have what you want, it doesn't pay."

"Thank you for making the operation so nearly painless. I haven't had a photograph taken since I was a medical student, and I wasn't prepared for so short a trial. But, even so, I felt the desperateness of the situation. Doubtless that will show plainly in the final result."

"Mine is a discreet camera, and doesn't tell all it sees, so it is possible it may keep your reluctance disguised."

She took away the plate, left him for a few minutes alone among the photographs, and returned.

"It is quite all right, I think, Dr. Leaver," she said, "and the agony is over. You are leaving town to-day?"

He rose. "I go to-night. I should have come to say good-bye, in any case, but, as I go out to Sunny Farm for one more look at the boy, I must be off. So — I'll make this the good-bye."

"I hope you'll have the busiest, happiest sort of

winter," she said, in the charming, friendly way which was naturally her own. "So busy and so happy you'll forget this long, trying time of waiting to be well. Surely, the rest — and Dr. Burns — have done the work. When you see the portrait I hope it will show you, better than looking at yourself in any mirror, what good has been done."

"Thank you. I know a great change has been wrought, somehow, thanks to a man who insisted on having his own way when I didn't want to let him. You expect to stay in this cottage all winter?"

"All winter, and all spring. Imagine us by a splendid fire in this good fireplace."

"I hope it won't smoke on windy days." Leaver looked doubtfully at it. "It strikes me as better photographic material than as practical defence against the cold."

"I shall demonstrate that it is entirely practical. And Granny's little feet will seldom touch the floor. I have a beautiful foot-warmer for her, which will keep her snug as comfort."

"I know you have a strong courage, and will face any discomfort bravely."

His eyes were dwelling upon her face, noting each outline, as if he meant to take the memory of it with him.

"All the courage in the world. What would life be without it? With it, one can do anything."

"I believe you." He was silent for a moment, still looking at her intently. "I wonder," he said then, "if you would be willing to give me something I very much want. I have no right to ask it, and yet, for the sake of many pleasant hours we have spent together — that's a tame phrase for me to use of them, from my standpoint — for their sake would you be willing to let me have — a picture of yourself? I promise you it shall be seen by no one but myself. It would mean a good deal to me. Yet, if you are not entirely willing, I won't ask it."

He spoke in the quietest, grave way. After a moment's hesitation she answered him as quietly.

"I don't know why I should mind, Dr. Leaver, and yet, somehow, I find I do. Will you believe it's not because I don't want to please you?"

His face showed, in spite of him, that the denial hurt him. He held out his hand.

"You are quite right to be frank. Shall we say good-bye? All kinds of success to you this winter — and always."

"Thank you, Dr. Leaver. I give you back the wish."

They shook hands, the two faces smiling at each other. Then he went quickly away. Looking after him she saw that he carried his hat in his hand until he had reached the gate in the hedge.

He closed the gate without a backward glance, and in a minute more was out of sight.

She went into her dark-room and examined again the plate she had just developed. Holding it in a certain light, against darkness, she was able to obtain a faint view of the picture as it would be in the print. Unquestionably she had made a lifelike and extraordinarily attractive portrait of a man of distinguished features, caught at a moment when he had had no notion that the thing was happening. She studied it long and attentively.

"It would have been better if I hadn't made it," she said slowly to herself. "For now I shall have it to look at, and I shall have to look at it. I'm not strong enough — not strong enough — I don't *want* to be strong enough — to forego that!"

After nightfall, on that September evening, Leaver took his departure. Burns was to convey him in the Imp to the city station, because his train did not stop in the suburban village. For a half-hour before his going Burns's porch was full, the Macauleys and the Chesters having come over to do Dr. Leaver honour. They found less chance for talking with him than they might have done if he had not gone off with Miss Mathewson for a short walk.

"Something in it, possibly, do you think?"

James Macauley asked, in an aside, of Mrs. Burns.
"Miss Mathewson certainly has developed a lot
of good looks this summer that I, for one, never
suspected her of before.   Whether she could interest
a man like him I don't know and can't guess.   He's
no ordinary man.   I didn't like him much at first,
but as he's improved in health he's shown up for
what he is, and I can understand Red's interest in
getting him on his feet again.   He's certainly on
'em now.   That was a great stunt he did for the
little chap, according to Red.   Looks a bit suggestive
of interest, his going off with Miss Amy for a walk,
at the last minute, don't you think?   Still, I can't
imagine any man's looking in that direction when
there's what there is across the street.   He hasn't
shown any signs of life, there, has he?"

"Jimmy, you're a sad gossip.   If I knew all these
people's affairs, or if I knew none of them, I shouldn't
discuss them with you.   But I'm quite willing to
agree with you that both Amy and Charlotte are
delightful, each in her way."

"Never did get any satisfaction out of you,"
grumbled James Macauley, good humouredly.   "I
didn't suppose women had such a fine sense of
honour when it came to talking over other women."

"Then it's time you found it out."

"What's this? Ellen giving you hot shot?"
Burns came up, watch in hand.   "It's time those

people were back. They've probably fallen into
a discussion of surgical methods, and forgotten the
time."

The missing pair presently appeared. James
Macauley looked curiously at them, but could
detect no sign of sentiment about them. Indeed,
as they came up the walk Leaver's voice was heard
saying in a most matter-of-fact way:

"I'll send you a reprint on that subject. You'll
find the German notion has completely changed —
completely. Nothing has happened in a long time
that so marks advance in research along those lines."

"He's safe," the observer whispered to Mrs.
Burns. "No fun to be had out of that. Unless —
he was clever enough to change his line when he
came within earshot. It has been done, you know.
I've done it myself, though I never jumped to
German reprints as a safety station. But, you
can usually tell by the woman. She looks as if
she had merely been out for a nice walk. Not a hair
out of place, no high colour, no —— "

Ellen moved away from him. She was conscious
that she, too, had been noting signs, but she would
not join him further in discussing them.

"I am not good at farewell speeches," said
John Leaver, holding Ellen's hand in both his own,
when he had taken leave of every one else. "I only
hope I can show you, somehow, how I feel about

what you and your husband have done for me.
I tried to tell Miss Mathewson something of the
same thing, but she wouldn't have it, which was
fortunate, for the words stuck in my throat."

Burns took him away. "If they hadn't, you'd
have missed your train. We've got to make time,
now."

As he took his place in the Green Imp Leaver
looked across the street at the cottage back among
the trees. Its windows were quite dark, although the
hour was barely ten o'clock. Burns looked over, too.

"By the way," he said, as they moved away,
"why wasn't Miss Ruston among the crowd assem-
bled to see you off? As an acquaintance of yours
in Baltimore she ought to join in the send-off back
to that town."

"She gave me her good wishes this afternoon,
after taking the photograph. Red, speaking of
Baltimore, when are you coming down?"

"When I get a card saying you are holding a
clinic on a subject I'm anxious to see demonstrated."

"Do you expect me to go to holding clinics?"

"Surest thing in the world. You can't keep
out of them."

"Do you suppose the men who saw my break-
down will be eager to welcome me back?"

"No question of it. Good Lord, man, you're
not the first nor the ten-thousandth man who has

broken down from overwork. Because my axe becomes dull I'm not going to refuse to use it when it comes back from the grindstone with a brighter edge than ever on it, am I? Wait till you see your reception. Some of those fellows have been making a lot of mistakes in your absence — have been trying to do things too big for them. They'll be only too glad to turn some of their stunts over to you. And the big ones, who are your friends, will rejoice at sight of you. Of course you have rivals; you don't expect them to welcome you with open arms. They'll be sorry to see you back. Let them be sorry, and be hanged to them! Go in and show them that they're the ones who need a rest now, and that you'll take care of their work in their absence."

Leaver laughed. "Red, there's nobody just like you," he said.

"That's lucky. Too many explosives aren't safe to have around. I know, and have known all along, Jack, that it's been like a cat lecturing a king, my advice to you. A better simile would be the old one of the mouse gnawing the lion out of the net. If I've done anything for you, that's what I've done."

Leaver turned in his seat. "Red," said he — and his voice had a deep ring in it as he spoke — "you're about the biggest sized mouse I ever saw.

I want to tell you this: Since I've been watching
your work up here I've conceived a tremendous
admiration for your standards. There are none
finer, anywhere. I've come to feel that you couldn't
do anything bigger or better in the largest place
you could find. Indeed, this, for you, is the largest
place, for you fill it as another man couldn't."

"The frog, in the marsh, where he lived, was
king," Burns quoted, in an effort at lightness, for
he was deeply touched.

"That's not the sort of king you are. You would
be king anywhere. But you're willing to rule over
a kingdom that may look small to some, but looks
big as an empire to me, now that I understand.
I've reached this point: I am almost — and some-
time I expect to be entirely — glad that the thing
happened to me which brought me here to you.
You have done more for me than any man ever did.
And there's one thing I think I owe to you to tell
you. The greatest thing I've learned from you,
though you haven't said much about it, is faith
in the God above us. I'd about let go of that when
I came here. Thanks to you, I've got hold of it
again, and I mean never to let go. No man can
afford to let go of that — permanently.'

Burns was silent for a moment, in answer to this
most unexpected tribute, silent because he could
find no words. When he did speak there was a

trace of huskiness in his voice. "I'm mighty glad to know that, Jack," he said simply.

Then, presently, for they had flown fast over the smooth road, they were entering the city limits, traversing a crowded thoroughfare, and approaching the great station on whose tower the illuminated face of the clock warned them there was little time to spare. Arrived there, every moment was consumed in a rush for tickets and in checking baggage. Leaver secured his sleeper reservation with some difficulty, owing to a misunderstanding in the telegram engaging it, and at the last the two men had to run for the train. At the gate there was only space for a hasty grip of two warm hands, a smile of understanding and affection, and an exchange of arm-wavings at a distance as Leaver reached his car, already on the verge of moving out.

As Burns drove away he was feeling a sense of loneliness as unpleasant as it was unexpected, and found himself longing to get back to a certain pair of arms whose hold was a panacea for every ache.

"He thinks he owes it all to me," he was saying by and by, when this desirable condition had been fulfilled. "But maybe I don't owe something to him. If the sight of a plucky fight for self-control is a bracing tonic to any man I've had one in watching him. I never saw a finer display of will against heavy odds.   Another man in the shape he was in last spring would have gone under."

"It would be pretty difficult, I think, dear," said his wife, softly touching his thick locks, as his head lay on her lap, "for any man to go under with you pulling him out."

"I didn't pull him out.   No man in creation can pull another out, no matter how strong his effort. The chap that's in the current has got to do every last ounce of the pulling himself.   I don't say God can't help, for I'm positive He can, but I don't think a man can do much.   And it's my belief that even God helps chiefly through making the man realize that he can help himself."

"For which office he sometimes appoints a man as his human instrument, doesn't he?"

Burns turned his head and touched his lips to the hand which had laid itself against his cheek.

"Perhaps, when he can't find a woman.   As a power conductor she is the only, original, copper wire!"

The curiosity which James Macauley had freely expressed as to the probable degree of friendship between Leaver and Amy Mathewson, developed by months of close association, was, with him and with others, not unnatural.   But, in Ellen's case, the desire to know just how much the situation had meant to Amy herself, was a result of her increasingly warm affection for a young woman of character and personal attractiveness, mingled with a sense of her own and her husband's responsibility in bringing together two people who might be expected to emerge from the encounter not a little affected by it.

On the morning after John Leaver's departure, Ellen, standing at a window, found herself watching with more than ordinary intentness the face of Amy as she came up the walk to the house. Lest Leaver should realize to what an extent his presence had disturbed the regular routine of Burns's office, Amy had not been allowed to resume her position according to the old régime, but had spent only a portion of her time there, more as a guest of the house might assume certain duties than as a regularly hired assistant would attend to them. This was, therefore, the first time, since Leaver had left the confinement in his room, that Amy Mathewson had appeared in the office in her old rôle, announced by the donning of her uniform.

"I certainly don't see any unhappiness there," said Ellen to herself, watching Amy as she stooped to pick up an early fallen scarlet leaf upon the lawn. She fastened it upon the severe whiteness of her attire, then came on to the house with an alert step, as if she approached work she looked forward to with zest. Her colour was more vivid than it had been last June, when first she began to live the outdoor life with her patient, her eyes were brighter, her whole personality seemed somehow more significant. Ellen had noted in her these signs of enriched life many times before during these weeks; but the fact that Amy's aspect, on the day after the departure of her comrade of the summer, seemed to have suffered no change, but that her whole air, as she came to her old task, was that of one who hastens to a congenial appointment, gave to Ellen a distinct sense of relief from an anxiety she had suffered from time to time throughout the whole experience.

Burns had gone away early, summoned by an insistent call, and the office was empty. Knowing this, Ellen went in to greet her friend. There could be no other term, now, for the whole-hearted bond between the two.

"Isn't it glorious, this touch of frost in the air?" Amy came in smiling, her cheeks bright with the sting of the early October morning. "And to-day — to-day, at last, I am free to go to work as I like. I don't believe Dr. Burns has sent out a bill for three months. He would go bankrupt before he would tell a man what he owed him."

"Do you like sending out bills so well as that?" Ellen asked, incredulous.

"I like anything that means being at work again,

without having to play that I'm a lady of leisure
at any moment that anybody wants my company.
I like to have things methodical and systematic.
I don't even mind sending out bills, when I know
they should be sent."

She stirred about the office, getting out her type-
writer and oiling it, while the two talked of various
things. Her whole manner was consistent with
her words: she seemed to be full of the very joy
of living. It occurred to Ellen once to wonder if,
by any possibility, this could be the result of expecta-
tion of future continuance of her friendship with
Leaver. But something happened presently which,
though but a simple incident enough, and all in the
day's routine, made any such supposition seem most
unlikely.

The telephone bell rang. Ellen saw Amy's face
change at the first sound of her questioner's voice,
with that subtle change which sometimes tells more
than the person engaged in this form of communication realizes.

"Yes, Dr. Burns," she said. "Yes . . .
Yes . . . Yes . . . Yes, I can have every-
thing ready in an hour . . . I will . . .
I won't forget one thing. . . . Yes . . .
Good-bye!"

Not an illuminating set of replies, given at long
intervals which evidently spelled instructions from

the other end of the wire. But Amy's voice was eager, her concise replies by no means veiled that fact, and Ellen could read, as plainly as if Amy had said it, that the voice which spoke to her was the one of all voices, as it had been for so long, which could give the commands she loved to obey.

She turned from the desk and looked at Ellen with the same animated expression of face. But even as she explained, she was taking instruments from their cases, setting out certain hand-bags, and preparing to fill them.

"It is an emergency case — operation — out in the country. Impossible to take the patient to the hospital; everything must be made ready on the spot. Dr. Burns is to come for me in an hour. He will let me stay with the case. It's work, Mrs. Burns; real work again, at last!"

"You extraordinary girl! A débutante, going to a party again, after enforced confinement at home, couldn't be gayer about it. I knew you loved your work, but I didn't know you loved it like that!"

"Didn't you?" Her hands moving swiftly, she seemed not to stop and think what was going to be wanted, she went from one preparation to another with swift, sure knowledge. "I'm not sure I did, myself, until I had to stop and take what was really just a long vacation, with hardly a thing to do. Vacations are very pleasant — for a while — but they may last too long."

"Evidently Dr. Leaver thought so, too. He seemed ready enough for work again."

"Of course he was. And work — and only work — will put him quite back where he was before the breakdown. I fully believe, Mrs. Burns, that labour is a condition of healthy life. And of the two evils, too much labour or too much idleness, the latter is the greater."

"You make me feel a drone," Ellen declared.

Amy gave her a quick, understanding glance.

"You? Oh, no, Mrs. Burns. You do the prettiest work in the world, and the most necessary."

"But yours is fine — wonderful."

"Not fine, nor wonderful. Dr. Burns's work is that. Mine is just — supplementary."

"But absolutely essential. How many times has he told me what he has owed you all these years for perfection of detail. He says he doubts if he himself could secure such perfection if it all depended upon his care."

Amy Mathewson bent suddenly over a strange looking instrument, whose parts she had been examining before putting them into the bag. Her fair cheek flushed richly. "I am glad to give him the best I can do," she said, quietly, yet Ellen could detect an odd little thrill in her voice.

Within herself Ellen understood the truth, which she had long ago guessed. And with it came a fresh revelation. This was the reason why Amy Mathewson could see, unmoved, the departure of Leaver, who had been so closely thrown with her all that strange summer. With the deep loyalty of a few rare natures, having once given her love, even though she received nothing but friendship in return, she could care for no future which did not include that friendship, dearer than the love of other men.

Ellen was still in the office, held there by a curious fascination of interest in Amy's rapid, skillful preparations. It meant so much, this operating at a country house, she explained to Ellen. It meant the working out of all manner of difficult details, that the final conditions might as closely as possible resemble those which were to be had, ready to hand, in the operating-room of any hospital.

"It's a serious handicap to a surgeon's best work," she asserted, "when he has to do it at a home. With all my precautions, I can never feel so sure of giving him perfect cleanliness of surroundings."

"You can, if any one can," Ellen said, feeling for the first time as she spoke, a curious little twinge of envy of the one whom her husband had long called, with affectionate familiarity, his "right-hand man."

Often as she had seen the two drive away together it seemed to her to-day that she looked at them with new eyes. Just as Amy set out the closed hand-bags, with a box and a bundle beside them, and donned hat and driving-coat, the Green Imp came rushing up the road and stopped in front of the house. Burns ran in, fired half a dozen rapid questions at Amy, nodding his head with approval at her answers, said, "All right, we're off," and picked up the hand-bags. Then he dropped them, snatched off his cap and strode over to his wife.

"We're in a mess of a hurry," he apologized, and kissed her as if he were thinking of something else, as he undoubtedly was. Then he seized the bags, Amy the box and bundle, and the two hurried out. A moment later Ellen saw the car start, getting under headway in twice its own length, and disappearing down the road in a cloud of dust.

"She would rather stay where she can help him than go away to a home of her own with any other man," Ellen said to herself; and the little twinge of envy became almost a pang. She stood staring out of the window, her dark eyes heavy with her thoughts, her lips taking on a little twist of pain. Then, presently, she lifted her head. "She will never, never let him know. He will never discover it for himself. But if she can find happiness in being of use to him, and he can reward her by being her good friend, why should I mind? Can't I be generous enough for that, when I know I have his heart? Her love for him won't hurt him. She can't take it back, but she will never let it show so that he can feel more of it than is good for him. It is so little for me to spare her — so much for her to have.   I will be glad, I *will* be glad!"

She smiled at Bobby Burns, running up the walk, but, being a woman, she smiled through tears.

The little lad ran in. "Oh, Auntie Ellen," he cried, "do you care 'cause I gave my new ball away? It was a new boy came to school, all patched. He'd never had a ball in his life. Uncle Red said I had to be good to other boys, 'cause I've got so much more'n some of them. I sort o' wanted to keep the ball, too," he added, regretfully. "It was a dandy ball."

"But it was nice to give it away, too, wasn't it, Bob?"

He nodded, looking curiously up at her. "You're cryin', Auntie Ellen," he said, anxiously. "Does sumpin' hurt you?"

"Nothing that ought to hurt, dear. It's too bad that being generous does hurt sometimes. But it ought not to hurt, when we have so much more than some of the others, ought it, Bob?"

CHAPTER XV

FLASHLIGHTS

PLEASE tilt your parasol back the least bit more, Miss Austin. That's it! Now walk toward me, up this path, till you reach the rosebush."

Miss Austin, a tall, thin young woman clad in white muslin and wearing also a prim expression with which her photographer had been struggling for some time in vain, obeyed these directions to the letter. Her lips in lines of order and discretion, her skirts hanging in perfect folds, she advanced up the straggling path, the picture of maidenly composure. The nearer she drew to the rosebush the more fixed became the look of meeting a serious obstacle and overcoming it by sheer force of will.

Charlotte Ruston, standing by her camera focussed on the spot of path beside the rosebush, drew a stifled, impatient breath. "I'm going to scream at her in a minute," she thought, "or fall in a faint. I wonder which would startle her out of herself most."

"Do you mind," she said aloud, "if I tell you how perfectly charming you look?"

Miss Austin's lips tightened into a little set smile, more artificial than ever. But just as she reached the rosebush a motor car rushed up the street and came to a standstill before the gate in Charlotte's hedge. Out of the car—a conspicuous affair of a strong yellow colour, and hitherto unseen in the town—descended a figure in a dust-coat, a figure upon which Miss Edith Austin had never set eyes before. Pausing by the rosebush she looked toward the scene at the gate, and her face relaxed into an expression of alert interest.

The camera clicked unnoticed. Quicker than a flash Charlotte had gone through a series of motions and had made a second exposure, smiling delightedly to herself.

"It's a gentleman to see you," called Miss Austin, softly, as the heavily built figure in the dust-coat opened the gate and advanced up the path.

Miss Ruston made all secure about her camera, and turned to meet the full and smiling gaze of the newcomer, standing, cap in hand, just behind her. He was a man who might have been thirty or forty—it would not have been easy for a stranger to tell which at first glance, for his fair hair was thick upon his head, his face fresh and unwrinkled, and his eyes bright. Yet about him was an air of having been encountering men and things for a long time, and of understanding them pretty well.

"Mr. Brant!" Charlotte's tone was that of complete surprise.

"You were not expecting me?" He shook hands, gazing at her in undisguised pleasure. He was not much taller than she, and the afternoon sun was at his back, so he had the advantage.

"I certainly was not. How does it happen? A business journey?"

"A most luckily opportune one — for me. It brought me within a hundred miles, and my descriptions to my friend of an interesting region did the rest."

His eyes swerved to the figure of Miss Edith Austin, standing tensely by the rosebush, an observer whose whole aspect denoted eager absorption in the meeting before her. Charlotte presented him. Miss Austin expressed herself as assured of his being a stranger to the town the moment her eyes fell upon him.

"And a very dusty and disreputable one, I'm afraid," Mr. Brant declared. "I should have stopped at some hotel and made myself presentable," he explained to Charlotte, "if I had not been afraid I should lose a minute out of the short time Van Schoonhoven agrees to leave me here."

Charlotte took him to the house and left him politely trying to converse with her grandmother — at tremendous odds, for he was not a rival of Red

Pepper Burns in his fondness for old ladies, not to mention deaf ones. The photographer returned to her sitter.

"I have several pictures of you now, Miss Austin," she said, "and I think among them we shall find one you will like."

"But aren't you going to have one of this last pose?" Miss Austin inquired, anxiously. "Of course, I know you have company now——"

"That doesn't matter. But I have two exposures, by the rosebush, and I think they are both good. I have kept you standing for quite a long time, and I want you to see proofs of these before we try any more."

"I haven't once known when you were taking me. I can't help feeling that if you just let me know when you were going to take the picture I could be better prepared."

"One can be a bit too much prepared. The best one I ever had made of me was done an instant after I had carelessly taken a seat where the operator requested. I looked up and asked, 'How do you want me to sit?' He answered, 'Just as pleases you. I have already taken the picture.'"

"Dear me! How methods change! Our best photographer here is always so careful about every line of drapery, and just how you hold your chin.

I don't see how you can just snap a person and be sure of an artistic result."

"You can't. And perhaps you won't like these at all. But I will show you proofs to-morrow. And if they are not right we'll try again, if you are willing."

Miss Austin went away, parasol held stiffly above her head, though the sun was behind her. She was wondering, as she went, who the man was who had come to see Miss Ruston, and she arrived without much difficulty at the conclusion that he was probably going to marry her. His speech about being in such haste to reach her that he couldn't take time to go to a hotel and make himself neat seemed to her sure evidence that the two were upon a footing more intimate than that of mere friendship.

"If you are not too proud," said Miss Ruston to Mr. Eugene Brant, "you may come into the kitchen and wash your hands and face. Afterward you may stroll about my garden while I get supper."

"I am not too proud to wash my face in your kitchen," responded Mr. Brant, following her with alacrity, "but I shall not be willing to stroll about your garden while you get supper. After supper, if you like, we will explore it to its mystic end down by the currant bushes I see from the window here."

He accepted the basin of water Charlotte gave him, as gracefully as she presented it, dried his face upon the little towel she handed him, and declared himself much refreshed. She did not apologize for the lack of a guest-room where he might remove the signs of dusty travel, nor did she allude to the absence within the house of most of the appliances considered necessary in these days for creature comfort. But she dismissed him to the garden with a finality against which his pleadings to be allowed to be of use to her proved of no avail, and only when, after a half-hour, she appeared in the doorway with a pail, and approached the old well nearby, did he discover a chance to show his devotion.

"If you knew what fun I should consider it to be carrying plates and things around for you in there," said he, as he drew the water for her, "you wouldn't keep me out here. What do you imagine I came a hundred miles out of my way for—to study the possibilities of landscape gardening as applied to miniature estates like these of yours?"

"You might do much worse," she responded promptly. "I have spent not a little thought on just how much trimming to give my old shrubbery and how much to leave in a wild tangle. Will you come in now and have supper? We will take it with Granny in the front room."

Mr. Brant was hungry, after his long drive, and he eyed with satisfaction the small table by the door, set out with fine old china and linen. He consumed two juicy hot chops with keen relish, accompanied as they were by well-cooked rice. A simple salad followed, and gave way to a dish of choice peaches, upon which his hostess poured plenty of rich cream. She gave him also two cups of extremely good coffee, and he rose from the repast feeling content, though the fact that he had made a heartier meal than either of the ladies had not escaped him.

By and by he had his way, and took Charlotte out to the garden. Little Madam Chase had been put to bed at what she called "early candle-light," because such an hour best suited her.

"Well, are you going to do me the honour of telling me all about it?" Mr. Brant asked, as he settled himself upon the old bench by Charlotte's side. He scanned her closely once more in the waning light.

"What do you want me to tell you?"

"Just what I ask — all about your coming here. How you get on. What it means to you. Your hopes — your fears, if you have any. I realize, better than you do, perhaps, that this is not a small venture for you to make. I am interested — you understand how interested — to know just the situation."

His tone was that of a brother, warm and kind. She responded to it.

"I am doing as well as I could expect. Almost

every day I have a sitter — sometimes two. My friends are very good; they bring me every one who will come. People seem to like the things I do — some of them."

"Almost every day you have a sitter!" he repeated. "Do you call that doing well? How long have you been here?"

"Just seven weeks. Yes, I do call that doing well. It takes time to become established, of course. Now that I have made pictures of many of the prominent people others will follow, I'm confident. You know this isn't the portrait season — too many have cameras of their own and are taking snapshots of outdoor scenes, with themselves in the foreground."

"You don't find yourself wishing you had stayed in the city, as I advised?"

"Not a bit. I want more experience first. I want to be able to do work I needn't apologize for when I really begin with a city studio."

"You are doing finished work, in my opinion."

"Not in mine."

He laughed. "There is nothing weak about your will," said he.

"I hope not. I need a strong one.'

"Granted, if you mean to persist in making your own way. But I live in hope that when you have demonstrated to your own satisfaction that you are

perfectly competent to hew out that way for yourself, you will be willing to let some stouter pair of
arms take a turn with the axe."

His tone had meaning in it, but she turned it
aside.

"Could anybody take your studio away from you?
Even though you don't do it for a living, but only
because you adore it, could you be induced to give
it up?"

"I'm not trying to induce you to give yours up.
I'll build a separate one for you right beside mine,
any time you say the word, and you shall pursue
your avocation in perfect freedom. All I object to
is your making the thing your vocation. I know
of a better one for you."

She shook her head. "We went over all this
ground — over and over it — before I came away.
Why do you come out here and begin it all over
again? I don't want to talk about it."

"I came because I had to see for myself what
sort of a place you were in. I had a notion that it
wasn't good enough. It isn't. You can't be comfortable in it, through the most of the year. Neither
can Madam Chase."

"We can be perfectly comfortable." She spoke
quickly and decidedly. "You know absolutely that
I wouldn't sacrifice what is dearest to me in the
world for the sake of having my own way. The

little house is primitive, but Granny can be made as snug in it as in any stone mansion."

"The thing may tumble down about your ears in the first high wind."

"It will not. Dr. Burns went over it thoroughly, and says it is much more substantial than it looks."

"Dr. Burns! May I ask who the gentleman is?"

"My neighbour across the street. He is devoted to Granny, and had as many fears as you could have before he tested the house."

"Is he married?"

"Certainly." It was impossible to help laughing a little at his tone, which was that of a jealous boy.

"Thank heaven for that! I'm suspicious of men who are devoted to your grandmother, charming old lady though she is. But, in spite of Dr. Burns's invaluable opinion, I must beg to differ with him. You can't be comfortable in that chicken-coop through the winter."

"I don't know," Charlotte said slowly, sitting up very straight in the twilight, and looking steadily in front of her, "that you have any right to care whether we are comfortable or not."

"No right to care? Not the right of an old friend? Charlotte, you wouldn't deny me that? Why, child, I saw you grow up. I was your father's trusted friend, in spite of being much younger than

he. And I'm not so much older than you, after all
— only fifteen years. You might at least let me
play at being elder brother to you."

"I did let you play that for a long, long time.
It was only when ——"

She paused. He took her up.

"Only when I began to intimate that the relation
wasn't fully satisfying that you began to give me
the cold shoulder. You haven't even written to me
since you've been here. Are you aware of that?"

She nodded. "There was nothing to write. And
I've been very busy."

He drew in his breath, held it for a minute, and
let it go again explosively.

"Charlotte," said he, presently, "it seems to me
I've lost ground with you. I wish I knew why.
You know perfectly well that I won't bother you with
my suit if you won't listen to it,— at least, I won't
bother you with it all the time. I don't promise
to give up hope. But what I can't bear is to have
you treat me as if you wouldn't have even my friendship any longer. It hurts to hear you say I have
no right to care whether you live in a comfortable
home or not."

She turned impulsively. "Then I take it back.
You have a certain right, it's true. You have been
a good friend, and I owe you much. It's because I'm
foolishly sensitive about this little cottage. I can

see, of course, that it looks like a poor place to a man
who lives in one of the finest houses in the State of
Maryland, but I can't let that influence me.   If you
happened to be the sort of man who loves to go off
into the woods and live in a log shack for a whole
hunting-season you'd understand its charm for me.
I don't in the least mind washing my face in a tin
basin.   You do mind."

"Not when you offer it.   But it's not the tin
basin I object to.   That is —— "

"It *is* the tin basin.   You don't like to see a
woman live in such a plain way.   But I tell you
this, Mr. Brant: she can be just as much a woman of
refinement —— "

"My dear girl —— "

"Yes, I lost my temper for a minute," she admitted.   "I shouldn't have said that.   I shouldn't
offend you by implying that you don't know it.
What I mean is that the luxuries you consider
essential are not essential.   I was brought up among
them.   I loved them as you do.   It is good for me
to do without them — I am conscious of it every
day.   I shall be a stronger woman and a better
woman if I can learn not to care."

"But you haven't wholly learned yet."   He said
it with satisfaction.

"*I have learned!*"   She flung it at him.   "I don't
mind living in this simple way, except when a man

like you comes along and tries, deliberately tries, to make me conscious of it."

He leaned toward her with a sudden, passionate gesture. "Charlotte, forgive me! It is because I long so to take you away from it, to give you the sort of home you have known in the old days. It fits you so well — that sort of home. You were a princess in the old home; you would be a queen in a new one."

"Oh, don't!"

"All right, I won't.".

There was silence between them for some time after this. Brant sat with his hands clenched and resting upon his knees, his head bent a little. Charlotte had turned and laid one bended arm upon the high back of the old bench — her head rested against it. She was the first to speak, in the light tone with which her sex is accustomed to let a situation down from the heights of strong emotion to a more normal level.

"What do you do with a sitter who won't let you bring out her best points, but insists on making herself into the stiffest sort of a lay figure?"

"Chloroform her and relax the tension." Brant's tone was grim. Then, suddenly, he looked up. "Will you let me go in and make a flashlight of you by a new method I've worked out? I promise you you'll find it a trick worth knowing."

"I shall be delighted. You've taught me half I know, and I'm more grateful than I seem."

"I hope that's true," he said, still in the grim tone, as they went up the garden path toward the house.

Inside the house he became the exponent of the art of which he was past master. His study was to him only a diversion, but he had become distinguished in it as an amateur who played at being a professional for the interest of it, and who possessed a collection of photographic portraits of half the celebrities in the world. With eager interest Charlotte watched him manipulate improvised screens and devices for casting light and shadow, and when he posed her understood the result he meant to produce.

"Oh, that will give a new effect!" she said, delightedly. "I should never have thought of it in the world."

"It will almost absolutely overcome the flatness of the flashlight, as you will see when we develop it — if you will let me stay so long. Now —— "

The flash flared and died. Brant smiled with gratification. If he knew what he was doing he had a new portrait of Charlotte Ruston which would surpass anything he had yet made of her. It seemed to him that during these last weeks she had grown even more desirable than he had ever known her. There had always been a spirit and enchantment about her personality which had been his undoing, but there was now a quality in it which was well nigh his despair — the quality born of self-sacrifice and endeavour, those invisible but potent agencies in the creating of the highest type of womanly charm.

The pair went into the dark-room together. Here, at least, Mr. Brant was able to give sincere approval. Although the place was cramped no necessary detail was lacking. Charlotte had not spared expense in transporting material or in fitting the spot with the requisite conveniences for swift and sure work. In a very few minutes Brant was showing his pupil the negative, which her trained eye was fully able to appreciate.

"Oh, that will make a perfect print," she exclaimed, everything else forgotten in the joy of the artist over the overcoming of difficulties. "You certainly have conquered almost the last obstacle to the making of flashlight portraits. That will be soft as daylight. I will make the print to-morrow and let you know."

"You don't mean to send me merely a report of its appearance, I hope."

She laughed. "Of course I'll make a print for you, if you want it. Perhaps you'll admit, when you see the setting, that the old room isn't such an inartistic choice for a photographer."

"The old room is delightful — as a background. But when your feet are freezing on its cold floor, in the dead of next winter —— Never mind, we won't go back to that. I admit it's a September night, and there's no use in my borrowing trouble. Besides, I suppose I must be off in half an hour. Let's make the most of it."

They sat in the room in question and talked of developers and fixing-baths, of processes and results, and Charlotte found such interest in these technical topics that she glowed and sparkled as another woman might have done at talk of quite different things. She knew well enough that nobody could give her greater aid or inspiration in her work than Eugene Brant, whose signature upon any portrait meant approval in the large world where he was known.

In spite of his over-heaviness of outline he was not an uninteresting figure as he sat there. His face had not taken on superfluous flesh as his body had acquired weight, and its lines were good to the eye of the artist. His eye was clear, his smile full and not lacking in a certain winning quality which spoke of sympathy and understanding. One who had never before seen him would not doubt that here was a man worth acquaintance, in spite of the fact that his only labour was in the pursuit of a fancy rather than in the making of a living.

The hour came for his reluctant departure. Standing on Charlotte's shaky little porch he looked up at her as she stood on the threshold above him. Against the light in the room behind her the outlines of her lithe young figure were to him adorable. He took her hand and held it for a minute with a strong pressure which spoke for him of his longing to keep it in his permanent possession.

"Will you send me off with the assurance that at least my friendship is still something to you?" he asked her. "You can be as independent as you like, but you need friends. Or, if that has small weight with you, let me appeal to your generosity. I need your friendship even more than you need mine."

"Unhappy Mr. Brant." She was smiling. "So few friends, so few pleasures, he needs poor Charlotte Ruston's support!"

"Poor Charlotte Ruston is a greater inspiration to Eugene Brant's good work than any dozen of his fashionable patrons."

"I am honoured — truly. And, of course, we are friends, the best of friends. I will send you the print soon. Thank you for coming. You have helped me very much."

With which he was obliged to be content.

CHAPTER XVI

IN FEBRUARY

ONE cold December morning Charlotte Ruston, sweeping up her hearth after making her fire for the day, preparatory to bringing little Madam Chase downstairs, heard the knock upon her door which heralded Mrs. Redfield Pepper Burns. It was a peculiar knock, reminiscent of the days at boarding-school when certain signals conveyed deep meaning. This particular triple tattoo meant "I have something to tell you."

Charlotte opened the door, smiling at sight of her friend. "You are worth looking at, in those beautiful furs, with the frost on your cheeks," she said, drawing Ellen in to the fire, and passing a caressing hand over the rich softness of her sleeve. "Furry hat and furry gloves — and furry boots, too, probably — let me see? I thought so," as she examined Ellen's footgear. "You could start on a trip to Greenland, this minute, and not freeze so much as the tip of your nose, behind that wonderful muff."

"It will be Greenland on the Atlantic liner next

week," said Ellen, drawing off the enveloping coat at Charlotte's motion, and seating herself in Granny's winged chair. "The trip to Germany is on foot, at last. Red has had to put it off so many times I began to think we shouldn't get away this year at all. But he's taken our passage now, and vows that nothing shall hinder. So I'm packing in rather a hurry, for we mean to be off on Saturday, though we shall not sail until Tuesday. One can always use a day or two in New York."

"Lucky mortals. I wish I were going with you." Charlotte said it gayly, but her eyes were suddenly wistful. "How long shall you stay? I shall miss you horribly."

"I wish you were going, dear. Nothing could make me happier. We should be a great party then, for Dr. Leaver goes with us. It's a sudden decision on his part. Red wrote him of certain work he wanted to do in the clinics and urged him to go along, thinking it would be just the thing for him now, after plunging into work again with such a will You know they spent a year there together, ten years ago, and Dr. Leaver wrote that the thought of going over the old scenes with Red tempted him beyond resistance. He's been across twice since, but only for a special purpose of study. Of course both will do more or less observing in clinics now, but I imagine they will get in a bit of merrymaking together. If I only had you to go about with me while they were busy I should ask nothing better."

"Shall you be gone all winter?"

"Oh, no; only two months in all. Neither Red nor 'Jack'—as he always calls him—feel that they can spare longer than that, this time. So by the first of March you will see us returning to our own fireside, and probably glad enough to get back to it. German fires, as I remember them, are by no means as hot as American ones. And that brings me to my plan for you and Granny. I want you to come over and live in the house in our absence. There'll be only Cynthia there, for Bob is to stay with Martha. He will be happier over there with her boys than with Cynthia. So you will have the whole house to yourselves and can be as snug as possible all through the heaviest part of the winter."

She smiled confidently at Charlotte, seeing no possible reason why her friend should object to a plan so obviously for the comfort of all concerned. But to her surprise Charlotte slowly shook her head.

"It's a beautiful, kind plan, and exactly like you, but I couldn't think of accepting it."

"My dearest girl, will you tell me why? You would be doing me all kinds of a favour."

"No favour at all. Cynthia doesn't need us to help her take care of the house. We shall be perfectly comfortable here, and — my business is here."

"Charlotte, I'm afraid you won't be perfectly comfortable. This room isn't really warm this morning, and it's not an extremely cold morning. Through midwinter we're likely to have very heavy weather, as you don't know, not having spent a winter here."

"Have you? Isn't this your first winter North? You're just as much of a Southerner as I am. You don't a bit know about Northern winters. You just imagine they must be dreadful."

"I've heard about the snowdrifts over the fences, the terrific winds, and the intense cold. The storms will beat upon this little old house, and I shall think about it away off in Germany — and be anxious. Please, Charlotte, don't be unreasonable. Why in the world shouldn't you do me a favour like this? Red wants it just as much as I do, particularly on the grandmother's account. Think how comfortable she would be in my living-room, and in my guest-room. And I should so love to have her there."

"I suppose I'm an ungrateful person, but I truly don't want to do it, Len. Of course you know I wouldn't persist in a course that I thought would do Granny harm, but I don't see how this can. She stays in bed in the morning, as warm as toast, until I bring her down here, and I don't bring her until the room is thoroughly warm. I give her her breakfast here, and keep her perfectly comfortable all day, as she can tell you. At night I take her up to a nest as cosy as a kitten's, and she has her hot milk the last thing to send her off. Not a breath of discomfort touches her beloved head."

The two looked at each other, Charlotte's expression proudly sweet, Ellen's charmingly beseeching.

"I can see it's of no use," admitted Mrs. Burns, disappointedly, "but I'm very sorry. Will you promise me this? If at any time it seems to you that my plan is, after all, a better one for you than your own, you'll be good and come straight over?"

"I promise you that I'll take proper care of both of us, and love you for a devoted friend. That ought to satisfy you. Do you know that as you sit there, with that furry hat on your head and your cheeks glowing, you're the prettiest thing north of Mason-and-Dixon's line?"

"I know you're a flatterer, as you always were. If I can rival you in that blue cotton —— Charlotte, do you think you ought to wear cotton in December?"

"You wear gauze and low-cut gowns in the evening in January, don't you? — and would in Labrador, if you went out to dinner. What's the difference between silver tissue in the evening and blue cotton in the morning?"

"Considerable difference, as you very well know. But you're impossible to argue with this morning, and I must run back to my packing. Red won't hear of my taking more than a certain quite inadequate amount of luggage, and I have to plan pretty closely accordingly."

"That's good for you. You don't know the first thing about curtailing your desires, and he means to teach you. Perhaps he won't limit you as to how much you bring home."

"I hope not. We shall stop for a week in Paris before we sail, and I mean to bring you the loveliest evening frock you've had in a long time. It's no use forbidding me, for I shall do it just the same."

"I'm not going to forbid you," laughed Charlotte Ruston, with her cheek against the furry hat. "I know when not to forbid people to do things I want them to do. Only make it blue, my blue, and have a touch of silver on it, and I'll wear it and think of you with adoration."

"It's a bargain," and Ellen went away smiling, with the image of Charlotte in the sort of blue-and-silver gown she meant to bring her, effacing for the moment the other image of Charlotte in a blue cotton house-dress on a freezing winter morning, in a chilly house.

A few days later the travellers were off. When Red Pepper Burns and Ellen came in to say good-bye in the early evening they found the little house as warm as even the most solicitous person could desire, and both the elder and the younger inmate looking so rosy and happy that doubts of their continued welfare seemed unreasonable. Charlotte, expecting them, was wearing a picturesque, if old and oft-rejuvenated, trailing frock of dull-rose silk, whose effect was to heighten the already splendid colour in her face. It gave her also a certain air of grand lady which seemed hers by right, whether in the dignified old drawing-room Ellen remembered in the Ruston house, or in this small apartment, illumined by fire and candle-light, and graced by a little old lady in cap and kerchief of fine lace. There were flowers on the table under the candles, and a tray with delicate glasses and a plate of little cakes. Altogether, the whole atmosphere of the room was so comfortably hospitable, and the charm of Charlotte's gay manner so convincing, that both her guests went away with the pleasant sense that they left real home happiness under the patched shingles of the roof, and contentment greater than that found beside most hearths.

"Remember that James Macauley has promised to be a brother to you in my absence, and will see you through any difficulty that may arise," declared Burns, shaking hands. "Arthur Chester claims the same privilege and both will be only too happy to be called on. The small boys will vie with each other to keep your paths shovelled, and Bob wishes to be considered guard-in-chief."

"Cynthia will be flattered to be asked to help you in any way, dear," Ellen urged. "She will be lonely with no one to cook for,— do make her happy by letting her do things for you."

"You dear people," Charlotte responded, "be assured that Granny and I will remember all these counsels. Don't have us on your minds, but come back to us with the first crocuses, and know that we shall be wild with delight at seeing you."

Burns stooped over Madam Chase's chair, and took both her small hands in his. "What shall I bring you from Germany, dear lady?" he asked.

She always heard him better than she heard most people, and laughed like a pleased child at the question. "I spent a winter in Berlin, when I was a young woman," said she. "I remember it clearly enough. There was a little shop in one of the streets — I forget just which — where they sold pictures of the emperor, in little carved frames. William the First, it was then, grandfather of the present Emperor. I should like such another little picture of the present Kaiser — and thank you!"

"You shall have it — and something else, of my own choosing, if I may. Good-bye, dear lady. May I kiss you good-bye?"

She permitted the privilege, beaming with pleasure under the reverent touch of her fair cheek. Then she gave Burns a parting admonition.

"Take good care of that wife of yours; she is well worth it," she said.

"I realize that more every day, Madam Chase. I'll take care of her — with my life," he said, soberly, close to her ear. Then he bore Ellen away, both looking back with friendly eyes at the pair they left in the cottage, and wishing them well with all their warm hearts.

They had barely sailed when the first heavy snowfall of the season covered the world with a blanket of white, and this was the forerunner of almost continuous genuine winter weather. No severe storms such as Ellen had prophesied assailed the region until the first of February, but then came such a one as deserved no other name than the modern term of blizzard, a happening of which Madam Ruston and Charlotte had heard, but had never genuinely experienced.

"We're going to show you the real article this time," declared James Macauley, stamping his way in out of the snow one evening, when the storm had been in progress for twenty-four hours without intermission. "I came over to assure you that if in the morning your roof has disappeared under a drift you may rest easy in the knowledge that you will surely be shovelled out before noon. My wife sent me over to find out if you had plenty of supplies on hand."

"We weren't provided for quite so long a siege, but I was coming over to telephone from your house this morning. It's a great storm, isn't it? I think it's fun, for it's my first experience. Do tell your boys to come over and make a snow fort or something in my front yard."

"They'll be delighted, when the storm stops. There's no use making forts now, you know."

"No, I didn't know. I was prepared to go out this morning and play with them."

Macauley looked at her. "Not in that dress, I hope," he observed, bluntly. "It beats me, the way women wear their thinnest clothes in the coldest weather. I wonder how I'd feel with the kind of rig you're wearing. And it's none too warm here, it strikes me, if you don't mind my saying it, in spite of that good-looking fire."

"The room warms rather slowly in this extreme weather," Charlotte admitted. She was standing close to the fire, in the unquestionably summerlike dress of the blue cotton she chose for all her working frocks. With its low rolling collar and short sleeves it certainly did not suggest comfort. If Macauley had suspected that beneath it was no compensating protection, he would have been considerably more concerned than he was. His wife was accustomed to explain to him, when he criticised the inadequacy of her attire, that she fully made up for it by some extra, hidden warmth of clothing. And when he complained that anyhow she didn't look warm she invariably replied that nothing could be more deceiving than looks.

He walked over to the windows. They were rattling stormily with each gust of the tempest raging outside, and as he held his hand at their edges he could feel all the winds of heaven raging in.

"Jupiter!" he exclaimed. "No wonder you're cold. That stage fire of yours can't warm all out-doors. I'll send for some window strips and nail you up."

"Please don't bother, Mr. Macauley. I am going to stuff them with cotton myself, and that will do quite well. If you will be so kind as to telephone this order to the grocery for me I shall be grateful, though I hardly see how the delivery wagons can get about."

He took the paper she handed him, and absently, after the manner of the householder, his eyes scanned it.

"Why, you want to order in larger lots than these!" he exclaimed. Then, as he looked up and saw her smiling without reply, he reddened and stammered hastily: "I beg your pardon; I looked without thinking. But, if you don't mind my advising you, I'd say double each of these items, at least; it's economy in the end. And — where's the meat order? Have you forgotten?"

"There are eggs on the grocery list," said Charlotte, a little flame of colour rising in her own cheek. "Granny prefers those. But you may double each item, if you wish. Probably you don't realize that I'm not ordering for a family like yours, and things spoil quickly when kept in the kitchen, as we keep ours."

"Of course you know your own affairs," mumbled Macauley, in some embarrassment. "But, if you'd heard R. P. Burns charging me to look after you as if you belonged to me, you'd pardon my impertinence."

"I appreciate your interest," Charlotte assured him, lightly. "But I'm really enjoying the new experience of this storm and don't mind a bit how long it lasts. Granny is warm as can be upstairs with her little stove, and as she can't hear the wind howl her spirits aren't in the least depressed. I admit I don't just love to hear the wind howl. If it would be still about it I should like to see the snow bury my whole front lawn three feet deep."

"I'm glad you take it that way. Martha insists that such storms are very depressing,— principally, I believe, because they keep her from running in to see her neighbours. Well, I must be off. I'll send the youngsters over to shovel a path to your front door; I had to wallow through myself."

He went away, and the storm raged on. The boys did not come over; their labours would have been of small avail if they had worked never so valiantly, for the drifts formed faster than they could have been shovelled away. Night fell with Nature still unappeased, and the wind, contrary to the prediction of the grocer's boy, when in the late afternoon he fought his way in with his basket of supplies, did not go down with the sun.

In the middle of the night, Charlotte, waking from an uneasy sleep, felt the house rocking so violently with the tempest that she became alarmed. She wondered if the shaky frame could withstand the continued shocks. The air of the room felt very cold to her cheek, although she had, out of consideration for the unusual conditions, refrained from opening wide her window. The rush of cold seemed to be coming from the door which opened into her grandmother's room, and with a sudden fear she flew out of bed and ran to investigate. With the first step inside Madam Chase's door her bare foot encountered the icy touch of snow, and she realized that a window was undoubtedly open to the full force of the storm.

Without a thought of herself she rushed across

the room, understanding what must have happened:
the shaky little old window frame had blown in,
for the tempest came straight from that direction.
Yes, she stumbled upon it, lying on the floor. She
picked it up and tried to replace it, but an instant's
struggle convinced her that this was impossible.
With a cry she ran to the bed, herself chilled through,
her heart beating fast with fear. How long had
Granny been lying there in the onslaught of wind
and cold?

She seized upon the small figure huddled under
the blankets, lifted it, blankets and all, and bore it
into her own room. She laid it on her own cot,
covered it with a mountain of clothing, and crushed
into place the door between the two rooms. Then,
shaking with chill, her teeth chattering, she dressed,
answering the old lady's one shivering complaint:

"I thought I was very cold, in my dreams,
Charlotte. What has happened?"

"It's all right, Granny,— you are safe in my room.
I'll get you warm in a minute."

She ran down to the kitchen, heated water over
a spirit-lamp, and made a stiff little hot drink, which
she carried upstairs, with a hot-water bottle. The
bag at Granny's feet, the stimulating posset drunk,
Charlotte felt easier about her charge and went
next at the task of making her comfortable for the
remainder of the night. She ran down again and

made up the fire in the fireplace, convinced that she must get the old lady downstairs, now that with each blast the terrible wind was filling one room with the storm and battling at the little old door to make an entrance into the other. Then she put on a coat, and went up to wrestle with Granny's bed, while the wind swept round her, and the snow flew across the room and stung her cheeks. It was a hard task, getting the bed apart and down the stairs, but she accomplished it, and set it up in the living-room, far from the windows and with one side to the fire. Then she brought down springs and mattress, warmed the latter thoroughly at the blaze, and put it in place.

"Now, dear," she said presently, bending over the cot, "I'm going to take you down by the fire. It's too cold for you up here, and you'll be perfectly comfortable there."

Granny, wrapped in many blankets, was not quite so light a load as usual, but Charlotte staggered down with her, and soon had her at ease in her bed, freshly made up and warm with surrounding blankets. The room itself could not be so quickly warmed, but Granny knew no discomfort nor realized that her niece, with all her exertions, was still shaking now and then with chill and excitement. She had small notion of the anxiety Charlotte was suffering concerning her frail self.

"You must get the window replaced at once, my dear," she remarked, sleepily, from among her pillows. "It must be really quite a storm. I could feel the bed shake. Down here it seems quieter."

"Yes, Granny, much quieter. Go to sleep now, and make up for lost time."

Her charge forgot to ask her what she meant to do herself, and presently dropped comfortably off into a deep slumber. Charlotte piled on wood, making a rousing fire, and sat beside it for the rest of the night, wrapped in a blanket in the winged chair. She shivered away the hours, unable to become warm no matter how close to the fire she crouched, and in the morning was conscious that she had taken a severe cold, quite as might have been expected. But, as her chief anxiety was relieved by finding that Madam Chase awoke apparently in as good condition as ever and not in the least the worse for her exposure, Charlotte made light to herself of her own ill feelings.

She struggled across the street in the morning to telephone a carpenter, and as it was the dull season for workmen of his craft obtained one immediately. He proved a conscientious person, who shook his head over the ancient window frame and advised putting in a new one with a tightly fitting sash. By night the room was secure from the weather, and Madam Chase insisted on returning to it, in spite of Charlotte's entreaties that she remain downstairs until the storm should be over.

"Nonsense, child," she said firmly, "this is no place for me and my bed. Any of our friends are likely to come in at any time, and it is impossible to keep the room looking properly under such conditions. Besides, I much prefer my own room."

So at her bedtime Charlotte moved her back to her quarters, having heated them to a summer temperature with the small oil-stove.

"Poof!" said the little old lady, as she was brought into the room. "How unnecessarily warm it is here! Just because a storm rages outside, dear, why should it be necessary to heat this room so stuffily? The stove consumes the air. When I'm in bed you must open the window and give me something to breathe."

"I was so frightened last night," Charlotte explained hoarsely in Madam Chase's ear, "I feel like doing you up in cotton wool, lest such another icy wind blow on you."

"Why, what a cold you have, child!" cried her grandmother, recognizing this undoubted fact more fully than she had yet done. "You must make yourself some hot ginger tea, or some hot lemonade, and get to bed at once. Promise me you will do it, my dear."

Charlotte nodded, smiling in the candle-light. Then she tucked her charge in with more than

ordinary care, and spent some time in arranging the
ventilation of the room to her satisfaction. The
storm outside was still heavy, but the wind was less
violent, and it had changed its quarter.

She went downstairs again, finding it too early for
her own bedtime, weary though she was. Martha
Macauley presently sent over a maid who was com-
missioned to send Charlotte across for an evening
with the family, the maid herself to remain with
Madam Chase. "If you have the courage to come
out in the storm," the note read.

"I'm afraid I haven't, thank you," Charlotte
wrote back, and dismissed the maid with a word
of sympathy for her necessary breasting of the
drift-blown passage across the street.

"Oh, it's awful out," the girl said. "I don't
think Mrs. Macauley knows how bad it is, not being
out herself to-day, and Mr. Macauley away."

Charlotte made up her fire afresh, and pulling
the winged chair close sat down before it. She
was cold and weary, and her head felt very heavy.
She had put on a loose gown of a thin Japanese
silk — dull red in hue, a relic of other days. Her
hair was loosely braided and hung down her back
in a long, dark plait. Upon her feet were slippers,
about her shoulders a white shawl of Granny's.

All the gay and gallant aspect of her, as her
friends knew her, was gone from her to-night, as

she sat there staring into the fire. She still shivered, now and then, in the too-thin red silk robe, and drew the shawl closer. Her heart was as heavy as her head, her mind busy with retrospect and forecast, neither enlivening. The courage which had sustained her through almost four years of endeavour was at a singularly low ebb to-night. It had ebbed low at other times, but usually she had been able to summon it again by a mere act of the will, by a determination to be resolute, not to be downcast, never to allow herself so much as to imagine ultimate failure. To-night, although she told herself that her depression was the result of physical fatigue, and fought with all her strength to conquer the hopelessness of the mood, she found herself in the end prostrate under the weight of thoughts heavier than the spirit could bear.

She sat there for an hour; then, still shivering, prepared to rake the ashes over the remains of the fire and go to bed. It occurred to her suddenly that before closing things up below she would see if Madam Chase were asleep, or if she might need something hot to drink again, as sometimes happened. She went wearily upstairs, her candle flickering in the narrow passageway. It seemed, somehow, as if the whole house were full of small conflicting winds pressing into it through every loose window-frame and under each sunken threshold.

She stooped over the bed, the candle-light falling on the small, white face. White — how white! With all its delicate fairness, had it ever looked like this before? With a sudden fear clutching at her heart she held the little flame lower. . . .

She groped her way half-blindly down the stairs, the candle left behind. As she reached the foot a stamping sounded upon the porch outside the living-room door. She ran toward it,— never had sound of human approach been so madly welcome. Before she could reach the door a knock fell upon it.

She wrenched at the latch, finding the door frozen into place, as it had been all through this weather. She tugged in vain for a moment, then a voice called from the other side:

"Look out! I'm going to push!"

With a catch in her throat, her heart pounding even more wildly than it had done before, she stood aside. What voice was that? It couldn't be possible, of course, but it had sounded like one she knew in its every inflection, one which did not belong to any of her nearby friends. It could not be possible — it could not — but ——

The door crashed open, and a mound of snow fell in with it. Striding in over the snow came a tall figure in an enveloping great coat, covered with white from head to foot, the face ruddy and smiling.

CHAPTER XVII

FROM THE BEGINNING

JOHN LEAVER turned and tried to close the door, but the mound of snow prevented. The wind was sweeping in with fury. "Go away from it," he commanded. "I'll see to it."

He kicked the snow out with his foot, crowded the door into place, and turned about again. He stood still, looking at the figure before him, with its startled face, wide eyes staring at him, breath coming short. Charlotte's hands were pressed over her heart, she seemed unable to speak.

"Did I frighten you, rushing in upon you at this time of night?" The smile upon his face died, he looked as if she had put out a hand to hold him off. Then, as he regarded her more closely, he saw that which alarmed him.

"Is something wrong? Has something happened?" he asked hurriedly.

She nodded, still staring with a strange, wild look. Then, in a breath, she found speech and action.

"Oh, come!" she gasped. "Granny is — something has happened to Granny!" and ran to him and caught at his hand, like a child, pulling him.

"Just a minute," he said, quickly, releasing himself, and pulled off his snow-covered overcoat and frozen gloves, and threw them to one side. Then he put out his hand to her.

"Now!" he said, and they ran together to the stairs, and up them. At the top Charlotte paused.

"In there!" she whispered, and let him take the lead.

Her hand held very tight in his he crossed the room. He took up the candle from the dressing-table, approached the bed, and gave the candle to Charlotte. Letting go her hand then, he bent and looked closely into the still, peaceful old face . . . made a brief, quiet examination. . . .

He led her down the stairs again. She was fully blind now, seeing nothing, conscious of but two things — the sense of a great blow having fallen stunningly, and the sense of being held firmly by a warm, strong hand. She clung to that hand as if it were all that lay between sea and shore.

In the living-room, before the fire, she felt the hand draw itself gently away. But then she found herself clasped in two warm arms, her head pressed gently down upon a strong shoulder. A voice spoke with a throbbing tenderness which seemed to envelop her:

"Don't question anything, just let me take you to my heart — where you belong. God sent me to you at this hour, I'm sure of it. I felt it all the way — that you needed me. I am yours, body and soul. Let me serve you and take care of you as if it had all been settled long ago. Be big enough for that, dear."

She listened, and let him have his way. Whatever might come after, there seemed nothing else to do now. The Presence in the room above seemed to have changed everything. One could not speak or act as might have been possible an hour ago. Only the great realities counted now. Here were two of them confronting her at once — Death and Love. How could she be less primitively honest in the face of one than of the other?

He put her in the winged chair, drew the white shawl closely about her shoulders, dropped upon one knee by her side, and, taking possession once more of her hand, spoke low and decidedly:

"I will go over to the Macauleys and send Mrs. Macauley to you. Then Mr. Macauley and I will take everything in charge — with your permission?"

He waited for her assent. She gave it with closed eyes, her head tilted back against the wing of the chair, her lips pressed tight together that they might not tremble.

"You will want to take her to Washington, **or** on to South Carolina?"

"South Carolina — where she was born."

"We shall not be able to start till the storm is over. There is no train or trolley service out from the city to-night, and there will not be until the wind and drifting stops. My train was ten hours late. I should have been here this morning. Meanwhile, I will stay just where you want me. You and Mrs. Macauley can settle that. I wish for your sake Mrs. Burns were here — and Red."

"They are not here? Then — how did you come to —— "

"Come home before them? I couldn't stay away contentedly as long as they. I had had an all-summer's vacation, and wanted to be at work. But I came from the ship straight up here, to satisfy myself that all was well with you. I found you — needing me. Can I help being thankful that I came?"

"Dr. Leaver —— ?"

"Yes?"

Charlotte sat up suddenly, opening her eyes, pressing her free hand again over her heart with that unconscious gesture as old as suffering.

"If I had not insisted on keeping Granny here' she would not have — would not have —— "

She sank back, covering her face.

"What had her being here to do with it? You took every care of her.   She was old — ripe — ready to go.   The wonder is that she has lived so long, with such a frail hold on life."

"But — she had an exposure.   This dreadful weather — night before last — her window blew in — she was chilled ———— "

Her voice broke.   With difficulty she told him the story of the experience.   He lifted her hand to his lips and held it there.   After a minute he spoke very gently:

"I doubt if that had anything to do with it.   It was probably the crash of the window blowing in that woke you, although you did not know it; she may not have lain there but a moment.   You overcame the slight chill, if there was one, with your prompt measures.   You brought her downstairs, and carried her back.   There was no strain whatever upon her, it was all upon you.   Dr. Burns has told me that her heart-action was the weakest and most irregular he had encountered; that, at any hour, without seeming provocation, it might stop. Why should you mourn?   It was a happy way to go — merely to stop breathing, as her attitude and expression show she did.   Her hour had come — you had nothing to do with it.   Take that to your heart, and don't blame yourself for one moment more."

She lay back in the chair again, relaxing a little under the firm words.

"Shall I go now and send Mrs. Macauley? It is nearly ten o'clock, time we were letting them know. But before I go let me tell you one thing, then I will say no more to-night. There is no more now to come between us than there was a year ago when — listen, Charlotte — we knew — we both knew — that we belonged to each other, and nothing waited but the spoken word. I dare to say this to you, for I am sure, in my inmost soul, that you know as well as I do where we stood at that time. And — the thing is gone which came between us afterward."

He stood up, put on his coat, said quietly: "You shall be alone but a very short time," and went out.

Left alone Charlotte laid both arms suddenly down upon the arm of the chair — Granny's chair — and broke into a passion of weeping. It lasted only for a little while, then she raised herself suddenly, threw back her head, lifted both arms high — it was an old gesture of hers when she was commanding her own self-control — gripping the clenched fists tight. Then, as steps and the sound of voices were heard outside, she stood up, holding herself quietly.

When Mrs. Macauley came in, excitedly sympathetic and eager to comfort, she found a quiet

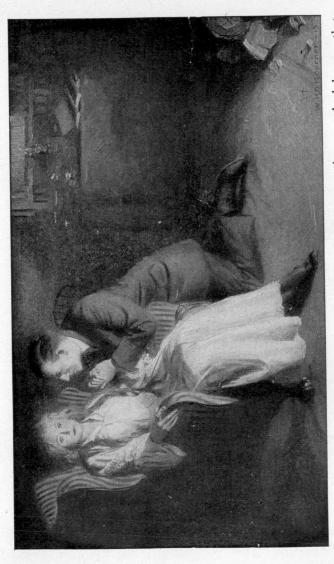

"There is no more now to come between us than there was a year ago when — we both knew — that we belonged to each other"

mourner ready to talk with her more composedly
than she herself was able to do. Martha, shocked
though she was by the sudden call, was full of curiosity as to the return of John Leaver, and only
Charlotte's reticent dignity of manner kept back a
torrent of eager questions.

"It's certainly very fortunate he's here," she
admitted. "He can take charge of the journey
South, knowing trains and routes much better than
Jim or I do. Of course we will go with you, dear.
I judge from what Dr. Leaver says he will go all
the way — which will certainly be a comfort. He
seems so strong and capable — so changed from the
way he acted when he first came here, languid and
indifferent. Oh, how sorry Red and Ellen will be
not to be here! Red was so fond of dear Madam
Chase."

Martha proved not unpleasant company for that
first night, for her practical nature was always getting the better of her notion that she must speak
only of things pertaining to the occasion. She went
out into Charlotte's kitchen and stirred about there,
returning with a tray of light, hot food. She had
been astonished at the meagreness of the supplies
she found, but made no comment.

"You must keep up your strength, my dear girl,"
she urged, when Charlotte faltered over the food.
"It's a long way between now and the time when

it will be all over. We may be delayed a day or two in getting off, and delayed all the way down. I hear this storm is raging all over the country."

Her words proved true. It was two days before the little party could be off. During that time Charlotte was overwhelmed with attention from her neighbours. The Macauleys and Chesters could not do enough. Either Winifred or Martha was constantly with her, and their presence was not ungrateful. John Leaver came and went upon errands, never seeing Charlotte alone, but making no effort to do so, conveying to her by his look or the grasp of his hand the comradeship which she felt more convincingly with every passing hour. His personality seemed somehow as vital and stirring as the course of a clear stream in a desert place.

At the short, private service which preceded the departure of the party for the train, he came and took his place beside her in a quiet way which had in it the quality of a right. Although he did not touch or speak to her the sense of his near presence was to her like a strong supporting arm. When the moment came to leave the room she heard his whisper in her ear and felt his hand upon her arm:

"Courage! You are not going alone, you know."

It went to her heart. On the threshold she suddenly looked up at him through her veil, and met in return such a look as a woman may lean upon. Her heart throbbed wildly in response, throbbed as only a sad heart may when it realizes that there is to be balm for its wounds.

All through the long journey Charlotte felt Leaver's constant support, although he made no further effort to define the relation between them, even when for a short space, now and then, the two were alone together. Instead he talked of his hurried trip abroad with the Burnses, and once, when they were pacing up and down a platform, at a long stop, he told her of his visit to a certain noted specialist in Berlin.

"I had had a breakdown in my work last spring," he said, in a quite simple way, as if he were speaking of something unimportant. "I had made up my mind that I could never hope fully to recover from its effects. Dr. Z—— told me that I was perfectly recovered, that I was as sound, mentally and physically, as I had ever been, and that, if I used ordinary common sense in the future about vacations at reasonable intervals, there was no reason why the experience should ever be repeated. This assurance was what sent me home. I found I couldn't stay in Germany and go sightseeing with my friends after that. I wanted to be at work again."

"I wonder that Dr. Burns didn't want to rush home with you," Charlotte observed — though it was not of Red Pepper she was thinking. This simple statement, she knew, was the explanation he was giving her of the thing he had said to her last August under her apple-tree. It made clear to her that which she had suspected before — it somehow seemed, also, to take away the last barrier between them.

"Burns needed the change — he hasn't had a vacation except his honeymoon for years. By the way, he's having a second honeymoon over there."

"I'm very glad," Charlotte responded.

Then the summons came for the return to the train, and Mr. and Mrs. Macauley, waving to them from the other end of the platform, met them at the step.

On the morning of the third day the party reached their destination. They were met at the small station by a staid but comfortable equipage, driven by an old family coachman with grizzled, kinky hair and a black face full of solemnity. They were taken to the hospitable home of the owner of the dignified old carriage and the fat, well-kept horses which had brought them to her door, and were there welcomed as only Southern hostesses can welcome. Mrs. Catesby's mother had been a friend of Madam Chase's youth, and for her sake the daughter had thrown open her house to do honour to the ashes of one whom she had never seen.

"How glad I am," Charlotte said, soon after

her arrival, standing by a window with kind Mrs. Catesby, "to come down here where it is spring. I could never have borne it — to put Granny away under the snow. She didn't like the snow, though she never said so. Are those camellias down by the hedge? Oh, may I go out and pick some — for Granny?"

"I thought you might like them — and might want to pick them yourself, or I should have had them ready. I sent for no other flowers. I remember my mother telling me how Madam Chase loved them — as she herself did."

From an upper window, in the room to which he had been assigned, Leaver saw Charlotte go down the garden path to the hedge, there to fill a small basket with the snowy blooms. When she turned to go back to the house she found him beside her.

"I see now why you wanted no other flowers," he said, as he took the basket. "These are like her — fair and pure and fragile."

"She was fond of them. She wore them in her hair when she was a girl. They have no fragrance; that is why I want them for her now. How people can bear strong, sweet flowers around their dead I can never understand."

"I have always wondered at that, too," Leaver admitted. "My mother had the same feeling." He looked closely at Charlotte's face, as the bright sunlight of the Southern spring morning fell upon it. "You are very tired," he said, and his voice was like a caress. "Not in body, but in mind — and heart. I wish, by some magic, I could secure for you two full hours' sleep before — the hour."

"I couldn't sleep. But I am strong, I shall not break down."

"No, you will not break down; that wouldn't be like you. And to-night — you shall sleep. I promise you that."

"I wish you could," Charlotte said, and her lips trembled ever so slightly. "But I shall not."

"You shall. Trust me that you shall. I know a way to make you sleep."

However that might be, she thought, his presence was now, as all through this ordeal, the thing which stood between her and utter desolation. A few hours later, when he stood beside her at the place which was to receive that which they had brought to it, she felt as if she could not have borne the knowledge that she was laying away her only remaining kinswoman, if it had not been for the sense of protection which, even at the supreme moment, he managed to convey to her. Her hand, as it lay upon his arm, was taken and held in a close clasp, which tightened possessively upon it, minute by minute, until it was as if the two were one in the deep emotion of the hour.

All the beauty of spring at her tenderest was in the air, as the little party turned slowly away, in the light of the late afternoon sun. Somewhere in the distance a bird was softly calling to its mate.

Behind Charlotte and Leaver, the kindly old clergyman who had been Madam Chase's lifelong friend was gently murmuring:

> "'Dust is dust, to dust returneth,
> Was not written of the soul.'"

Upon the evening of that day, spent as such evenings are, in subdued conversation at a hearthside, Leaver came across the room and spoke to Charlotte.

"I am wondering," he said, "if a short walk in the night air won't make you fitter for sleep than you look now. It is mild and fine outside. Will you come?"

"It will do you good, Miss Ruston," urged her hostess, who had taken a strong liking to Dr. Leaver. The Macauleys seconded the suggestion also, and Charlotte, somewhat reluctantly as to outward manner, but, in spite of sorrow and physical fatigue, with a strong leap of the heart, made ready.

As her companion closed the door behind them Charlotte understood that she was alone with him at last, as she had not been alone with him in all these days, even when no person was present. She had small time in which to recognize what was coming, for, almost instantly, it was at hand. There was a small park opposite the house, and to the deserted walk which circled it she found herself led.

"Dear," Leaver's voice began, in its tenderest inflection, "I have a curious feeling that no words can make it any clearer between us than it already is. Last winter we knew how it was with us — didn't we? Won't you tell me that you knew? It is my dearest belief that you did."

"Yes, I knew," Charlotte answered, very low.

"To me it was the most beautiful thing I had ever dreamed of, that two people could so under-stand and belong to each other before a word was said. When the time came to speak, and — the thing had happened that made it impossible, I can never tell you what it meant to me. When I found you there in the North it seemed as if the last ounce had been added to the burden I was bearing. I couldn't ask for your friendship; I couldn't have taken it if you had given it to me. I had to have all or nothing. Can you understand that?"

She nodded. She put up one hand and lifted the thin black veil she was wearing, and turned her face upward to the stars. They were very bright, that February night, down in South Carolina.

"But now," he went on, after a moment, "it is all plain before us. Charlotte, am I a strangely presumptuous lover to take so much for granted?

I don't even ask if you have changed. Knowing
you, that doesn't seem possible to me. I have never
wooed you, I have simply — recognized you! You
belonged to me. I was sure that you so recognized
me. It has been as I dreamed it would be, when
I was a boy, dreaming my first dreams about such
things. I have known many women — have had
a few of them for my very good friends. I never
cared to play at love with any one; it didn't interest
me. But when I saw you I loved you. I won't
say 'fell in love;' that's not the phrase. I loved
you. The love has grown with every day I have
known you — grown even when I thought it was
to be denied."

"I know," Charlotte said again, and now she was
smiling through tears at the friendly stars above
her.

"Yes, you know," he answered, happily. "That's
the wonderful thing to me — that you should know."

A little path wound through the park, as deserted
as the street. He led her into this, and, pausing
where a group of high-grown shrubs screened them
from all possible passers-by, he spoke with all the
passion he had hitherto restrained.

"Charlotte, are you my wife? Tell me so — *in
this !*"

He laid one arm about her shoulders, his hand
lifted her face as he stooped to meet it with his own.

When he raised his head again it was to look, as she had looked, toward the stars.

"That was worth," he said tensely, "all the pain I have ever known." Then as he led her on he spoke again with an odd wistfulness.

"Dearest, I have talked about our love not needing words, and yet, I find I want to hear your voice after all. Will you tell me, in words, how it is with you? I want to hear!"

After a moment she answered him, softly, yet with a vibrant sweetness in her tone. "John Leaver, it is as you say. I have known, from the first, that I — must love you. You made me, in spite of myself. I couldn't — couldn't help it!"

He bent his head, with a low murmur of happiness. Then: "And I thought I could do without words!" he said.

For the first time in many days Charlotte's lips curved suddenly into the little provoking, arch smile which was one of her greatest charms.

"I never thought I could!" she said.

He laughed. "You shall not! And now I'm going to speak some very definite words to which I want a very definite answer. Charlotte, you are — I can't bear to remind you — as far as kinspeople go, quite alone in the world. There is no reason why that should be true. The nearest of all relations can be yours to-morrow. Will you marry me

to-morrow, before we go North?   Then we shall be
quite free to stop in Baltimore or to go on as you
prefer.   I can go with you, at once, to close up the
little house, if you wish.   Is there any reason why
we should stay apart a day longer?"

"I don't know of any that would appeal to you.
But there is one."

"May I know it?"

She hesitated.   "I'm — very shabby," she said,
reluctantly; "much shabbier than you can guess."

"We'll go by the way of New York, and you can
buy all you need.   That's an objection which turns
into an argument for the other side, for I want very
much to see a certain old friend in New York, who
was out of town when I landed last week.   I can do
it while you shop.   Doesn't that convince you?"

"I can let it — if you really think it is best to be
in such haste."

"Why not?   Why should we waste another day
apart that we could spend together?   At its longest
life is too short for love."

"Yes," she murmured.

"I'm thankful, very thankful, that you are too
womanly to insist on any prolonging of what has
certainly been separation enough.   I felt that you
wouldn't.   Oh, all through, it has been your woman-
liness I have counted on, dear,— an inexhaustible,
rich mine of sense and sweetness."

"You rate me too high," Charlotte protested, softly. "I'm only a working-woman, now, you know. All the old traditions of the family have been set aside by me."

"You have lived up to their traditions of nobility understood in just a little different way. It is these years of effort which have made you what you are. If I had known you in the days before trouble came to you I might have admired your beauty, but I shouldn't have loved your soul."

"Then" — she looked up into his face — "I'm glad for everything I've suffered."

The sunlight was pouring in again, next morning, when Charlotte awoke. She lay, for a little, looking out into the treetops, holding the coming day against her heart.

"I can't believe it; oh, I can't believe it," she whispered to herself. "A week ago so heavy and forlorn and poor — to-day, in spite of losing Granny, so rich, rich. I'm to be — his wife — this day — his wife! O God! make me fit for him; make me fit to take his love!"

When she went downstairs she found him waiting at the foot, looking up at her with his heart in his eyes, though his manner was as quiet and composed as ever. At his side stood Martha Macauley, excited and eager. The moment that Leaver's hand had released Charlotte's Martha had her in her arms.

"You dear girl!" she cried. "Of all the romantic things I ever heard of! I'm so upset I don't know what to do or say, except that I think you're doing just exactly right. It's as Dr. Leaver says; there isn't a thing in the way. Why shouldn't you go back together? Only I wish Ellen and Red were here; they're certain to feel cheated."

"We'll try to make it up to them," Leaver said, smiling.

"It's all right," declared James Macauley, joining them. "I like the idea of getting these things over quietly, without any fuss over trunkfuls of clothes. If a lady always looks like a picture, whatever she wears, why should she need fairly to jump out of her frame because she's getting married?"

Upstairs, a little later, Martha, coming in upon Charlotte, as she bent over a tiny trunk, put a solicitous question:

"My dear, if there's anything in the world I can lend you, will you let me do it? I have a few quite pretty things with me, and I'd love to give them to you."

Lifting a flushed, smiling face Charlotte answered: "That's dear of you, but I think I have enough — of the things that really matter. I've only this one travelling dress, but as we shall go straight to New

York I can soon have the frock or two I need. It's so fortunate I brought a trunk at all. When I came away I was so uncertain just what would happen next, or how long I might want to stop on the way back, that I put in all the white things I had there."

"And beautiful white things they are, too, if that is a sample," said Martha, noting with feminine interest a dainty garment in Charlotte's hands. "You're lucky to have them."

"My mother left stores and stores of such things, and I've been making them into modern ones ever since. They are my one luxury," and Charlotte laid the delicate article of embroidered linen and lace in its place with a loving little pat, as if she were touching the mother to whom it had belonged. "Otherwise I'm pretty shabby. Yet, I can't seem to mind much."

"You don't look shabby. You look much trimmer and prettier in that suit and hat than I in mine, though mine were new this fall. If you knew how I envy you that look you would be quite satisfied with your old clothes," said Martha, generously. "And as for the husband you are getting — well — I suppose you know you're in the greatest sort of good fortune. All the way down here I've been watching him — Jim says I haven't done anything else — and I certainly never saw a man who seemed so always to know how and when to do the right thing. If ever there was a gentleman, born and bred, Dr. Leaver is certainly that one. And he's a man, too — a splendid one."

"I'm so glad you recognize that," said Charlotte, a joyous ring in her voice.

Ten o'clock, the hour set for the marriage, came on flying feet. Before Charlotte could fairly realize it she was walking down the street of the small Southern village to the little old church which Mrs. Rodney Rutherford Chase had attended as a girl. The old rector who met them there had been a life-long friend of the Chase family. Then, in a sort of strange dream, Charlotte found herself standing by John Leaver's side, listening to the familiar yet quite new and strange words of the marriage service. She heard his voice, gravely repeating the solemn vows, her own, following them with the vows which correspond, then the old rector's deep tones an-nouncing that they two were one in the sight of God and man.

She felt her husband's kiss upon her lips, and, turning, lifted her tear-wet, shining eyes to his. At that moment they two might have been alone in the world for all their consciousness of any other presence.

CHAPTER XVIII

THE COUNTRY SURGEON

R EDFIELD PEPPER BURNS and Mrs. Burns
returned from their stay in Germany just
three months later than they had intended. The
opportunities for extended study and observation
had proved so tempting to the surgeon who had
taken only a fortnight's vacation in several years
that he had decided to make the most of them.
The pair had been kept fully informed of the progress
of events, had wept tears of gentle grief over the
news of Granny's sudden passing, and had smiled
with satisfaction over that which shortly followed
it — the news of the marriage which had immediately
taken place.

Charlotte had written to her friend a brief description, which — Ellen reading it aloud to her husband
— had called forth his sparkling-eyed comment:

"It's rather refreshing to find a woman who doesn't
make clothes the most important part of the ceremony, isn't it? No doubt at all but Jack's found
the right woman, eh?"

"No doubt in the world," and Ellen's eyes silently

went over the few paragraphs again, reading between the lines, as a woman will, and as Charlotte had known she would.

"I thought I couldn't possibly sleep that night, when it had all been arranged," — the letter ran — "though I was so tired with all I had been through. But in an hour I had gone straight off, and slept like a child, my head on such a soft, soft pillow of confidence and rest. O Len, — to lie on a pillow like that, after months of laying my unhappy head on stones!

"At ten next morning we went to the little stone church, all overgrown with ivy, where Granny was a communicant so many years, and there we were married, with Mrs. Catesby, Mr. Macauley and Martha for witnesses, and Dr. Markham, the dear old rector, to give us his blessing. After that John and I walked over to the place where we had laid dear Granny the day before.

"It wasn't sad, Len; how could it be? The flowers were still fresh over her, and that blessed sunshine was so bright, — as it is in South Carolina, I think, when all the rest of the world is dark. When we came away I felt as I often have when I have put that little frail body to bed and tucked her in and blown out her candle — as if she must surely sleep well till morning. I am sure she will — sure!

"Our whole party came North together as far as Harrisburg, then John and I said good-bye to them and came over to New York, where I am writing to you, now. I am buying a few simple clothes, just enough to begin to live with in my new home. In a few days we go to Baltimore, where we shall settle down in the house, which is just as it was left when John's mother died, five years ago. He says I may change anything I wish, but from all I know of his mother and himself I imagine that I shall not care to make many changes in so fine an old place. He has his offices in a wing — I'm so glad of that. She wanted him at home, and so shall I.

"Len, you will want to know if I am happy. Do I need to tell you? All my old readiness of speech fails me when I come to this. In spite of the way talk bubbles from me, on ordinary subjects, you know I have never said much of the big things of my life. I didn't tell you a word of all there was between your guest of last summer and me. Neither can I talk about it now.

"Just this, to satisfy you, dear. Every time I look at his beautifully strong, sweet, grave face, at his splendid quiet confidence of manner, as he leaves me to go away to do some of the wonderful work he does, or comes back to me after having done that work, I realize what it means to be the wife of such a man. Oh, yes, I am happy, Len, so gloriously happy I can't tell you another word about it!"

When Burns and Ellen landed in New York in late May they were met by a telegram. Burns read it hurriedly, re-read it with a laugh, and handed it to his wife.

"Seems peremptory," he commented. "Shall we let Jack dictate? It will mean only a short delay, and though I'm anxious to get home I'd like mighty well to see them, shouldn't you?"

The despatch read:

"Important clinic on Thursday should like your assistance my wife urges the necessity of seeing Mrs. Burns without further delay please take first train for Baltimore.

"LEAVER."

"Yes, I want to see them," Ellen agreed. "I'm quite willing to delay if you will send Bob a telegram, all to himself, explaining and telling him to tell the rest."

"That will please him enough to make up for our failure to arrive on the promised day. We'll run down for twenty-four hours with them, at least. . . . I confess I'm eager to see Jack do one of his big stunts again. And I'll wager I can show him one trick that even he doesn't know — the last thing I got at Vienna, under W —— "

He sent off the message to Bobby Burns without delay, and despatched another to Leaver, announcing their arrival that evening. In two hours more they were on their way, and at six o'clock they were met in the Baltimore station by Leaver himself.

"See the old chap grin!" said Burns in his wife's ear, when they descried the tall figure in the distance, coming toward them with smiling face and alert step. "Can that be the desperately down person who came to us last June? He looks as if — in a perfectly quiet way — he owned the city of Baltimore!"

"How well, how splendidly well, he looks!" Ellen agreed.

Then they were shaking hands with Dr. John Leaver and listening to his hearty greeting:

"This is great of you two — great. We certainly appreciate it. Come, I'll have you at home before you know it. Charlotte is waiting with the warmest welcome you will find on this side of the Atlantic!"

He hurried them away, but not so fast that Red Pepper Burns did not find time to chuckle: "The power of association is beginning to tell already, Jack. That was the most impetuous speech I ever heard from your lips. I don't call such language really restrained — not from you."

Leaver turned, laughing, to Ellen. "One would

think I had been the most solemn fellow known to history," said he.

In two minutes he had bestowed his guests in a small but luxuriously appointed closed car, had given the word to his chauffeur, and had taken his place facing them. Burns examined the landau's interior with interest.

"The evidence of a slight but unmistakable odour tells me that this is the jewel-box in which Baltimore's gem of a surgeon keeps his appointments," said he. "Well, the Green Imp's beginning to show traces of her age, but her successor will be no aristocrat of this type. I'd rather drive myself and freeze my face to a granite image than be transported in cotton-wool, like this."

Leaver and Ellen laughed at his expression.

"Of course you would," Leaver agreed. "And equally of course every friend and patient of yours would grieve to see you shut up behind glass windows with another hand on the steering-wheel. It's unthinkable and out of the question for you, but for me — it's rather practical."

Burns nodded. "Saves time — and carries prestige. I understand. You city fellows have to play to the galleries a bit, particularly when you've reached the top-notch and people demand that you live up to it. It's all right. But I should feel smothered. And as for letting any young man in a

livery manage my spark and throttle,— well, not
for mine, as I have already remarked."

Leaver looked at him as one man looks at another
when he loves him better than a brother. Then he
put a question to Red Pepper's wife: "Can any
one wonder that there seems something missing
in America when he spends the winter in Germany?"

She shook her head. "I never mean to find out
what America is like when he is out of it," said she.

Burns regarded them both. "And I suppose
you think you and Mrs. John Leaver are just such
another pair?" he said then, to his friend.

"Just such another," was the decided answer.

The car came to a standstill before a stately
stone house, its walls heavy with English ivy.
In another minute the entrance doors were open,
and the party were inside. A radiant figure in
white was clasping Ellen Burns in eager arms, while
a blithe voice cried:

"Oh, my dear, this is so good, so good of you!
We couldn't be entirely satisfied until we had seen
you here!"

"Seeing *you* here," declared Burns, shaking hands
vigorously, when his turn came, and regarding
Charlotte with approving eyes, "reminds me of one
of Jack Leaver's favourite old maxims, which he
used unsparingly while he was chumming with me:
'A place for everything and everything in its place.'

The demonstration of that, raised to the nth power, is certainly what I now see before me!"

Charlotte's glowing eyes met her husband's fixed upon her. She gave him back his smile before she answered Burns:

"Thank you, Dr. Red Pepper. Your approval was all that was lacking."

"Didn't I cable my approval with a reckless disregard of expense?"

"Indeed you did. But you couldn't cable the italics that are in your face — and it was the italics that we wanted!"

Upstairs in the rooms of old-time elegance and comfort to which Charlotte assigned them, Burns demanded to know how such quarters looked to his wife.

"You could put our whole house into that great living-room of theirs," he asserted. "As for these two rooms, they would take in our whole upper story. Don't you suppose stopping here will make you feel cramped at home?"

Ellen, arranging her hair before a low dressing-table of priceless old mahogany, shook her head at him in the mirror.

"Not a bit," she denied.

"You used to live in a home like this one."

"Not nearly so fine. Dr. Leaver is a rich man by inheritance, entirely apart from his practice.

Between the two he must have a very large yearly income. My family was not a rich one, only —— "

"Only old and distinguished. Leaver has both — family and money. Not to mention power. Your friend Charlotte ought to be a happy woman."

"She surely ought, and is. But not happier than the woman you see before you."

Burns came close, lifted a strand of silky dark hair and drew it through his fingers. Then he stooped and put it to his lips.

"You stand by the country doctor, do you?" he murmured.

"Always and forever, dear."

"And yet you are a city woman, born and bred."

"What has that to do with it? I should rather drive in the Green Imp over the country hills with you than ride in the most superb limousine in Baltimore — with any one else."

He gathered her close in his arms for a minute. "Begone, dull envy," said he. "From this moment I'll rejoice with Jack over every worldly possession and envy him nothing, not even the power to give his wife everything the world counts riches."

They went down to such a dinner as such homes are famous for. The candle-light from the fine old family candelabra fell upon four faces brilliant with the mature youthfulness which marks the years about the early thirties, the richest years of all yet lived. The splendid colour of the crimson roses in the centre of the table was not richer in its bloom than that in Charlotte's cheeks, nor the sparkle of the lights more attractive than that in Ellen's dark eyes. As for the two men — all the possible achievement of forceful manhood seemed written in their faces, so different in feature and colouring, so alike in the look of dominant purpose and the power born of will and untiring labour.

During dinner a telephone call summoned Leaver to a consultation. Immediately at its close he went away, carrying Burns with him.

"You can't take me to a consultation, Jack," Burns had objected, with, however, a betraying light of eagerness in his eye. He had been four months away from work — he was hungry for it as a starving man for food.

"Can't I?" Leaver answered, coolly. "Come along and see. It's a chance to give the patient the opinion of an eminent specialist just back from Berlin."

"I'm no specialist."

"Aren't you? I think you are. Specialist in human nature, which, if the reports of this case are true, is the particular sort of diagnosis called for. Trust me, Red, and — put on your gloves!"

Burns had grinned over this suggestion. He hated gloves and seldom wore them, but out of consideration for his friend — and Baltimore — he extracted a pair of irreproachable ones, fresh from Berlin, and donned them, with only a derisive word for the uselessness of externals as practised by city professionals.

Left alone with Charlotte, in a pleasant corner of a stately library, by an open window through which she had watched the departure of the two men in the landau, Ellen turned to her.

"I can't tell you," she said, "how happy it makes me to see your happiness. John Leaver is so exactly the man, out of all the world, who is the husband for you. From all I know of you both, it seems to me I never saw a pair more perfectly mated."

"I'm glad it looks so from the outside," breathed Charlotte, softly. She too had watched the departing pair; waving her hand as her husband, under the electric light at the entrance, had turned to lift his hat and signal farewell. She still stood by the window, through which the soft air of the May night touched her warm cheek and stirred the lace about her white shoulders. "From the inside — O Len, — I can't tell you how it looks! I didn't know there was such glory in the world!"

"What do you think this fellow has done?" cried Red Pepper Burns, returning with his host at midnight. He towered in the doorway, looking

in at his wife and Charlotte. From over his shoulder
Leaver looked in also, smiling. "He's arranged
for me to operate on one of his most critical cases
to-morrow morning at his clinic. The country
surgeon! Did you ever hear of such effrontery?
I may be ridden out of town on a rail by to-morrow
noon!"

"Hear the man! He looks like a country surgeon,
doesn't he?" challenged Leaver, advancing. "Lon-
don-made clothes, Bond-street neckwear, scarfpin
from Rome, general air of confidence and calm.
I assure you I was nowhere, when the family of my
patient saw the lately arrived specialist from Berlin."

"It's not on that patient I'm to do violence,"
Burns explained, at Ellen's look of astonishment.
"He's just mixing things up on purpose. It's a
charity case for mine — but none the less honour, on
that account. I have a chance to try out a certain
new method, adapted from one I saw used for the
first time abroad. If it doesn't work I'll — drop
several pegs in my own estimation, and in self-
confidence."

"It will work," said Leaver, "in your hands.
The country surgeon is going to surprise one or two
of my colleagues to-morrow."

The morrow came. Charlotte and Ellen drove
with the two men to the hospital, and watched
them disappear within its bare but kindly walls.

"How they can do it!" observed Charlotte, as the car went on. "I'm proud of them that they can, but the eagerness with which they approach such work, the quiet and coolness, and the way they bear the suspense afterward when the result is still doubtful,— oh, isn't it a wonderful profession?"

At noon they returned in the car to the hospital. It was some time before Leaver and Burns emerged, but when they did it was easy for the two who awaited them to infer that all had gone well.

"It's a pity to bring this suggestive odour out to you untainted ones," said Burns, as he took his place opposite Charlotte, "but it can't be helped. And as we bring also the news that Jack Leaver has brought down the hospital roof with applause this morning, you won't mind."

"What did he do?" Charlotte asked, eagerly.

Burns briefly described the case — without describing it at all — after the manner of the profession when enlightening the laity. He brought out clearly, however, the fact that Leaver had attacked with great skill and success several exceedingly difficult problems, and that his fellow surgeons had been generous enough to concede to him all the honour which was his due.

"And now — what about your case?" Charlotte asked, realizing suddenly what the morning's experience was to have been to Burns himself.

"Died on the table," said Burns, with entire coolness. His face had sobered at the question, but his expression was by no means crestfallen.

"Oh, I'm so sorry!" Charlotte began, earnestly.

But her husband interrupted her. "No condolences are due, dear. He gave a dying man the most merciful sort of euthanasia, and at the same time demonstrated a new method as daring as it was triumphant. With a case taken a month earlier it would have saved a life. The demonstration is a contribution to science. If he received no applause it was because we don't applaud in the presence of death, but there was not a man there who didn't realize that in certain lines the country surgeon could give them a long handicap and still win."

Burns looked out of the window without speaking. His sea-tanned face showed a deeper shade under Leaver's praise. Leaver himself smiled at the averted profile of his friend, and went on, while Ellen looked at him as if he had given her something which money could not buy.

"I wish," said John Leaver, laying a firm-knit hand on Burns's knee, "you'd come to Baltimore, Red. Between us we'd do some things pretty well worth doing. Without undue conceit I think I could promise you a backing to start on that would give you a place in a twelvemonth that couldn't be taken away from you in a decade. Why not? It's a beautiful city to live in. Your wife is a Southerner, born and bred; it would be home to her among our people. My wife and I care more for your friendship than for that of any other people on earth. What is friendship for, if not to make the most of?"

Burns turned and looked at him, then at his wife, then back at Leaver. There was a strange expression in his hazel eyes; they seemed suddenly on fire beneath the heavy dark eyebrows. He took off his hat and ran his hand through his coppery thick locks. Then:

"Are you serious, Jack?" he questioned. "Or are you trying the biggest kind of a bluff?"

"Absolutely serious. How should I be anything else? You taught me certain values up at your home last summer — you and Mrs. Burns. One was, as I have said, the worth of a big, true friendship. I've been thinking of this thing a long time. It's not the result of your performance this morning. If you had failed entirely in that particular attempt my faith in you would not have been shaken a particle, nor my desire to have you associated with me here. But there's no denying that what you did this morning would easily make an entering wedge for you. Why not take advantage of it? Will you think it over?"

Burns looked again at his wife. Her eyes held an expression as beautiful as it was inscrutable. He could not read it.

He turned back to Leaver. "Yes, we'll think it over," he said briefly. Then he looked out of the window again. "What's the name of this park?" he asked.

The conversation veered to follow his lead. It was not resumed during the drive home, nor again that day, between the four. It cannot be denied that the subject was discussed by John Leaver and Charlotte through varying degrees of hopefulness and enthusiasm. As for Burns and Ellen ——

In their own quarters that night Burns threw a plump silk couch-pillow upon the floor at Ellen's feet, and himself upon it, by her knee, as she sat in a big chair by the open window. She was still wearing the Parisian-made gown of the evening, with which she had delighted the eyes of them all. It was the one such gown she had allowed herself to bring home, treating herself to its beauty for its own sake, rather than because she could find much use for it in her quiet home.

Burns put up one hand and gently smoothed the silken fabric upon Ellen's knee.

"This is a beauty of a frock," said he. "I can't tell you what you look like in it; I've been trying to find a simile all the evening. Yet it's not the clothes that become you; you become the clothes."

"Thank you. That's a dear compliment — from a husband."

"It's sincere. You've worn such clothes a lot, in your life, before I knew you. You are used to them — at home in them. If we came to Baltimore, and I made good, you would have plenty of use for dresses like this. You would queen it, here."

She smiled, shaking her head. "Taking one's place in society in any Southern city isn't quite such a foregone conclusion, dear," she said. "Not for strangers from the North."

"With the Leavers to vouch for us, and your own personality, I don't imagine it would be a matter of tremendous difficulty. Even the country surgeon could get along without smashing many usages, under your tuition. Besides, you have the acquaintance of some of the — what do they call them? — 'best people,' was the term, I believe, Jack used to me. It's a curious phrase, by the way, isn't it? Doesn't mean at all what it says!"

"Not quite — always."

He looked at her. "Would you like to come?" he asked, bluntly.

"What about you?"

"I would rather you answered first."

"I decline to answer first. The offer is made to

you, not me.   You are the head of the house, the breadwinner.   It is for you to decide."

"I can't decide without reference to you."

"You needn't.   When you tell me what you want I will tell you what I want."

He was silent for a little.   Then suddenly he got to his feet, walked up and down the room a few times, and came back to stand before her.

"My little wife," he said, "if I thought you would be happier ——"

"I shouldn't."

"Are you sure?"

"Absolutely.   If you wanted very much to come it would influence me, of course.   But doubting that ——"

"Why do you doubt it?   Shouldn't I be lacking in ambition if I failed to take advantage of such a chance?   It is a chance, Ellen,— the chance of a lifetime.   Jack means precisely what he says, and he could give me such a backing as would insure me a tremendous start."

"Just the same, Red, you don't want to come!"

"No, I don't," he owned, bluntly.   "But why don't I?   Is something wrong with me?"

"Not at all.   You have made a large place for yourself at home; you do all any man could do anywhere.   And you are happy there.   You wouldn't be happy here, because you would have to alter your simple way of living. And if you were not happy, neither should I be. Why should we change conditions in which we are both entirely content, and in which you are accomplishing just as much benefit to humanity as you could anywhere?"

"Ah, but that's the question. Couldn't I accomplish more here?"

"Is human life more valuable here than there?"

"Not a whit."

"Could you save more of it?"

"I doubt it."

"We should have to leave Sunny Farm." She looked up at him with a smile.

"We should." He shook his head. "You would be sorry to do that?"

"So sorry that I can't possibly think of it. Dear, — make your decision!"

"I will. We will stay where we are."

He gathered her close and kissed her tenderly.

"A place for everything, and everything in its place," he quoted once more. "The place for Jack and Charlotte is here — unquestionably. The place for Ellen and Red is there. I believe it. Jack's offer didn't shake my belief for a minute, as far as I am concerned. It did put into my mind the question whether I ought not to make the change for your sake."

"I don't believe," she said slowly, "that a man

is often called upon to leave the place where he can be most useful, on account of his wife's tastes or preferences — providing nothing more serious is involved. And, when her tastes and preferences are on his side of the question, there can be no doubt at all. You may be at rest, Red, for I'm sure I'm happiest to live your life with you, just as it is best for you to live it. And I love my country surgeon so well I don't want him made over into anything else. I can't believe he'd be so satisfactory in any other shape!"

Red Pepper Burns gently released himself from his wife's arms, walked over to the window, and stood there looking out into the thick branches of a magnolia tree, the ends of which came so close he could almost put out a hand into the night and touch them. There was suddenly upon him a deep realization of just how much her words meant. He felt unworthy of a love like that, even though he knew that all there was of him to give was wholly hers.

She stood, motionless, looking after him, her eyes touched with a lovely light, but she did not move. And, presently, when he had conquered the curious stricture which had unexpectedly attacked his throat, he turned and saw her there, an exquisite figure in the French gown which she could seldom have occasion to wear where she had chosen to live out her life with him. Both understood that the decision they had made was made for a lifetime, as such decisions are.

"I believe I could take it better," said he, somewhat unsteadily, "if you weren't wearing that confounded dress. It makes me feel like what Jim Macauley dubbed me once — a Turk. Who am I, that I should keep you hidden away in my little old brick house?"

She turned and caught up a long gauzy scarf of white silk with heavy fringed ends. She drew it lightly about her shoulders, veiling the delicate flesh from his sight. Then she flung one end of the scarf up over her head and face, and came toward him, her dark eyes showing mistily through the drapery, her lips smiling.

"I'm not sure I don't like being guarded by my Turk, Red," she said. "And — about the frock." She came closer still, standing before him with downbent head, and speaking low, through the veiling, silken gauze. "Please don't mind about that. I'm going to leave it behind with Charlotte. I shall not care to wear it. When next May comes I hope I shall be wearing only simple frocks that — little hands can't spoil!"

With a low ejaculation he tore off the scarf, seizing her head in both his hands and gently forcing her face upward that he might look into it. For a minute his eyes questioned hers, then ——

"And you're happy about it?" he asked of her, breathlessly.

"I was never so happy in my life. . . . O Red —are you so glad as that?"

"I think I've been waiting for that all my life," confessed Red Pepper Burns.

THE END